"Nothing and no one can make me stay away from you,"

Nick said as he grabbed her upper arms, and roughly pulled her to him.

He gentled his hold on her and she closed her eyes, feeling his kiss at her temple, a soft nuzzle against her neck. *It would be so easy to give in to this pleasure, this passion he evoked.* His gaze drifted over her, heat sizzling in the depths of his brown eyes. "As enticing as that outfit is, maybe you should get dressed."

The fire in his eyes seemed to blaze brighter, and Desire's body started to respond.

"Unless you plan on us showering together, I'd suggest you'd hurry."

"I'll be sure to use all the hot water, Nick. A cold shower is definitely on your agenda this morning."

"It would take more than a cold shower to make me stop wanting you, Desire."

Dear Harlequin Intrigue Reader,

Welcome again to another action-packed month of exceptional romantic suspense. We are especially pleased to bring you the first of a trilogy of new books from Rebecca York's 43 LIGHT STREET series. You've loved this author and her stories for years...and—you ain't seen nothin' yet! The MINE TO KEEP stories kick off this month with *The Man from Texas*. Danger lurks around every corner for these heroes and heroines, but there's no threat too great when you have the one you love by your side.

The EDEN'S CHILDREN miniseries by Amanda Stevens continues with *The Tempted*. A frantic mother will fight the devil himself to find her little girl, but she'll have to face a more formidable foe first—the child's *secret* father.

Adrianne Lee contributes a terrific twin tale to the DOUBLE EXPOSURE promotion. Look for *His Only Desire* and see what happens when a stalker sees double!

Finally, Harper Allen takes you on a journey of the heart in her powerful two-book miniseries, THE AVENGERS. *Guarding Jane Doe* is a profound story about a soldier for hire and a woman in desperate need of his services. What they find together is everlasting love the likes of which is rarely—if ever—seen.

So join us once again for a fantastic reading experience.

Enjoy!

Sincerely,

Denise O'Sullivan
Associate Senior Editor
Harlequin Intrigue

HIS ONLY DESIRE

ADRIANNE LEE

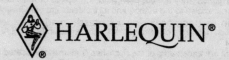

HARLEQUIN®

TORONTO • NEW YORK • LONDON
AMSTERDAM • PARIS • SYDNEY • HAMBURG
STOCKHOLM • ATHENS • TOKYO • MILAN • MADRID
PRAGUE • WARSAW • BUDAPEST • AUCKLAND

ISBN 0-373-22627-6

HIS ONLY DESIRE

ABOUT THE AUTHOR

When asked why she wanted to write romance fiction, Adrianne Lee replied, "I wanted to be Doris Day when I grew up. You know, singing my way through one wonderful romance after another. And I did. I fell in love with and married my high school sweetheart and became the mother of three beautiful daughters. Family and love are very important to me and I hope you enjoy the way I weave them through my stories."

Books by Adrianne Lee

HARLEQUIN INTRIGUE
296—SOMETHING BORROWED, SOMETHING BLUE
354—MIDNIGHT COWBOY
383—EDEN'S BABY
422—ALIAS: DADDY
438—LITTLE GIRL LOST
479—THE RUNAWAY BRIDE
496—THE BEST-KEPT SECRET
524—THE BRIDE'S SECRET
580—LITTLE BOY LOST
609—UNDERCOVER BABY
627—HIS ONLY DESIRE

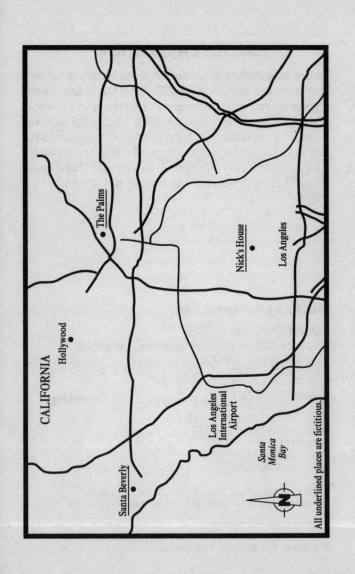

CALIFORNIA

Hollywood

The Palms

Nick's House

Los Angeles

Santa Beverly

Los Angeles
International
Airport

Santa
Monica
Bay

N

All underlined places are fictitious.

CAST OF CHARACTERS

Desire Hamilton—This tough Assistant District Attorney lost her twin sister to a deadly stalker who now has his sights set on her.

Nick Rossetti—A tough cop! He knew the moment he met Desire that he'd married the wrong twin.

Dare Hamilton—Desire's twin was literally scared into having a fatal accident.

Michael Pride—The man Dare had been about to marry before her untimely death wants Nick to investigate Dare's accident and find the stalker so he can exact his own brand of justice.

Ted Gunderson—Desire is determined to nail this creep for stalking and eventually murdering an innocent kindergarten teacher.

Ron Whiting—Ex-husband of the slain kindergarten teacher is an angel in cop's uniform.

Conner Gregg—Desire's boss is tidy to a fault.

Breena Falls—The famous psychologist seems too hostile. What secret is she hiding?

Eager Eddie—A pest with a camera, or something more?

SPECIAL THANKS to Larry
for all you do for me always,
and to Ed and Jackie Heater for the years of friendship
and love, we're going to miss you something awful.

For Anne Martin and Evelyn Gayle Webster.
For all that you both are and all that you give me.
For opening my mind to the possibilities
and for always, always believing in me.

Prologue

He liked small, dark places. Liked the way the tightness sheathed him—the way he wanted her body to sheathe him. He sank onto his haunches, invincible in this space that smelled of her. Of his sweet Dare. Of that mind-teasing scent she was making famous, the one in those pretty bottles on her bathroom counter, the one that lingered on her creamy skin. On her clothes. And in his mind. Forever.

He nuzzled his nose against the hem of her dresses, drawing the fragrance into him as he wanted to draw her into him.

Soon now, he would.

A smile crooked his mouth at both corners and his insides heated with anticipation. She'd looked perfect this morning in that TV commercial, the one for this very perfume, a haunting fragrance that called to him. Her cascading blond hair had waved around her perfect oval face, her wide aqua eyes beckoning him. A siren call of promises.

Dare Hamilton. His Dare. Straight off a ranch somewhere in Texas. As wholesome as an angel. Innocent and pure. But quick success was fraught with pitfalls. Even now, fame threatened her virtue with its evil temptations. Resolve swept through him. He would save her. His love would save her.

Thank God, she was finally willing to accept their destiny.

His smile widened as he saw again her eyes looking directly at him, her lush lips speaking to him alone, delivering her private message through the TV commercial. "I'm ready for you. I want you. Today. Come to my home. To my bedroom. Wait in my closet."

And so he waited.

DARE HAMILTON CHEWED her bottom lip and glanced out the rear window of the taxi. The ad campaign and rapidly growing popularity of Dare to Love perfume had made hers a recognizable face. At first she'd thought it was fun. But lately, she'd had the feeling she was being followed. Watched.

Stalked.

Not by that paparazzi-wannabe she'd dubbed Eager Eddie, who had actually aided her career. But by someone she'd never seen, just sensed—like one who senses something foreboding on the horizon. The sensation had her nerves frayed; the two huge glasses of wine she'd just downed at lunch hadn't helped.

As the taxi pulled to her destination, she felt frantic, half expecting to spot *him* lurking behind one of the old palms that lined the busy avenue of this once-prosperous area in the shadow of the Hollywood Hills. But she saw nothing to account for the edginess in her belly. Even her aging Volkswagen sat undisturbed at the curb where she'd left it.

She paid the driver and turned to face the Pacific Palms. Home sweet home no longer. She was leaving for Las Vegas, getting married today.

Dare hurried to the bungalow apartment she'd called home for the past three years, shoved the key into the lock and was greeted by the usual musty stench of the place, a combination of mildew and dust. She shut the door and tossed her keys onto the desk. They landed near a photograph of her and her twin sister, Desire. She stared at it and scowled. They'd been estranged for the past five years since Dare's first marriage. Dare hadn't been able to forgive Desire. Maybe after she returned from her honeymoon, she'd attempt a reconciliation. She did miss Desire, wanted to share her new-found happiness with her twin, the one person who'd known her best her whole life.

She moved to the small closet in the living-room corner, tugged open the cloth that served as a door and extracted her carry-on. She had only a few things to collect. She wished the unease that kept climbing her throat would go away. Nothing bad was going to happen. She was on the verge of real happiness. Deserved happiness.

Feeling an inexplicable need to hurry, she carted the carry-on into the bathroom, scooped her cosmetics into it, gathered toothbrush and paste, then realized she didn't have her hairbrush. Where was it? She scanned the counter. Hadn't she left it there earlier today? She checked the drawer. Not there either.

Giving up, she went into the bedroom and opened the dresser. Just one thing she wanted here. A gentle breeze grazed her face as she gathered up the brand-new French-bra-and-panty set she'd purchased for the honeymoon and nestled them into the carry-on. She zipped the bag, then debated whether or not to relent and take her favorite comfortable old jeans. Why not? New jeans were nice but took a while to break in.

She crossed to the closet.

Something crunched beneath her feet, staying her hand halfway to the knob of the louvered door. She glanced down. Glass littered the rug. Fear crashed through her. Dear God, the breeze she'd felt. Her gaze flew to the window. The pane was shattered. The frame shoved wide open. She gasped. Was someone here?

The closet door started to open.

With a yelp, she snatched the carry-on, tore through the apartment and outside. She ran to her VW, clambered inside, shaking so hard it took three tries to get the key in the ignition. She locked the doors, punched her fiancé's phone number into the cell phone and hit dial. As he answered, she peeled into traffic, the phone pressed to her ear.

HE BANGED the closet doors open and scrambled up out of the tight space. He raced after her, into the living room. The door slammed in his face, bringing him up short. He stared at it, stunned, shaken. She'd been about to open the closet and welcome him into her life. Acknowledge their relationship. Instead, she'd run away. His heart shrank at her betrayal and fury tightened his grip on the handle of her plastic hairbrush.

He pulled back the curtain. She was in her car, driving away. Away from him. Away from them. Her tiny car was moving too fast, weaving badly, as though she were drunk. As he watched in horror, it veered into the path of a semitruck. "No!"

The collision sounded like a bomb going off. The VW buckled, then burst into flames.

"No!" he screamed, snapping the hairbrush in two. His cries turned to whimpers, then he fell silent. The quiet resonated through the apartment, echoing the loss deep inside his brain. His knees wobbled and he grabbed for support, clutching the desk. He knocked over a gilt frame. He lifted it, gazing at it absently. Two women were caught for posterity with their arms around one another, their smiling faces peered up at him. They were identical. Yet somehow different.

Dare and… He noticed the plaque on the bottom edge. It read, Dare and Desire.

Desire seemed to be smiling at him, offering him comfort and love with that smile. Understanding. Empathy. They had both lost Dare, were both grieving that loss. They should grieve together. Hold each other. Love each other.

As sirens filled the street outside, he broke the glass covering the picture and ran his fingertip down her cheek.

Desire.

Yes. *His Desire.*

Chapter One

Santa Beverly, California—a suburb of Los Angeles County, situated north of Torrence near Santa Monica Bay—seemed a sleepy, peaceful little town, but Deputy District Attorney Desire Hamilton was a living example that looks could be deceiving. She'd learned early on that to beat men at their macho games a woman sometimes had to play underhanded with her feminine wiles. In Desire's case, her name was the biggest asset at her disposal.

Desire, the name given to her by her father, was pronounced exactly as it was spelled—not Desiree—but desire…as in passion.

She'd thought of shortening it to Dee when she started law school, but she'd discovered immediately that if you were a pretty blue-eyed blonde with a name best suited to a stripper, most people underestimated you. She'd used that to her advantage.

Used it still. For despite her name and appearance, two things she owed directly to her parents, she was not a bit of fluff. She considered herself no-nonsense, dedicated, fair-minded. She knew when to take it light and when to come down hard.

And peaceful-looking little Santa Beverly provided

her more than enough crime to prosecute week in and week out. Not that justice always prevailed; today it had taken a direct hit to the heart. Another murderer found not guilty. Cindy Whiting, kindergarten teacher, had been stalked and slain because she'd dared say no to a man. If that were a reason to murder, Desire thought, *she* would have been struck down years ago.

She'd sat at the back of the courtroom, unnoticed by colleagues, and watched Ron Whiting's stunned face when the verdict was read. One of Santa Beverly's best police officers, Ron was Cindy's ex-husband. He and Cindy had remained friends after their divorce. Good friends. Desire had wanted this conviction as badly as Ron. He would be inconsolable.

She understood inconsolable.

This had been the worst ten days of her life—the phone call from the LAPD, the call she'd had to make to her parents, flying to Laredo, the funeral, the wake, dealing with her parents, the whole Hamilton clan, everyone weeping, upset, stunned by the sudden loss of Dare, and she, more shell-shocked than anyone, was the one everyone else leaned on.

She felt ready to collapse from the weight.

She shouldn't have come to the courthouse today, but she'd had to hear the verdict, had to get away from her small house, the four walls closing in on her. She'd thought she'd feel better after the verdict. She felt worse.

She had nothing else to do here today, but she was in no hurry to return home. She needed something to anchor her—perhaps a moment or two alone in her office upstairs.

As she left the heavily populated courtroom floor and entered the elevator, she felt a prickling at her nape, as though someone was watching her, following her with

their eyes. She scanned the crowd. Spotted no one staring. Nerves, she supposed. The verdict. Dare's death.
The awful knowledge that their estrangement could now
never be breached, healed.

A face filled her mind and her pulse tripped. *No, she
wouldn't think of him.* But just the flash of memory
roused all the guilt she felt for the hurt she'd caused her
twin.

On the third floor, she proceeded down the hall to the
district attorney's suite, unlocked the door to her private
office and stepped inside. Her shoe came down on something soft. An envelope. She scooped it up. It was stan-
dard greeting card size, her name printed in plain block
letters as though written by a child. Another expression
of sympathy. She didn't want more pity. She wanted her
sister alive, wanted the rift between them mended,
wanted it never to have happened, wanted back all the
years they'd lost, wanted Dare there for all the years
ahead.

She poked her index finger into the fold of the envelope. The ensuing rip was overridden by a noise in
the doorway. She spun around with a start. Her boss.
She blew out a taut breath.

"I thought you were in Laredo." Everything about
District Attorney Connor Gregg screamed neat-freak,
from his Perez of Rodeo Drive haircut to his gleaming
Italian wingtips. Everything about him commanded attention, from his steely blue eyes, to his ramrod stance
and monochromatic suits. Even his voice, deep and res-
onant, was perfect for the career he'd chosen and rel-
ished.

"It's nice to see you, too, Connor." Desire dropped
the hand holding the card to her side. Her chin shot up,
a reflexive response whenever her emotions threatened

to reduce her to a blubbering female. *Never let them see you sweat. Or cry.* Judd and Marvel Hamilton had wanted her to do more than just survive in a man's world. She swallowed against the dryness in her throat.

"You're on a six-week leave of absence." Connor's tone was not unlike her father's: gruff, chiding. He was a runner, a fat counter, his face lean, all planes and hollows as though the skin was stretched taut over his bones. He was only a couple of years her senior, but his serious nature made him seem much older to Desire. Connor was like the brother she never had. "What are you doing here?"

"I was in the courtroom."

He inhaled noisily. "Complete waste of taxpayers' money."

"Bull. The case was rock solid. Cindy told us he was stalking her."

"Cindy Whiting was our only witness, but dead women can't testify. No matter how much you and I believe Gunderson did her, the case was circumstantial at best. Full of reasonable doubt. You let your emotions carry you on this one, Hamilton. I shouldn't have allowed you to talk me into prosecuting."

Her emotions? Desire gritted her teeth at the insult. If there was one thing she prided herself on it was her ability to control and hide her emotions. At the moment, however, she failed to keep the sarcasm from her voice. "If the passion to see stalkers brought to justice is a sin, then get me to a church before the devil takes me down."

Connor made a face and shook his head, his dark hair remaining undisturbed. "Hamilton, you're one of the best prosecutors I have. We win some, we lose some. We don't get to choose which. Forget Gunderson. He's no longer our concern." The glint in his icy eyes softened with sympathy. "Go home. Grieve for your sister."

Desire was too upset to listen to good advice. "What about the phone calls I've been getting?" *To my private, unlisted number.* "I know Gunderson is making them."

"From jail?" Connor looked unconvinced. "Why would he risk that?"

"How do I know? Maybe it gives him some kind of rush, thinking he can get to me even from behind bars."

"I've heard of stranger things. You have proof, do you? The kind I can use in court?"

"No. But I know it's him. They're the same kind of creepy calls Cindy was getting. I had another last night."

"Did you record it?"

"Yes, but all I got was the usual heavy breathing."

Concern washed Connor's face, softening the normally stern visage. "Gunderson is not the only creep you've indicted, not the only one who might enjoy seeing you end up like Cindy Whiting. I don't have to tell you to be careful, do I?"

She'd known the risks before deciding to become a prosecutor. She'd grown up with a mother and father who devoted time and money helping women and children escape from abusive situations and relationships. Her dream had been to put those abusers, and others like them, behind bars where they belonged. And yes, sometimes accomplishing that put her own well-being at risk. "I'm always careful."

"Yeah, but some heavy breather found out your unlisted phone number. You might consider changing it."

The suggestion irritated Desire. She slapped the edge of the card against her thigh. "If I start running scared every time I successfully prosecute some slimeball, or receive threats from someone under indictment, I might as well hand you my walking papers here and now.''

His expression suggested she was being inappropriately stubborn. He nodded at the envelope she held. ''What's that?''

''A card. Someone must have shoved it under the door.''

His eyebrows knit together in a frown. ''No postmark on it?''

She showed it to him. ''No.''

''Open it.''

Desire didn't like the leery tone that had crept into his voice. She continued tearing the flap where she'd left off.

''I'm sure it's just another sympathy card. I've gotten dozens of—'' She broke off as she tugged the card free and stared at it with lifted eyebrows. ''It—it's a valentine.''

''In April? Who sent it, does it say?''

She opened the card. ''It's signed, 'Your one true love.' ''

Her heart had begun to hammer uneasily.

''I didn't know you were seriously seeing anyone these days,'' Connor said quizzically.

''I'm not.'' There had only ever been one man who'd owned her heart, a man who'd belonged to her sister, a man she would never be with—not even now that Dare was gone. *Especially now that she was gone. He* wouldn't have sent her a valentine. ''I haven't dated anyone in six months.''

''Then who?''

''Gunderson?'' she suggested.

''He was in jail until this morning.''

''He could have delivered it after getting acquitted.''

"Yeah, but when could he have purchased it? They don't sell these in lock-up."

"His lawyer could have bought it for him."

"Yeah, maybe." Connor lifted a clean hankie from his pocket. "Whoever it's from was probably too smart to leave prints on the card or envelope, but I'll have both items dusted anyway. Meanwhile, I want you to go home and pack and get the hell out of town for a while. Rest. Grieve. You're needed here, but not in this condition."

Needed? Desire stepped back at his declaration, bemused. "No one is indispensable, Connor." It was his favorite expression. "You've told me that from the moment I darkened your doorstep, green from law school."

"You were never green, just sassy and smart with a name that belongs on the Hollywood strip."

For the first time in ten days she grinned.

Connor checked his watch. "I'm due in court. Get out of here. Go home. Go away. I'll have the card and envelope sent to the lab."

Though she would never tell him, Connor's suspicions that the card might have been from someone other than Gunderson rattled Desire. She supposed it had something to do with knowing one's enemies. It was the unknown quantity that was dangerous. The last thing she wanted was to have become the target of an obsessed stalker. Like Cindy Whiting. The thought made her stomach roil. Too much coffee and little else, she supposed.

She locked her office and went to the ladies' room. In the mirror, she saw her cheeks were a blotchy red and felt hot to the touch. She dampened a paper towel with cold water, daubed her face and pulled in a wobbly breath, getting a noseful of the awful room deodorizer, some stinky artificial flowery scent unrecognizable from anything in nature. It seemed to press in from all sides, gagging her. Her stomach heaved.

Fresh air. Now. But the room had no window.

She hurried out into the hallway, finding it all but deserted, and moved to the elevator. When it arrived, she stepped to the back wall, gripping the handrail. The doors began to close. A hand snapped between the shrinking gap. Large fingers with grimy black nails wrapped the gleaming chrome. The doors bounced open.

A man appeared as if she'd conjured him with her dark thoughts, an evil man. Cindy Whiting's worst nightmare. He grinned at her, a lopsided, icy-white grin that emphasized every good feature on his handsome face. Some might find it disarming. She found it vile, all the more terrifying for the fact that it seemed just the opposite. He was wiry of build, a few inches taller than she, and moved with a disjointed ease that kept a person off balance. He still wore his trial suit, a dirty-brown gabardine, the same color as his hair. A ruby stud glinted in his left ear.

Ted Gunderson.

Desire's heart kicked. His hard gaze raked scathingly over her. "Well, well, well, the lady D.A. is looking a little green around the gills."

Desire's chin arched a notch higher. She stepped forward, hit the Lobby button and stepped back.

He chuckled, a nasty gloating rumble in his throat. "I told you I was innocent."

"You're as innocent as I am purple."

Ted Gunderson's eyes narrowed and hate flashed at her. "No matter what you think, there is nothing you can do about it now."

She met his gaze, feeling a bit reckless—her emotions

loosened from their usual restraints—not in the mood to pick a fight, but not about to back down from one either.

As the elevator began to descend, Ted leaned close enough for his hot, sour breath to fan her face. "If I was a vindictive man, I'd think about paying you back for everything you put me through."

Desire matched his nasty grin with one of her own. "Since that would give me reason to put you back in jail, please go with your inclinations."

He grinned and dragged an oil-stained finger down her cheek. "I just might take you up on that invitation, sweet Desire."

The elevator slid open on the first floor. Voices and activity intruded. Desire stalked out without looking back, keeping her shoulders squared, her head high. Inside she shook like the ground during a temblor.

She left the building, grateful for the warm, calming sun, and climbed into her car. At the moment, home was the last place she wanted to go, even if it was only to pack. Pack. That's what she'd do. Pick up some boxes and go to Dare's; her belongings needed to be packed and sent to Laredo. Daddy had suggested she hire someone for the dreaded task, but Desire couldn't bear the thought of strangers pawing through her sister's personal belongings.

Checking to make sure Gunderson's old white pickup wasn't following her, she drove out of the parking lot and turned for the freeway. She was soon weaving through the heavy traffic, eastbound toward Hollywood. She arrived half an hour later in the rundown section of L.A.

In the three years Dare had resided here, Desire had visited only twice. She'd tried to make amends. Dare had refused to speak to her. She should have tried again…and again, kept trying until she'd made her sister listen.

She carried the boxes along the breezeway, past neglected flower beds, over a walkway that was cracked and grooved from years of wear and numerous earthquakes.

The Pacific Palms had started out as a secluded getaway for movie-industry hotshots and their paramours. As L.A. spread her greedy arms in all directions, encroaching even here, the retreat had lost its allure. The rich and adulterous found other playgrounds for infidelity.

Eventually, the Palms—as it was called by locals—was sold, the individual cottages expanded and linked into an apartment complex that looked as though a child had shoved all her dollhouses into a heap and glued them together.

Actually, the effect was not without charm, even if the stucco was a dingy yellowed-white, the roofs and window wells a darker, indefinable color that might once have been a brilliant red.

Desire got a key from the landlady.

THE SOUND of the front door opening stilled his hand on the silken lingerie. His pulse kicked a notch higher. He swore under his breath and eased the drawer shut. He was trapped. Had to hide. But where? The bed? No, too short. The bathroom? No, he'd be seen crossing to it. He spun around. The closet.

He shoved the dresses to one side and wriggled into the cramped space. Gingerly, he maneuvered the louvered door shut. Hunched over, his shoulders feeling as if they were in a vise, he peered through the slats and waited, breathing shallowly.

The flowery scent Dare had been promoting at the time of her death floated into his nostrils, the fragrance as stirring as some long-forgotten memory. God, he wished he could forget, but some memories lingered forever.

Feminine footsteps clicked tentatively through the living room and into the bedroom. All he could see was the top of a blond head and slender arms hugging some cardboard boxes. She came through the doorway, immediately turning her back on him as she dropped the boxes onto the bed.

Relief swept him. She seemed to be alone. Hopefully she'd do whatever she'd come for quickly and leave. Ignoring the ache in his shoulder blades, he breathed shallowly as he gave her shapely backside an appreciative once-over. She was wearing a short skirt and high heels that did great things for her legs, and his libido.

Then the woman moved slightly, giving him the full force of her profile. Shock jammed the length of him.

Desire!

He swore to himself. He should have realized from the boxes. She was the logical one to pack up Dare's belongings. Hell. That also meant the dresses in this closet. It was only a matter of minutes before she discovered him. He imagined a wild scenario, Desire opening the closet, spotting him, screaming an ear-piercing shriek like some human alarm system…even after her mind relayed the message that he wasn't some psycho killer of women.

Someone would either come to her aid, or when she calmed down she'd throw him out without hearing him out. Neither idea appealed to him nor fit his plans.

She began emptying the contents of the chest of drawers into a box. He eased the closet door open and stepped silently from its depths. He caught Desire by the shoulders, spun her toward him. Her eyes were wide with terror, but as he yanked her close, her pliant curves melding his hard length as though she were a missing piece of his anatomy, he saw the terror slipping into stunned recognition.

As he'd predicted, a scream was rolling off her tongue. His mouth found hers, effectively squelching her cry for help.

This woman needed no help subduing him.

Kissing her was doing that…as it always had.

Chapter Two

As though she'd lit a fire in his veins, his blood began to heat, growing thick and heavy, turning him stone hard and breathless and senseless.

D didn't struggle in his arms, instead he felt her hand go to her side, and sweet anticipation swished through him. It was followed by the worst pain he'd ever felt— her knee connecting with his groin.

Nick Rossetti released his former sister-in-law and stumbled back, clutching himself, trying to maintain some dignity while sinking to his knees, groaning. He should have known she wouldn't tolerate his brash approach. Should have expected retaliation. But every time he was near her he lost whatever good sense God had given him and ended up pissing her off.

Eventually, he glanced up at her. "I probably deserved a slap in the face, but was *this* really necessary, D?"

She sounded as out of breath as he. Her cheeks were rosy, her lips swollen. He felt his good sense slipping again…then realized her eyes blazed not with lust, but fury. It took him a moment more to register that she was aiming something eye level at him. He swore silently. Pepper spray. Her thumb tapped the pressure valve.

"What are you doing here, Nick?" she said.

"Don't discharge that thing!" Nick held out his palm to ward off her attack, not doubting for a minute that she would use the pepper spray on him if he pulled another fresh move. "Okay, look…I'm…ah…"

"Yes…?" Her voice was sweet, the steel beneath it as subtle as a stiletto heel slicing over his nerves. "Go ahead. Convince me not to reduce you to a weeping mass of masculinity."

"There's no need to act rashly."

"Why are you sneaking around Dare's apartment?"

"I'm not sneaking." She knew damn good and well that he was an LAPD detective. "This is my case."

"Case? Dare's death was an *accident*." As she said this last, he saw her confidence falter. "Wasn't it?"

"That's the official line."

"Then why would homicide need to investigate an accident?"

He ignored her question, asking one of his own. "Had she spoken to you lately, told you she was nervous about…anything?"

D blanched. "No. She was *still* not speaking to me, thank *you* very much."

He blinked at the dig. Dare had been estranged from her whole family thanks to him. He felt bad enough about it without being reminded every time he saw D. But maybe that was why he wanted to find out all he could about what had happened to Dare, to make up to her in some small way the hurt he'd caused her, caused her family. He glanced away from D.

"What was Dare nervous about?" she demanded. "Obviously you know, or have an idea, or you wouldn't have asked."

He dug his hand through his thick raven hair, lifted

his gaze from the pepper container and stood, gazing down at D. She wouldn't give up until he leveled with her. "There is no official homicide investigation. No investigation at all."

"You're doing this on your own?"

"That's right."

She blew out an exasperated breath. "Why? What the hell do you hope to prove?"

"I don't know exactly. I guess I'm trying to understand why it happened. So, I'm checking on...a few things."

"Like?"

"Well, like that shattered bedroom window." She looked where he pointed. "The glass is on the inside, which means it was broken from the outside. The sash was raised and there are marks on the sill that appear to have been made from a shoe or boot."

"You think someone broke in here?"

"Yeah, I do."

"Some ghoul who read about her death in the papers and wanted souvenirs?" She winced as she said this, the thought repulsive.

"Not really. Nothing has been taken as far as I can tell. Nothing the *normal abnormal* fan would covet." He waved his hand to emphasize his point. "Not her underwear, her dresses, T-shirts, shoes or her hairbrush—which is on the floor in the other room, broken in half, and still has some strands of her hair caught in the bristles."

D's face had gotten whiter with each item he ticked off as she obviously drew conclusions similar to his own.

He continued, "I've been trying to understand what would have had Dare in such a tear that she'd been so reckless as to pull out into traffic without looking."

"*That's* what witnesses claim she did?"

"Yes. They say she ran to her car as though the devil himself were after her, and veered into traffic with her cell phone pressed to her ear."

"You think she was running from someone in this apartment?"

"According to her fiancé, Michael Pride, that's exactly what she was doing."

"*That's* who she was speaking to at the time of the accident?"

Nick nodded. "Have you met him?"

"No. I heard about him for the first time last week." She had that accusatory look again. "In the tabloids."

He'd seen those papers, all with varying headlines on the same theme: Bride-To-Be Dies On Way To Elopement.

She said, "He wasn't at the funeral, but he sent a huge wreath of yellow roses, Dare's favorite. As far as I know he's spoken to no one in the family. Where did she meet him? At his place in Santa Barbara?"

She would know from the tabloids that Pride was a restaurateur, his bar and grill one of the elite Santa Barbara eateries. He shook his head. "No. They met at a divorce survivors' meeting put on by the counselor Dare was seeing after our divor…" He trailed off. Why did everything he said to D raise the wall between them a notch higher?

"Dare was seeing a counselor?" She lifted her eyebrows, genuinely surprised, and he could see she was hating the constant surprises. Hating that she and her sister had grown so far apart that they were strangers at her death. "Who?"

"Breena Falls. She's a shrink of some note."

"Psychologist," D corrected. "I've never met her, but

I've heard of her. Area police departments send officers to her after a shooting or burnout. She's on the payroll of the Santa Beverly P.D.''

"LAPD, too."

D refolded a sweater she'd taken from the drawer, smoothing her hand over it as though it were the last time she'd be petting a favorite cat. "I'd think the LAPD would keep her in business full-time."

"She's not the only shrink they use."

"Of course." She shut the empty drawer and opened the next. "Was Dare seeing her privately as well as in the divorce survivors' sessions?"

"Yes."

She drew a shaky breath. "What about Michael Pride?"

"What do you mean?"

"Was Pride also seeing the doctor privately?"

"Oh." He shrugged. "I don't know. He didn't volunteer that information."

"Can you find out?"

"Why?"

"I just want to know more about him." She glanced up from her task, pushing her hair back from her face. Her eyes were sad, full of grief. His heart wrenched for her. "I've called him a few times over the past few days, but he's always unavailable and, though I've left my numbers, has yet to return any of my calls. I assume his reluctance to speak to me is because of Dare's and my estrangement, but maybe it's something else."

"He's been eager enough to talk to me." Nick wanted to touch her, hold her, take her grief into himself and away from her, wanted to make her accept his apology, and to finally forgive herself. "He seems genuinely upset about her death."

She nodded as though grateful to hear that Dare had found someone who apparently really loved her. "What exactly did he tell you about the day she died?"

"He said Dare called him from her car seconds before the accident. She was hysterical. Said someone was in her apartment and then the line went—" He broke off, realizing the crassness of what he'd almost said. "They were cut off."

"Was it Pride who told you Dare had been nervous about something lately?"

"Yes."

"Did he say what or who, in particular, was making her uneasy?"

Nick grinned. She was too good at turning the tables on him, questioning him when he'd intended on being the one asking the questions. "You and I always did make a great pair."

The pepper spray reappeared in her hand as if by magic. "Don't go there, Nick. We were never a pair of anything. We were nothing more than a moment of mistaken identity and a heady dose of lust that you seem to think entitles you to attack me whenever we meet."

"We belong together, D." Why couldn't he convince her of this? God knew he'd been trying for three years.

"We broke my sister's heart."

"It was a damn kiss." He leaned closer to her, pulled by some magnetic lure he couldn't deny. "That's all."

Her cheeks flared red, and he knew she was remembering, too. Remembering how good that kiss had been. How revealing. "That kiss ruined your marriage. I can't forgive either of us for that. Neither could Dare."

She went back to emptying the dresser, transferring Dare's clothes to the boxes on the bed. He leaned against the door frame and watched her. He wanted to wring her beautiful, stubborn neck. They hadn't committed adultery. He'd grabbed her—thinking she was Dare, not knowing Dare had a twin sister.

Dare and he had met in Nuevo Laredo, across the Mexican-American border from Laredo, at Pepe's, a favorite watering hole for him and his pals. Dare had waltzed in looking hotter than Pepe's tamales, a couple of girlfriends in tow, and the party was on. He and she had paired off. Soon, someone, he couldn't recall who, was taunting Dare, challenging her about her name. Asking whether she was coward or daredevil.

It seemed to touch off something wild in her. One thing led to another, mixed with too many tequilas, and they found themselves married.

He still could not explain how or why he'd gone along with it. Stupid, stupid move. Not thinking with his brains, that was for sure. They knew almost nothing about one another and had spent the wedding night engaged in pursuits that hadn't involved clearing up that situation.

The next morning, she'd brought him to the Hamilton ranch outside Dallas to meet the family. Dare had said she had a surprise for him. Unfortunately, he'd surprised her.

Surprised them all.

The moment his lips had met D's, he'd felt something that hadn't ever happened to him before…or since. He'd fallen head over heels in love. With his wife, he'd thought. But he hadn't been kissing his wife. The woman in his arms had felt it, too—that thunderbolt through the heart.

Dare had seen it on their faces. He'd leveled with her. It was the right thing, no matter how painful for them all. They couldn't live a lie. Dare was a great gal. She deserved better than he'd given her. He was sorry as hell. Wouldn't have hurt her for the world. But he had wounded her deeply.

He'd tried apologizing…to the whole Hamilton family. Granted, it was a hell of a mess, but he'd figured they'd be able to work through it someday.

D had seen it differently. She wouldn't answer his calls, even when the divorce was final. It was not as though they had had an affair, gone behind Dare's back. Nor was it as though either of them had meant for it to happen. It just had.

She glanced up at him. "Why don't you go investigate or something?"

"Do I make you nervous, D?" *Do I get under your skin? The way you get under mine?*

She glared at him. "Leave me alone, Nick."

She asked the impossible. He could no more leave her alone than he could stop eating, stop breathing. What he couldn't seem to do was make her accept that they were meant to be together. Especially now that Dare was dead. While she lived, there had been the hope that the three of them might one day work through their guilt and pain. But now, they were further apart than ever.

He fought the urge to go to her. He had to respect her request. She wanted him to stay away. He feared he wasn't that strong, not when just looking at her had his good senses slipping and his resolve weakening, but by God, he would try. Not because he wanted it, but because she did.

He strode away, leaving her to the packing. He stood in the kitchen/living room for a few minutes, centering his equilibrium, concentrating on the reasons he'd come here in the first place. The main thing he noticed was the smell, a damp, mildewy odor. The furniture was all secondhand junk.

Having refused financial help from her parents and Nick, Dare had had little money when she'd moved to Los Angeles, or during the immediate years following as she struggled to get noticed in a town and in an industry with more hopefuls than jobs. But why hadn't she moved out of this dump the minute she signed the contract to be the spokesperson for Dare To Love perfume? Maybe *that* was another question for Dr. Falls, or for Michael Pride. Come to that, why hadn't Pride insisted his fiancée move in with him, given that she suspected someone was stalking her?

Too many questions. Too few answers. How much, if any of it, was his business? He didn't care. He had to know. Had to understand what had happened to Dare. *To clear your conscience?*

He ignored the tiny voice in his head and glanced at the desk. She'd probably taken her personal papers with her, but it couldn't hurt to check. As he strode to it, a glint of light poked his eye. The sun, angling in through a gap in the curtains, had reflected off something. Chips of glass.

For a moment, he thought the glass might be from the window in the other room, then he spotted a chrome photograph frame facedown on the desktop. He lifted it. The glass was broken, the frame empty. Someone had removed the picture. Dare? There was a plaque at the bottom etched with D's and Dare's names.

Nick frowned. Despite the fact that she'd stopped speaking to her twin, Dare had kept a frame with both of their names on it, kept that frame on this desk. A woman who'd done that would not likely have left the frame empty or smashed the glass to remove the picture.

So, who had? The intruder? Had he also taken the photograph? Maybe. There was every hybrid pervert known to man roaming the world these days, a good number of whom called L.A. home. But why a photograph and nothing else? Had he taken it for a trophy, like a serial killer, or because he was grieving Dare's loss, never appreciating his part in her death? Either way, it was grisly.

He didn't want D to see it. At least not yet. And he'd like to dust it for prints. He opened the top drawer, thinking to hide the frame and glass. The drawer was empty, except for a card.

He lifted it, staring at the romantic images and words. Likely from Pride, of sentimental value only to Dare. It was signed "Your one true love."

He heard a gasp and pivoted. She had crept up on him and was gaping at the card as though it were a ghost. "D," he asked. "What is it?"

"That valentine." She was as pale as the envelope still nestled in the drawer. "I received one this morning exactly like it."

Chapter Three

"What kind of cupid sends valentines in April?" Nick was incredulous, all warmth gone from his dark-chocolate eyes.

Desire felt a shiver down her spine as though a cold wind had blown through the stuffy, musty-smelling room. "That's what my boss and I wondered. He's having the one I received fingerprinted."

Nick had collected the envelope from the drawer and was examining it. "Was yours addressed by hand, like this?"

Dare's name was written in block printing, the lettering similar to that on the valentine left under her office door. "Yes."

"You've no idea who might have sent it?"

She shook her head. "None."

"And we've no way of knowing when this was sent to Dare. Wonder if she mentioned it to Pride."

"You don't think he sent it?"

"I'm not ready to eliminate him as a possibility, but it doesn't seem likely he'd have sent its twin to you."

"What are you suggesting?"

"Pride said Dare thought someone was watching her, stalking her." Nick's full mouth tightened and the tiny creases on either side deepened. He had a sharp mind, a high "case-solved rate," and he was an expert at deciding which two should be added to an original two to reach four. She felt exposed beneath his stare. She wasn't prepared for his question. "Have you been having the same experience?"

"No." Denial sprang from her, but she knew she'd responded too quickly, could see Nick thought the same. *What about the sensation that someone had been watching her in the courthouse that morning? What about the heavy-breather phone calls to her private, unlisted phone?* Were they from Gunderson, the jerk in the elevator? Or was she wrong about that? Was someone else making those calls—that "unknown factor" she'd pondered earlier? Was the same person who'd stalked Dare now stalking her?

She didn't know what to think. Or how much to tell Nick. She did not want *him* involved, not in any way. "I've prosecuted some angry men in my three years in California, some for stalking. It's possible someone has a grudge against me and would try to scare me with, say, spooky phone calls...or something."

His eyebrows arched. "Some pervert has been making spooky phone calls to you, D?"

Oh, damn. She didn't want Nick concerned. She didn't want him worrying about her. Deciding to protect her. The last thing she needed was Nick Rossetti sticking to her like Velcro. She couldn't trust him. Couldn't trust her traitorous body near him. Like now. She thought again of his kiss and felt a long tug of yearning, a deep thrust of passion, a sharp stab of guilt, of shame. No. She *would* not build happiness on her sister's heartache. "Just some late-night heavy breather. Nothing serious. Nothing to warrant that look in your eyes."

"And yet, someone has sent the same valentine, in probably the same handwriting, to you and your sister and signed both 'Your one true love.' It has to mean something, D, probably something bad."

"Don't look for devils where there are none."

"Oh, I'd say there's a devil here all right—one who imagined Dare was in love with him." He looked at her with worried eyes. "One who apparently now imagines *you* are in love with him."

She shook her head and stepped away from Nick as though putting distance between them would put the lie to his supposition. "That's crazy."

"Yes, it is. That's what worries me."

She felt riveted. Immobile. It couldn't be true. She couldn't have attracted the attention of some pervert who had been stalking Dare. That didn't even make sense.

"There are such people, D," Nick said as though he'd read her thoughts. "Dr. Breena Falls might give us a line on this one. I think I'll talk to her about this valentine. You want to come along?"

"Yes, but only because I want to hear her tell you that you're wrong." But how could he be wrong? She couldn't deny that she'd received the very same valentine in an envelope addressed in a similar script. Desire felt a twinge of real fear, and wondered if this was what Cindy Whiting had felt, what Dare had felt.

Nick held the door open, waiting for her to move.

She glanced back toward the bedroom, then at this man who haunted her dreams and was now slipping on the cloak of knight in shining armor with an ease that made her wince. Despite what he thought, he was not going to control this situation. She couldn't risk that. "We also need these envelopes to be compared by a handwriting expert."

"Sure." He nodded hard and a lock of his too long, raven hair swept his tanned forehead, giving him a mussed, boyish look. His black eyebrows lowered to ebony slashes above intense brown eyes. His gleaming white teeth caught at his lower lip. Her heart beat faster at the memory of his lips on hers... No.

"And," she added, swallowing hard as she tore her gaze from his mouth, that damn tempting mouth, "we need to tell the landlord about that broken window. I want it boarded up before we leave. I don't want to risk some of those 'normal abnormal' fans you mentioned getting in here and ripping the place off—not until I've packed all of Dare's personal things. Then they'll be welcome to the rest of this junk."

LORELEI COLLINS, manager of the Pacific Palms, was a reed-thin black woman with shoulder-length microbraids and a mouthful of perfect white teeth. She'd been startled when she opened the door to Desire an hour or so ago, perhaps thinking she was face-to-face with a ghost, but a light had quickly dawned in her eyes and she'd exclaimed, "Oh, yer the sister."

Her unschooled voice had held none of the disdain Desire half expected from everyone who knew or was close to Dare, and she'd been oddly relieved. Perhaps Dare hadn't told *everyone* that her sister had ruined her marriage. Perhaps only Desire's guilt made it feel as though she had.

Lorelei yanked the door to her apartment open; the sounds of her television blasted into the hot afternoon. She appeared to think Desire was back to return Dare's key, but when she saw Desire wasn't alone, she moved into the open doorway like a guard taking up a post, her eyes narrowing on Nick. The stench of fried fish clung to her shorts and halter top.

Nick flashed his police badge, and Lorelei reached back, snagged the doorknob and tugged the door closer to her backside. "Somethin' wrong?"

Desire frowned. Lorelei was the one acting as though something was wrong. Chances were, however, that it had nothing to do with Dare, but with the woman's own distrust of police. She'd seen this often enough and wished Nick had kept his ID in his pocket. They could have questioned the woman without being official about it. Why had he done that? Habit? Because he wanted to play by the rules?

It galled her that he couldn't play by the rules with her, that he always crossed the line, acted on emotion, ignored propriety…and her repeated warnings to keep his distance. But she supposed what bothered her most was her response to his advances. How could she blame Nick when she apparently kept sending him mixed signals?

Nick told Lorelei about the broken window. Lorelei cursed. "Now who gone and done that?"

"We were hoping you could clear that up." Nick's voice was low, but his tone held suspicion, a reaction, Desire suspected, to the landlady's guarded behavior.

Lorelei bristled. "The Palms mightn't meet yer high standards, mister cop man, but I got my ethics and one of 'em is not snoopin' on neighbors."

"I assumed in your official duty as the landlady—" Nick's neck was growing red, not from the unrelenting sun, but from anger "—that you might have been over there to check out the place since Ms. Hamilton's accident."

"Forgive my tall, dark and *dense* friend." Desire

smiled sweetly at them both, trying to put the woman at ease, trying to get through to Nick to back off a bit. "He doesn't mean we think you *know* who did it. We just wondered if maybe you'd noticed anyone snooping around Dare or her apartment?"

Lorelei studied her for a moment, then seemed to accept her apology. "You talkin' 'bout that Eager Eddie...or the other 'un?"

"The other one?" Nick prodded, gently this time.

Desire's breath caught. Suppositions were one thing, but hearing that there actually was a man who might have been stalking her sister, who might be stalking *her,* a man that this person had seen and might be able to identify, raised gooseflesh across every inch of her. On the other hand, perhaps Lorelei held the key to their finding him, having him arrested, prosecuted, if necessary, and this whole nightmare would end.

"That day she had the axkident," Lorelei drawled, "some dude was here askin' 'bout her. Han'some. Ya know? Like he mighta been in one of 'em commercials of hers. I figured mebbe that was what he was doin' here, but he looked like I'd 'sinuated he was a condom salesman 'stead of a actor, and hurried off."

"What did the guy look like?" Nick asked.

She shook her head as though she understood why Desire had called him dense. "*I said* he was han'some."

Nick blew out a breath, and Desire could see he was grappling with his patience again. "Yes, but how tall was he? Was he Caucasian, Latino, African-American, Asian, Native American, what?"

"Oh." She squinted, pondering that. "Guess he was white of some kind. Wore a cap so as I couldn't see his hair, and dark glasses. 'Em mirrored ones like pilots use." She looked pleased with herself at this last detail.

"So, you couldn't see his eyes either," Desire pointed out.

She frowned. "Don't s'pose so."

"But you could tell he was handsome?" Nick's tone rang with sarcasm, his bleak opinion of eyewitnesses stark on his face.

Desire didn't blame him, but she believed this woman could help. The Unibomber had been disguised, but they'd caught him based on a sketch. "Could you describe this man for a police artist?"

"Ya mean go down to the po-leece station…?" Her eyes widened and she shook her head. "Oh, I don't know 'bout that."

Nick ran his hand through his hair. The heat was getting to them both, not to mention the frustration. "Don't you want the vandal who broke into Ms. Hamilton's apartment caught?"

"Why?" Lorelei shifted her weight from one narrow hip to the other, her gaze darting between them. "You said he didn't do nothin' 'cept bust the window. Right?"

"That's correct," Nick answered.

Lorelei eyed him with disdain. "Well, then, lest he fixes windows fer a livin', what good is catchin' him to me?"

Nick looked ready to blow a gasket. Desire touched his arm, catching his attention, cutting off any retort he might have been going to make. Keeping her voice gentle, she asked, "Have you seen this man since Dare died?"

Lorelei wiped sweat from her forehead and considered for a while. "Nope. Only 'un I seen is that popper-ratzy scuzzer Dare called Eager Eddie."

Eager Eddie. Hearing this name a second time brought back a memory of an old boyfriend Dare had dubbed Eager Eddie after breaking up with him. He'd had a thing for cameras, too. "Tell me about this Eager Eddie."

"Oh, he was followin' her everwhere. All the time snappin' pictures, makin' her nuts. He was here the day she died. The next day, too. That's how the Palms ended up in the *Celebrity Crier*."

"Is Eddie his real name?" Nick asked, looking hopeful as he dragged out a hand-size notebook from his pocket.

Lorelei shrugged. "Yer guess is good as mine."

"What does he look like?" Nick pressed.

"Shorter than you. 'Bout as tall as her." She pointed to Desire. "A scuzzer wit' oily black hair pokin' out from a hat looks like a towel and cameras hangin' 'round his neck."

"An Arab?" Definitely not Dare's other Eddie. "East Indian?"

"I guess." She shrugged again.

"Any facial hair?"

"Huh?"

"Beard? Mustache?"

"Oh, yes. A nasty bushy thang hang clear down to here." Lorelei touched the middle of her chest and shuddered. "Looks lice-infested."

"Is that all you remember?"

"Well, I recollect what Dare said 'bout him."

"What was that?"

She scrunched her sharp features into a thoughtful expression. "If'n Eager Eddie comed back, I was to tell him I was callin' the cops. But I tole her that ya can't call the cops on a guy ain't doin' ya no harm. Now, if'n he beat ya up or killed ya—" she glanced pointedly at

Nick "—well, then, the cops'd be more'n happy to help. Right, mister cop man?"

Nick didn't answer, and Lorelei smirked, then continued, "She tole me, 'In that case, if'n he shows up again, shoot him.'" Lorelei flinched at her own words. "Not that I got no gun or nothin'. But I tole her, if'n I shoot that scuzzer the cops'd come help *me* off to jail."

Nick made a disgusted face and shoved his tablet back into his shirt pocket. "Thank you, Ms. Collins. If we think of anything else, we'll be back."

Desire thanked her, too, then said, "Would you please have that bedroom window boarded up or fixed right away?"

"'Course I will. Tha's my job."

"Dr. Falls can spare us ten minutes at five. We should make it with fifteen minutes to spare." Nick put his cell phone away and concentrated on his driving.

Desire sat beside him, lost in thought, trying to make sense of everything she'd learned today. *Had a stalker scared Dare so badly he'd precipitated her accident?* The possibility sickened her.

Dare had never had *her* courage. *Her nerve. Her sass. Her survivor's instincts.* Dare's biggest asset was her shyness, the reason she loved being someone else and probably why she would have succeeded as an actor. But in the real world this weakness served her ill, may have contributed to her death.

And now that same stalker might be after me.

No. Supposition was not fact. She knew better than to leap at some half-baked hypothesis and run with it. If she was being stalked—and, as far as she was concerned, that was a mighty big "if" at this point—she would deal with it differently than Dare. Differently than Cindy Whiting. *She would not end up dead.*

Suppressing a shudder, she asked, "What do you think the chances are that we can find this Eager Eddie?"

He glanced at her. "Why would we want to?"

"Because it occurs to me that if he was at the Palms the day Dare died, he may have inadvertently snapped a photo of the stalker."

"Good point." He sounded impressed. "Between the two of us, we might use our official pull to get the *Crier* to cough up his name...maybe even an address. They have to send the checks somewhere."

The Falls Clinic loomed ahead, a large black pyramid—three walls of black glass rising four stories into the smog-heavy air. They parked in the lot behind it and stepped out into the hazy heat. Nick walked close to her, leaning down near her ear. She could smell his aftershave. Her throat tightened. He said, "What do you make of this?"

It took a moment for Desire to realize he meant the building and not her reaction to him. She dared not look at him for fear he would see in her eyes the need he roused in her. "It seems to me that it might be a clue to the doctor herself. Maybe she believes in all methods of healing, ancient and New Age, and wants to use every possible mode available to ensure her patients' mental health."

"You have such wonderful insight into others, D. Why don't you use that on our situation?"

She ignored his question and pushed through the double doors into the cool lobby, grateful that the doors swishing shut had cut out the cruel outside glare, encapsulated them in a marble and glass tower, and silenced her yearning for a man she could not have, should not want.

There was no receptionist at the outer office desk, but the door to Dr. Falls's office was open. They peered inside. The furnishings were all clean lines and subdued hues undoubtedly selected to allow her patients to focus on their problems instead of their surroundings. A woman with red hair sat behind a wide desk. She glanced up as Nick called her name and ushered Desire in.

Breena Falls had clear gray eyes and the kind of movie-star beauty that is rarely nature-given, but can be bought from any good plastic surgeon through several long, painful, expensive operations. Even wrapped in professional demeanor, she was the warmest thing in her air-conditioned offices.

Her gaze fell on Desire, searing through her layers of self-protective defenses, exposing her sins for exhibit to anyone who cared to look. Was it the doctor's personality? Or did the sensation come from knowing that Dare had confided to this person her most private thoughts and heartaches—confidences she'd once shared with Desire—every detail of the destruction of her marriage, every transgression Desire had committed against the sister she had loved and would forever miss?

The doctor said, "It is startling, your resemblance. Of course, I knew Dare was an identical twin, but one is seldom prepared for meeting their friend's double."

Friend was an odd choice to label a patient, in Desire's opinion. She moved toward the woman who stood behind an enormous desk, an arboretum at her back. The sound of a gentle waterfall issued from somewhere overhead. It was as though they'd stepped onto a remote tropical island, and Desire suspected the building was soundproofed against the traffic noises on the busy streets outside. "Was Dare your 'friend'?"

"I like my patients to consider me their friend. It seems less restrictive that way, puts them at ease." Her smile gave the impression that this woman was kind and honest and gentle and open, but the light in those gray eyes was cool, the heat not reaching that high, giving Desire the impression it was all a facade, that Dr. Breena Falls was as warm and fake as a gas log.

The doctor turned her smile on Nick. "Detective Rossetti, why is your name so familiar? Have I seen you before...perhaps, professionally?"

"No." Nick waited a beat, then added, "Maybe Dare mentioned me? I was her ex-husband."

The doctor's pleasant expression faltered for a second. She didn't like surprises, Desire noted. Breena said, "I'm sorry to offer you such a short amount of time, but I have another session in half an hour and I need to eat before the meeting." She motioned for them to take the two low-slung leather chairs facing her desk.

The doctor asked, "Now, how may I help you?"

Desire leaned forward in her chair, feeling as though the doctor's huge desk was a moat between them, that it had been selected for the purpose of keeping a distance between the doctor and her "friends." She said, "We think Dare was being stalked."

Nick showed her the valentine and envelope that he'd placed in large evidence bags, and asked if she knew anything about who might have sent them to Dare.

The doctor shook her head and sighed wistfully. "Obsessive fans are a hazard for celebrities these days, and Dare was definitely a celebrity. Her face on billboards, in magazines. Her commercial airing constantly on television."

"You knew about the stalker?" Nick asked.

"Let's say I'm not surprised, but I cannot tell you anything about Dare's sessions with me. That is privileged information."

"We understand that. But we hoped—"

"I'm a touch confused, Detective." She cut Nick off, staring at him exclusively. "I believe Dare told me you were with the LAPD homicide division. Is that correct?"

"Yes."

"I understood she died in a traffic accident. Is that wrong?"

"No."

Breena studied him. "Then, why are you doing what I can only call investigating?"

Nick blanched, as though it had only just occurred to him that the doctor might inform his boss he was misusing his authority. Would she?

"Because." Desire spared him from answering. "I hoped you might appreciate a family's need, a twin's need to comprehend everything that was going on that led up to Dare's accident."

She gazed at Desire for a long moment, her expression practiced sympathy. "I'm sorry. I really cannot help you. Now, if you'll excuse me."

She started to stand. Desire said, "Please, we just want to know whether or not Dare told you someone was stalking her and if she knew who it was."

The doctor shook her head, the sympathetic look deepening. "I repeat, my sessions with your sister were confidential. I will not tell you more than that."

Desire rose and leaned across the desk. "We think this man, whoever he was, broke into Dare's apartment. We think he frightened her so badly he precipitated her accident."

The doctor stood, the "I'm sorry" smile plastered on her perfect face, walking to the door, dismissing them, their ten minutes over, counted to the second. "I cannot help you."

"But you must." Nick called after the doctor. "We think this creep is now focusing on Desire."

HE PULLED into the parking-lot space and turned off his car. His gaze skipped to the couple coming down the steps of the Falls Clinic. *It couldn't be. It was. Desire.* His pulse hammered against his temples. It was a sign, an omen. Or was it? Confusion crashed through his certainty, through his excitement at this chance encounter. What was she doing here? Had she learned somehow that he was a patient at the clinic?

The throbbing at his temples began to ache. Even if she had discovered that, Dr. Falls wouldn't tell her anything about him. Confidentiality was the doctor's mantra.

He shifted his gaze to the large, strong-looking man beside Desire. Anger licked through the man in the car, a hot disturbing flame. How dare that jackal glance at *his Desire* in a proprietorial manner? How dare the fiend try to keep Desire from *him*?

Why did being with the one he loved—the one who loved him—always present a challenge?

Perhaps he would ask Dr. Falls that in their session today.

But for now, all he could do was stare at Desire, unaware that his hands white-knuckled the steering wheel. God, she was beautiful. She turned and in that flash of an instant her gaze met his, and she smiled—that same smile in the photograph on the seat beside him—reassuring him, acknowledging him…*acknowledging them*.

He savored the moment, drawing the warmth of it into

his cold, empty heart. Letting it fill him. He ached to leap out, to rush to Desire, to offer his condolences over their mutual loss, to knock the interloper to the ground, to smash his smug handsome face with the heel of his shoes.

Then take Desire into his arms. *She belonged to him!*

Her being here was all the proof he needed that she felt the same way about him that he felt about her. After all, he'd been to her house in Santa Beverly, to her office at the courthouse, but he'd found her at neither place. He'd wanted to stay at her house and wait for her, but he didn't have that option. He couldn't afford to alter his routine so much it gave others reason to question his comings and goings, his whereabouts.

Who he loved was *his* business.

He made a decision, dialed a number on his cell phone. A woman answered, "The Falls Clinic."

He identified himself and apologized for canceling his appointment at such late notice, was told how much it would cost him, and laughed. "Cheap at half the price."

He hung up and started his car, following Desire and the man, merging into traffic behind them. Desire was *his*. No one else's. Anyone who tried to keep them apart—including the guy in that car with her—would be eliminated, permanently. Fatally.

"Soon, my sweet Desire. Soon."

Chapter Four

"I can't believe she wouldn't tell us anything," Desire grumbled. They were back in Nick's car, with him careening crazily through the early-evening traffic. The days were getting longer, staying light later. She was angled toward Nick, tension gripping her limbs as she vented. "Not that I expected her to violate her professional ethics, but couldn't she have at least confirmed that she knew this guy existed?"

"She did. Not in words, but that phony grin of hers slipped a dimple when you said we thought Dare was being stalked. She knew it, all right. But if she knows or suspects who he is, she won't cough it up—not without official documents that no judge is going to sign for us on what we have to offer as cause."

She hated this. Her sister's stalker might have decided to come after *her* and she had no "cause," no legal recourse or action. At least, not yet. "*If* it pans out there *is* a stalker after me, I'll approach a couple of judges I know who happen to respect me professionally, each of whom owes me a favor."

"I could use a favor, myself. Especially if Dr. Falls decides to call my boss and put a bug in his ear about the unofficial little visit we paid her." He turned to face her; his expression had lost some of its usual cockiness.

She almost felt sorry for him. Almost. "You're a big boy, Rossetti. You had to have weighed the risks when you decided to involve yourself in finding the cause of Dare's accident."

"Touché." A sheepish grin dug deep attractive grooves along both sides of his sensuous mouth. "I'm not good at following convention, D."

"Are you saying you color outside the lines, Rossetti? That the good and wise homicide detective stretches the rules to suit his needs at any given moment?"

His cheeks seemed to tighten as though she'd struck a nerve. He said grimly, "It's not that simple. Nothing is black and white."

"Really?" She was surprised. He was a cop, dedicated to upholding the letter of the law. Wasn't he? What didn't she know about him? Why did she care? "How do you decide what falls into that gray area?"

"I play it by ear." He dropped the dour expression, flashing a wicked, teasing grin meant, she suspected, to put her off.

Despite that suspicion, her body reacted with a warm tingling through her lower belly, a quickening of her heartbeat. "I guess that explains your impulsive nature...."

The way you're always grabbing me and kissing me.

They were stopped at a traffic light. Nick reached across to her, touched her hair, his gaze a sensuous caress. "Let's be friends, D."

His fingers brushed her cheek and the tingling in her belly flared to a delicious heat. She flinched, shifting away from him, jamming herself against the door, her back toward him. That was when she realized he was not driving her to her car. "Where are you going, Nick? Dare's apartment is in the opposite direction."

"It's dinnertime and even tough lady deputy D.A.'s have to eat."

She rounded on him, anger flaring through her. "I'm not having dinner with you."

"Really?" He drove through the green light and up a freeway ramp, merging with the crush of vehicles creeping southward. He smirked as though he knew he had the bait that would make her change her mind. "Even if there's more than one way to skin this particular cat?"

She fumed. "At the first exit, get off and take me back to my car."

"Are you sure?" The smile had reached his eyes and bounced through his words. "I thought you might like to try the Flamingo Bar and Grill in Santa Barbara."

She started to protest again, then it dawned on her that the Flamingo was the name of one of Michael Pride's restaurants. Nick's smile fell away, his focus on the heavy traffic. "But if you insist, there is an exit coming up..."

Desire sighed. "Do we have a reservation?"

"No, but I doubt that will be a problem."

She sank back in the seat, anxious yet uneasy. Michael Pride hadn't returned any of her calls. Hadn't shown up for Dare's funeral. Why? She did want to meet him, wanted to see for herself whether or not he had really loved Dare as she'd deserved. But could she face the shock on his face when they strode in unannounced, unexpected? "Are you sure he'll even be there? If he's grieving for Dare, as you suggest, he might have taken a few days off."

Nick shook his head with confidence. "He seems to practically live at the Flamingo."

But Michael Pride wasn't there when they arrived, though he was expected soon. They decided to have a drink and wait. They chose a table near the bar where they could watch the entrance. The Flamingo was alive and jumping, music and chatter blaring into the high ceiling, thrust down by the overhead fans to ricochet against wallpaper that was reminiscent of a tropical jungle. The waitress wore a super-short, hot-pink sarong and a fresh flower over one ear. Nick ordered two iced teas.

Their drinks had been served, and Desire was squeezing lemon into hers when she sensed someone staring at her. The tiny hairs on her arms lifted. Unconsciously, she inched closer to Nick, her head jerking up, her gaze darting across the room. Then she saw him. In the entrance. His gaze locked on her, his stance as still as the palm trees throughout the restaurant.

"That's him," Nick murmured. "Michael Pride."

He was medium height, athletically built, in khakis, a floral shirt and sandals, an unlit cigar clenched in his mouth. His hair was thick and golden, his skin darkly tanned, his eyes the blue of a lagoon, the perfect beachcomber in the perfect setting. For a single fleeting second, such hope filled his eyes it tore at Desire's heart.

She knew that look, had felt that flash of hope several times the past two weeks when she'd glimpsed her own reflection in the mirror, before realizing it wasn't Dare. Confusion quickly overtook the hope on his face, replaced it with the realization that she was Dare's twin, the woman he'd been avoiding.

He wasn't flat-out handsome like Nick, but even from across the room he exuded a raw sensuality that had women's heads turning as he wove between the tables to reach theirs. His voice was edged with annoyance.

"Detective Rossetti, I pray this means you've discovered something."

Nick gestured toward Desire. "This is—"

"I'm neither stupid nor blind. I know who she is." He kept his voice low.

Desire stiffened. His glance said he wished she was the one who was dead and Dare alive. How often she'd wished the same. She forced herself to smile. "Mr. Pride, I'm glad to finally meet you."

"Are you?"

Desire bristled. No matter what he thought of her, or had been told about her, he had no right to treat her like a pariah. She countered his rudeness with politeness, offering her hand this time. "I wanted to thank you for the beautiful roses you sent to Laredo and to offer my condolences to you as well. I'm sorry that circumstances have prevented us from meeting until—"

"Dare didn't want anything to do with you and neither do I." He looked at her hand as though it might bite him, then shook his cigar at Nick. "What is this, an ambush?"

Nick's face had hardened, his eyes were black with outrage. "Apparently, you don't seem to realize, Pride, that *I* was the man who caused the rift between Dare and her sister."

"What? *You're* Nick?" He said the name as though he had a mouthful of dirt. His expression raced between fury and disbelief. He plunked the cigar into his mouth, sucking on it furiously. Apparently in his grief he hadn't connected Detective Rossetti with Nick Rossetti. He didn't like finding out now.

His gaze sliced to Desire and she could see that most of his disdain was for her. As Dare's had been. Desire supposed if she'd been in Dare's shoes, the greater hurt would have been caused by her sister, not by any man, any outsider. Since childhood on, they'd been inseparable, close on every level. She was the big sister, the brave one, the strong one, the one Dare had learned to rely on, to trust to take care of her. And the betrayal she felt by Desire was all the worse for it.

Pride pulled a chair from an adjoining table and sat, his angry glare directed at Nick. "Why the hell are you the one investigating Dare's accident?"

"Because I cared about her, too." Nick struggled to keep his voice even. "And because no one else is going to look into this matter or check out your concerns."

"Why not?" he demanded.

Nick took a long swallow of iced tea and set the glass down with a muted thump. "As far as the police are concerned, her death was just what it appears—an accident."

"It *was* an accident, Mr. Pride," Desire added. "Besides the three of us, no one else cares to find out if something or someone precipitated the accident."

He regarded her with narrowing eyes. "*Was* there something to find out?"

"Her apartment was broken into," Nick confirmed. "The bedroom window smashed, the sash opened, someone's heavy black heel marks on the sill."

"That proves it, then." Excitement flared in Pride's eyes.

"But it doesn't tell us *who* was there," Desire cautioned him.

"I'd like to ask you a few more questions," Nick said, glancing at the rapidly filling restaurant. "But not here. Could we use your office?"

Pride looked at Desire as if to say, "Her, too?" But thought better of actually saying it. He nodded, then led them to a walkway behind the bar that was stacked high with liquor boxes, and up a single flight of stairs to his private office. The door opened on a ten-by-twelve room with a one-way mirror that overlooked the main dining area and the entrance.

The furniture was masculine and comfortable, leather and oak, the office laid out for the business side of keeping a restaurant running. His desk faced the mirror. He was, apparently, a man who liked his finger on the pulse of every aspect of Pride Enterprises. The only thing that struck her as odd was how tidy the room appeared. Almost too neat. Stalkers were orderly. Methodical. She shivered.

As she strode to the sofa and sat, Desire scanned the room, noting a photo of Dare on the desk. It was a head shot that looked like a publicity still. The photographer had captured Dare at her best, her makeup subtle and artistically done. She had an innocence that seemed to shine from within. Life had robbed her of her naiveté, but here she seemed to have recovered it. Had Michael managed that? Or Dr. Falls?

Had the stalker ruined that? The possibility infuriated her.

Pride took the overstuffed chair behind his desk. "I already told you, Dare said someone was in her apartment, so, if a broken window is all you've discovered, then asking me more questions won't get us any further in finding who broke in."

"That's not all." Nick had noticed Dare's photo, too. He lifted the frame, stared at the picture. Desire could only wonder at his thoughts, at the dark shadow that had fallen across his handsome face. "There were a couple of other things."

She expected him to mention Eager Eddie and the

valentine. Instead, Nick said, "I didn't tell Desire about one of them."

"What?" She stiffened and glared at him. "Dammit, Rossetti."

He blinked, his eyes warm with contrition and apology, his voice a gentle stroke of tenderness and concern...for her, for her feelings, she realized, feeling flustered as well as ticked. Damn it all. Why did it have to be Nick Rossetti who stirred her blood?

He set the photograph down with care. "It was a picture frame. The glass was broken, the photo missing."

Desire had noticed no such thing. "What frame? Where?"

"The one on her desk?" Pride supplied, frowning at her. "The one of the two of you?"

"What is he talking about?" she demanded of Nick.

"It was an eight-by-ten chrome frame with Dare's and your names etched on the lower bar." Nick sat beside Desire, his thigh grazing hers, the contact both reassuring and disturbing her, but she made no effort to move. He leaned forward, laying his strong forearms on his muscled thighs. He seemed barely able to keep from touching her, his hands gripped together on his knees, a pulse beating at his temple. His gaze heavy on her. "Does that ring a bell?"

Heat rushed into her cheeks and the image of the described frame filled her mind. She had one exactly like it. "It was a gift for our sixteenth birthdays. Mother gave us each one. The photograph was taken at the country club after we'd won a doubles tennis tournament match."

Michael Pride's frown intensified. "That's the picture Dare kept in that frame all right. Maybe she removed the photograph when she packed."

Nick shook his head. "Why would she do that? The frame had to have held sentimental value for her to have kept it despite her estrangement from her sister. Why would she suddenly destroy the frame and photograph in a fit of rage when she was on the verge of a happy new life with you? It doesn't wash."

"You think the stalker broke the glass and stole the photograph for a...what do they call it?" Pride asked around the cigar. "A trophy? A souvenir?"

"To remember her," Nick stated harshly.

Pride looked ill. "Damn him. If I could get my hands on this bastard..." He yanked the cigar from his mouth. The tip was wet and unappetizing, making Desire wonder how long ago he'd quit smoking.

Nick continued, "We've also discovered there was a paparazzi photographer tailing her."

"Yeah, *that* guy." Pride nodded; his grip tightened on the cigar.

"You knew about Eager Eddie?" Disbelief widened Nick's eyes.

"Knew about him? I've been his victim on more than one occasion."

Nick half rose. "Why didn't you tell me about him?"

Pride leaned back in his chair. "If I'd told you about the photographer, you might have dismissed my concerns about Dare, might have thought he was the one stalking her. Now you know he wasn't."

"I don't know any such thing."

"Sure you do. Eager Eddie wouldn't risk breaking into Dare's apartment and getting arrested. Think about it. If he'd broken in, there would have been photos of the interior of her apartment in *Celebrity Crier*. There were none."

Desire had had enough of this macho spitting contest. "Mr. Pride, do *you* know who was stalking my sister?"

"If I knew that, I'd find the guy and kill him."

"That wouldn't be wise," Nick warned. Jerking the bagged valentine out of his pocket, he showed it to Michael. "Have you seen this before?"

Pride studied the valentine and envelope for a few minutes. "Not that one, but others like it."

"Others, huh?" Nick's annoyance was turning his neck red.

"Yeah, signed the same as that, but this is a new one."

"How long has she been getting these?"

"Since we first became aware of him. About two and a half months ago."

"But you've never seen this one?" Desire pressed.

He shook his head. "She must have gotten it in the last day or so that she was alive."

"What did Dare do with the others?" Nick asked.

"We've been keeping them in a file."

"Where?" he pressed.

Michael Pride grunted. "You know, I don't know why you'd want to see them. We went to the police and were told there was nothing they could do about this guy if we didn't know who he was. You can't get a restraining order against a man without knowing his name. We couldn't give them that."

Nick exhaled loudly, impatience lifting his shoulders. "Then why didn't you hire someone to watch over Dare?"

"Like a private detective?" Pride suggested. "I did that. But the investigator the agency assigned the job was an idiot. He thought the one following Dare was that—that Eager Eddie."

Nick looked more exasperated than ever. "Then how can we be sure he's *not* the stalker?"

Pride broke his cigar in half, bits of tobacco flew across his desk in a fragrant burst. "I should have known going to the police again was a waste of time. Inefficient bunch of—"

"*This* is getting us nowhere," Nick broke off Pride's tirade, running both hands through his hair. "Tell me something, Pride, if you were so damn concerned about Dare that you went to the police twice about this stalker and hired a private investigator, why in hell didn't you have her move in with you to keep her safe?"

Michael Pride had lost some of the summer freshness of his appearance. He began gathering the remains of his cigar into a little pile. "We were buying a house in Denver. I'd lined up a buyer for my restaurants who would pay enough to foot our disappearance."

"Disappearance? Dare's career was just taking off."

"You think I wanted to walk away from Pride Enterprises?" He raised his voice. "No way in hell. But we had no choice."

"There are always choices." Desire rose and went to the mirror. Everywhere she looked she saw affluence. This man had a lot of money. "You should have insisted she move in with you. She would have been safe. She would have been alive."

Guilt grabbed his features, deflating his bluster. "I wanted to do exactly that, but we…were advised against it."

"Advised?" Desire was incredulous. "By whom?"

"Dr. Falls."

Desire and Nick exchanged a glance. Shock and outrage stripped the fragile hold she had on her temper. She charged toward Pride, reacting, wanting to pounce on the guy, shake him until his teeth rattled, make him pay for not keeping her sister safe.

Nick caught her, pulled her gently but firmly against him, her back clasped to his front. "You'd better explain, Pride, or I'll let D show you a little Texas retribution."

Michael Pride swallowed hard and nodded. "The man who was stalking Dare is an erotomaniac."

"An a-rot-a-what-iac?" Nick choked out.

"Erotomaniac," Desire corrected, reining in her temper with every ounce of will she possessed. "What is that?"

"An erotomaniac is someone who imagines a romantic relationship that does not exist. In his mind the object of his affection is in love with him, wants to be with him. He lives as though they share a life."

Most stalkers Desire knew imagined something similar. "How did this man target or become focused on Dare?"

Pride had formed the cigar remnants into a tiny pile. He poked at it absently. "Maybe from watching her on TV. Maybe somewhere else. We don't know."

"You still haven't explained why you didn't insist Dare move in with you," Nick reminded him.

"Why you didn't order round-the-clock bodyguards," Desire said from between clenched teeth.

"Because people like the one obsessed with Dare often kill their perceived competition—me, in this case, or anyone who might have been guarding her, keeping her from him in the stalker's view. I couldn't, wouldn't risk the life of any bodyguard no matter how well trained. The erotomaniac can be bold and clever. Do the unexpected."

"Are you saying *you* were in more danger from this

man than Dare?'' Nick gripped Desire's shoulders, his heat infusing her, but not reaching the cold that wrapped her heart.

"Yes." Pride stared at the remains of his cigar a long moment. "Dare was all set to move in with me, but Dr. Falls advised against it."

"We visited Dr. Falls earlier," Nick informed him. "She said nothing about any erotomaniac."

Pride ignored that. "Dr. Falls insisted that we not change our routines, that we stay living where we were for the sake of keeping the stalker off balance, hopefully to keep him from knowing about our plans."

"Your plans?"

"We were going to elope and leave the state before he knew we were gone. We were leaving the day she…the day she…"

A shiver rushed over Desire, a fear similar, she was certain, to that which her sister must have felt. The music from below reached into her consciousness, something Latin, rhythmic and upbeat, the exact opposite of how she felt at the moment. Everything seemed to have conspired to end Dare's life, all those who should have kept her safe were prevented from doing so. This man, more frightened for his own life than hers, the doctor with her advice to keep to the usual routine, she, herself, for not mending the rift with her twin.

The room, the noise, the guilt and frustration stripped the air from her lungs. She needed to get outside, to breathe. Cool, sobering oxygen. Slipping from Nick's hold, she rushed from the office, down the stairs and out the double glass-and-bronze front doors.

Nick caught up with her near his parked car. "What is it, D?"

She bent over at the waist, drawing in fresh gulps of

night air. She was trembling, shaking from deep within herself. As he touched her shoulders, he seemed to understand the emotions and fear that gripped her. He pulled her into his arms, embracing her, his hold neither too tight nor too loose, just a safe, warm circle of heat and reassurance. "Don't worry, love. I won't let the stalker get you."

She leaned into Nick, glad he was a large man and that folding herself against him seemed to dissolve her fear, as though he could really protect her and keep her safe from someone whom neither of them had ever seen, just an anonymous no one with the power to destroy. It struck through her like a shaft. He didn't want to destroy *her,* but he wouldn't hesitate to eliminate someone close to her. Someone the man perceived was a threat to his imagined relationship with her. And here she was on a public street where everyone, anyone, could observe and assume the wrong thing.

She shoved Nick away. Feeling more alone, more isolated than ever. She would not be the source of his being in jeopardy, the cause of another person she cared about losing his life. She would stay away from Nick. For his sake.

She started towards his sedan. "Please, take me to my car, Nick. Then stay far, far away from me."

Chapter Five

Nick planned on sticking to D like a second skin—whether she liked it or not. He would not let what had happened to Dare happen to her. He dropped her off at her car, figuring to circle the block, then tail her back to Santa Beverly, make certain she arrived home safe, unmolested.

Instead of getting into her car, she started across the street and up the path toward Dare's apartment.

"What the hell is she doing?" Nick abandoned his car and chased after her, catching her arm. "Where do you think you're going?"

"To finish packing." She pulled free of his grip. "Go home, Rossetti. Don't you have to work or something?"

"No. I—" He clenched his jaw. "I'm not leaving you here alone."

She stiffened. "Yes, you are."

Like hell he was. She couldn't really want to face that creepy apartment alone. He fell into step beside her.

"Go away," she growled.

"Not a chance." He leaned near her as she unlocked the door and dropped the key into her purse, then he stepped around her, entering first. "Geez, it's like a hot box in here, and it's only April. It must feel like Hades in summer.''

"It *is* a miserable little hovel."

D glanced at the living room/kitchen combination with such guilt in her glorious eyes, it roused his own guilt. Had Dare been punishing herself by living in this hellhole? Had he done that to her? Driven her to think she didn't deserve anything better? Maybe. Maybe he had.

But, dammit, she'd continued playing the martyr after she'd gotten that lucrative contract from the perfume company. *That* wasn't *his* fault. No. She'd kept living here on the advice of her psychologist. Over two years of weekly, private sessions with that woman doctor hadn't given Dare the power or the inclination to forgive D or him. What kind of therapist was Dr. Falls anyway?

"Stay here," he told D. He walked through the three rooms, turning on the lights, making sure no one was hiding in any corners or in the closet, then came back to her in the living room. "No one but us."

She looked as though she'd expected nothing more. "Go home, Rossetti."

He shook his head and plopped onto the sofa, crossing his arms over his chest and staring up at her beautiful furious face. "I'll just park myself on the couch and when you're done packing I'll help carry the boxes to your car."

She blew out a heavy breath. "Are you so damn insensitive and thick-headed you can't understand that I need to do this alone?"

Insensitive? Thick-headed? Did she really expect she could insult him out of her life? He stifled a grin, realizing it would be less appreciated than his so-called insensitivity. Okay, he could understand her needing some private time to complete this grievous task. In fact, he could and would allow her some space—in small increments. He levered himself off the couch and crossed to her. "Okay, fine. I'll go. But only to get some coffee."

"Just go away."

"No. You've had a hell of a day, D. You're running on nerves. They'll let you down the minute this chore is complete. Maybe on the long drive back to Santa Beverly." He let this sink in a moment, then added, "Your folks don't need another call from the LAPD."

"Damn you, Nick." Her eyes narrowed and he'd swear she'd like to strike him. She lifted her arm, pointed toward the door, the fight gone from her. "Go get some coffee. But take your time."

He wanted to apologize for his tactics, but she'd needed shaking up, needed to face the realities of her situation. She had too much pride. Was too stubborn. Both dangerous attributes given the current circumstances. He could live with her hating him—if it kept her safe. Alive.

She held the door open for him. Her expression stern, but there was a softening in her aqua eyes. "I like my coffee with cream and three sugars."

He strode toward the door, stopping even with her, leaning close enough to feel her sweet breath on his mouth. "I remember."

The words came out husky. Their gazes locked for a long moment, and he couldn't speak for her, but he was remembering more than the way she liked her coffee. He felt his resolve not to touch her slipping like a toboggan on ice. Damn but she had kissable lips. No. Don't go there. That kind of thinking would be his undoing. He straightened, reined in the temptation, willed his thoughts elsewhere and stepped outside. "Lock it behind me."

She began closing the door, then called, "Hey, Rossetti, you promised me dinner. Why don't you pick up some burgers to go with that coffee?"

He grinned. "Good idea."

DESIRE CHECKED the lock, then turned and leaned against the door. The bungalow had come furnished, everything from the silverware to the bed. The oddest thing to her about this place was not that Dare had lived here, but that she'd never put a personal mark on it. No imprint of her personality. Nothing. Not in three years. As though she only came here between interviews and auditions and dates and sessions with that strange Dr. Falls, as though she didn't want to "own" it in any way that might make her care about losing it.

That her sister might actually have felt that way saddened Desire, immobilized her. Why were they all stuck in the same emotional rut three years later?

The sudden rattling hum of a tired motor broke her dark musing. Her gaze fell on the refrigerator, a dented, white, noisy box. Since the landlady hadn't known the window was broken, she likely hadn't disposed of the contents of the refrigerator either. She made herself cross to it. Her nose wrinkled reflexively as she tugged open the door. Cool air wafted out, but no foul smells. There were three bottles of designer water, one furry tomato, and stuck to a couple of shelves what looked like yellow rose petals whose edges were browning.

Again, less than she would have expected.

She shut the door, decided the landlady could clean this along with the rest of the place before she leased it again. She scanned the room once more, her gaze landing on the desk. The photograph frame. She found it in the top drawer, atop a clutter of glass chips.

She'd felt a warm glow learning that Dare had kept this with their photo in it, despite everything. But she hadn't taken it when she left. Had she meant to? Desire would never know, thanks to the stalker. The frame was as broken as her relationship with her twin. Irreparable. She touched a fingertip to their names and yelped at the unexpected chill that shot up her arm.

It was as though the chrome retained the essence of cold and evil that had ripped the photograph from it, as though she'd somehow connected with the man who had scared her sister to her death. She hugged her hand to her thundering heart and berated her foolish thoughts.

Nick needed to stick this in one of his evidence bags. She doubted there would be fingerprints that would lead them to the stalker, but sometimes long shots paid off. Criminals, she discovered on a daily basis, were often tripped up by stupid mistakes.

She closed the drawer and retreated to Dare's bedroom. The boxes were where she'd left them, the things she'd packed undisturbed, as far as she could tell. But there was a difference. Boards crisscrossed the window, a clumsy job that gave bugs access, allowed very little air and fewer patches of moonlight.

She set about her task, anxious to finish and leave. Nick was right. The stress and grief, along with every other rotten thing this day had handed her, was taking its toll on her energy. Skipping meals, consciously or unconsciously, exacerbated the problem. The dresser was quickly emptied. To her disappointment, there was nothing much there. No treasures or keepsakes. Had Dare, perhaps, mailed all her personal items to her new address in Denver?

If so, then why not the photograph?

It was a question without answer.

She began removing clothes from the closet, leaving dresses on their hangers, folding them all into the boxes. She studied the emptied closet, wondering if the stalker might have left a clue there. Nick suspected the stalker had been hiding there because it was the only place to hide in the three-room apartment.

She hunkered down and scanned the tiny space from one corner to another, seeking a hair, or thread, or fiber of some kind. After several minutes of searching, she gave up. If the stalker had left anything behind, it was too minuscule to see with the naked eye. Besides, Nick had hidden in there, too, and likely destroyed whatever evidence there might have been. Not that it mattered. The police frowned on spending taxpayers' money running tests for crimes without victims.

She could get her boss to run the picture frame for fingerprints only because of the possible connection with the valentine she'd been sent. The LAPD would not be involved in Nick's and her investigation into Dare's death in any way.

Frustrated, she rose from her haunches. Outside the window she heard a crunch. Then another. As though someone had stepped on the dried weeds that poked from around the foundation of the bungalow. Her heart leaped. Her gaze flew to the window.

Shadows moved on the wall. Her pulse skipped. Someone was out there. She ducked back, but couldn't tear her gaze from the window.

The boards were too close together for her to see who it was. It had to be the man who'd been stalking Dare. Who had caused her death. A blast of rage exploded through her. He wasn't getting away this time. She ran through the apartment and outside.

As the door slammed behind her, Desire sobered. Her heart kicked hard. What the hell was she thinking? Confronting, unarmed, a stalker she wanted and needed to see was dangerous enough, but what if the person outside Dare's bedroom window wasn't the stalker? This was a crime-riddled neighborhood. What if it was a mugger? A rapist? A murderer?

Breathing rapidly, she glanced up and down the path lit by the moon and alive with specters that might be shrubs, that might be predators lying in wait. Her heart pounded. Approaching footsteps sounded, coming from around the side of the apartment. She lunged for the doorknob. It was locked. Oh, God, no. The key was in her purse on Dare's bed.

"I DAMN NEAR TOLD HER the truth," Nick thought, berating himself as he pulled out of the drive-through window. The aroma of hot French fries had his stomach juices moving. *That would have been a mistake,* he suspected. She thought little enough of him as it was. She saw everything in black and white. Life wasn't that tidy. Sometimes a man had to do the right thing—even if the rules said otherwise.

He figured as long as a person realized there would be consequences, and expected to pay the price for insubordination, then he had no right to grouse. Or to feel discriminated against, even when his so-called recklessness had resulted in the happy and successful outcome of a case.

But right now, he was pushing his luck. He had no business pretending his investigation into his former wife's accident was official. If the captain found out, his ass would be grass. Instead of putting out the fire he'd created, he was adding fuel to it, making sure it burned high enough to draw notice.

Trouble was, he had nothing but free time on his hands, a savage curiosity and a deeper need for justice. He wanted the guy who'd precipitated Dare's death, wanted to look him in the eye, wanted to make him pay some way or other for his sick obsession.

But if the creep was now after D, there was no telling what Nick might do to him. He sure as hell wouldn't run and hide like that coward Pride. Crudballs who scared women and children didn't deserve to walk the streets, free to carry on their nasty little games. If catching him meant breaking the rules...well, so be it. This guy had stalked his last victim.

The thought made him suddenly anxious about leaving D alone in Dare's apartment, even though he was only a few blocks away. He decided to take a shortcut down an alley. He'd driven less than a car length into it when the sedan gave a lurch to the right and wobbled. Then he heard it, felt it. Flat tire. Passenger side. Nick swore. Garbage was strewn everywhere. Must have run over broken glass or a nail or something.

He stopped and banged out of the car. The neighborhood was three blocks from the Palms, littered with low-income housing and shabbily kept residences, all going to weed in the heat and smog. Giant palm trees were peppered between the buildings.

Why the hell had Dare really stayed in this area? There had to be a reason, something more than bad advice from her psychologist? But what?

Nick rounded the front bumper and knelt beside the damaged tire. In the dying daylight between dusk and dark, the tall buildings and taller trees, light was in short supply. He could see the air had all but drained from the tire, but could not find the cause.

Nick frowned. He hadn't heard the tire blow and he doubted he could have made it to Santa Barbara and back without noticing a slow leak. Mulling this over, he went to the trunk and popped the lid, grabbed the jack and the spare.

His car wasn't police issue, but his own private two-door sedan with one of those temporary tires. He was saving for a truck, something roomy so that his dog—when he got a dog—could ride around with him. Nick loved dogs, but he'd been working too many long days since moving to Tinseltown. It wouldn't be fair to a dog to leave it home alone so much. So, he'd been waiting until his life settled down, but his life seemed more complicated and less satisfying every day.

He'd been feeling more and more lonely. He didn't like admitting he needed anyone. But he did. He needed D.

She, however, might never admit she needed him. Might never allow herself to be with him. That would be a crime, one that no amount of rule bending could fix, or bring about a happy ending.

As he wrenched off the mag bolts, he pushed the unhappy thought aside. It had been a hell of an afternoon since finding D in Dare's apartment. They had learned a few new things, but nothing that put them closer to catching the stalker. Or to identifying him.

He tugged the tire off the wheel and replaced it with the spare, laying the damaged one on the road beside him. He'd hoped to find a clue or two in the closet today, but there'd been nothing. He secured the bolts, puzzling this. Usually he could spread out details like jigsaw pieces on a card table, then fit the tiny, seemingly unconnected bits to their adjoining pieces until the whole began revealing itself.

But today, D kept intruding on his thoughts, scattering them into an incoherent mess. Seeing her again, kissing her, holding her... Damn, the woman could rattle him as no one else ever had. He carried the damaged tire to the trunk.

The light from the lifted lid shone on it, revealing an inch-long slit. His chest tightened. Someone had sabotaged this tire. When? While they were in Santa Barbara? No. A hole this large would have lost air quickly. Outside Dare's place, then. Someone had been very quick. Very daring.

The stalker?

Michael Pride's words about erotomaniacs being unpredictable and daring came back to him in a rush. D! He'd left her alone—with the damn maniac prowling nearby. He slammed down the lid, leaped into his car and peeled out, tipping the sacks over. Hot, hot coffee poured from the brown paper, draining against his hip, saturating his chinos. Nick didn't notice.

Chapter Six

D's car was still curbside. Lights still blazed from within Dare's apartment. Neither calmed Nick. He jumped out of his sedan and hurried up the walk. With every step, he cautioned himself against overreacting, grappled for the detached mental state that saw him through the average L.A. day on homicide duty.

But he couldn't remain detached. Not where D was concerned. He grabbed the doorknob. *Locked. Good, that was good. Take a deep breath. Let it out.* He rapped his knuckles against the weathered wood. Gently. Then harder. Why didn't she answer? The apartment was only three rooms large. She had to have heard him.

His pulse skipped. He pounded the door, shouted her name. No response came from inside. ''D. Where are you?''

Fear scraped along his nerves. He circled the apartment, around to the back to the boarded-over window, his rapid footfalls crunching dried twigs and dead flowers. His gaze zeroed in on the window. The boards were intact. ''D, are you in there? For God's sake, if you can hear me, say something.''

Was she lying inside, injured, unable to respond? He grabbed hold of one of the boards and wrenched it off.

Although the intruder had broken the window to unlatch the lock, he had not removed all of the glass. As Nick tugged loose another board, shards came with it. The night erupted with the discordant song of splintering wood and clinking glass.

"God, why did I leave her alone?" He could see the bedroom now. The boxes were on the bed, along with D's purse. But he couldn't see her anywhere. He called again, "D!"

The bathroom door was open, but from this window he could see no farther into it than the doorjamb, could see next to nothing of the living-room area. Dread spread through his gut. He had to get inside. He shoved up the sash, lodged one of the sticks of wood as a brace to keep it up, then lifted his leg to pull himself through.

A movement to his left stopped him. As he turned to see what was there, something with the force of a freight train slammed into him, tearing him out of the window and knocking him to the ground. Whatever had hit him landed on him, weighing, he judged, as much as a caboose and knocking the wind from him. Nick groaned, acutely aware of the broken glass and splintered bits of wood beneath him poking through his chinos and T-shirt.

He realized, too, that it was a man who'd hit him and was now squashing the life out of him. Nick was not a small man, but this guy was huge.

"You like snoopin' 'round ladies' 'partments, bub?" the man growled, his breath fishy, garlicky.

"No, no!" a woman called. *D! Alive. Speaking.* If Nick could have breathed, he would have released a sigh of relief. She shouted at the mountain that was sitting on him. "He's not the one! Let him up!"

"Huh? Not the one?" The big man lifted himself off

Nick's chest, and Nick sucked a long breath, the first deep one in several minutes. The man, he saw in the light coming through the bedroom window, had skin the color of Michael Pride's cigar, and a body built for football.

He glanced over his massive shoulder at the two women—D and the landlady—coming nearer. "What you mean he ain't the one?" He spoke in a mellow southern drawl. "He tore off the boards I put up and was tryin' to get in your sister's place when I stopped him."

"Oh, my God Keray, thas the policeman I tole ya was here earlier." Lorelei Collins's eyes were wide. "This here's my husband, Keray Collins."

As Keray lifted completely off Nick, Lorelei bent over him, shaking her head as though he were daft. "If'n ya wanted that window boarded up, hows come ya ripped the slats back off?"

Nick rolled his eyes and stifled a moan. He was bruised and bleeding and being bawled out. Anger burned at the depth of him, but he held his tongue, fearing he'd verbally slice this woman to shreds, and abusing women, verbally or otherwise, was something he did not tolerate. Besides, he'd had all the tussles he wanted with Keray Collins, who might not take kindly to any man berating his wife.

Gingerly, he sat up. His back felt like a pincushion; minuscule pricks of pain radiated from neck to tailbone. D knelt down and put a hand under his elbow. "I'm so sorry, Nick. Are you okay?"

"I'm not sure. If Refrigerator Perry there didn't crack a rib or two, he bruised them. Not to mention slamming me onto the splintered wood and shards of glass, half of which now seem to be protruding from my back."

"How was I s'pose to know?" Keray questioned. "She said someone was tryin' to get in here and there you'all was, just like she said."

"Yeah, we was jes' tryin' to help," Lorelei added, defending her husband, as though he couldn't manage that himself. She turned to Desire. "Here's the spare key. Don't lose this one 'cause I don't got no more."

She looped her arm through Keray's and they stalked away, leaving Desire and Nick alone. Desire helped him to his feet. "Can you walk?"

"I think so." He leaned on her, hobbling, his legs still weak from Keray's bulk slamming him to the ground. Needing her support embarrassed him a bit, but damn, she felt wonderful, smelled wonderful.

They returned to the front door of the apartment and were quickly inside. She locked the door behind them and set the key on the desk. She released him and surveyed his back. "Your shirt and pants are torn and—"

D was grinning at him. "What's so funny?" he demanded.

"Well, your pants…are wet and ripped and…barely covering your, um, shall we say, your…assets."

Nick glanced down. He looked as though he'd wet himself. Heat flashed into his face, heat and annoyance. But she laughed, and the sound warmed him from the inside out. He grinned wryly. Knowing that she was okay made everything else tolerable. "I had a flat. The tire was slashed, as though with a knife. If it had happened in Santa Barbara we'd have had the flat on the freeway. Since that didn't happen, it had to have been done while we were in here. It was probably some street punk, but I leaped to the conclusion that it was *him*, and in my hurry to get back here I must have upended the coffee."

Her smile fell. "Someone *was* outside the bedroom window. I ran out to see who it was and locked myself out. I heard someone coming from around the apartment and dashed over to the landlady's."

Nick swore. "D, how could you take such a chance?"

Her chin shot up and her hands landed on her hips. "Judd and Marvel Hamilton didn't raise me to be a coward. I wanted to see who it was."

"So you ran outside?" He felt like shaking her, like counting off all the reasons why that action had been the most foolish she could have chosen.

"I just reacted." The contrition on her face told him she'd already berated herself enough on that score.

"Well, for God's sake, why didn't you use your cell phone and call me or someone else for help?"

"My phone is in my purse on Dare's bed, along with the key to the front door. Sometimes, Nick, I'm as rash and impulsive as you—with the same bad results."

"Oh, the results aren't always bad...." He stepped closer to her, lured by the challenge of her, by the need for her. But moving brought the awareness that he was not only wet but had perhaps been burned in a few sensitive areas by the hot coffee that had spilled in his car. He not only looked ridiculous, he hurt. He tried to stifle a grimace. "*Did* you see who was outside the window?"

"No. Not a glimpse."

He sighed. "And the 'Refrigerator' and I obliterated any and all evidence we might have culled from beneath that window."

She caught his arm. "Come into the bathroom. Dare left behind a tube of antiseptic cream and Band-Aids. You need ministering."

She dug something from her purse—tweezers, he

saw—and joined him in the bathroom. "Take off your shirt."

He grinned broadly. "I thought you'd never ask."

She glared at him. Still smirking, he did as ordered, but he paid for his cheekiness. Using the tweezers, she plucked out, none too gently, slivers of glass and wood from his skin. Then cleansed each wound with peroxide and smoothed in the cream. He alternated between flinching in pain and wallowing in the pleasure of her fingertip massage, fighting always the demon of wanting her.

"Okay," she said after a while. "Drop your pants."

He tensed, no smart-ass comments springing to mind or tongue. He glanced over his shoulder at her, searching her eyes for some hidden meanings, but all he found was concern and detachment, which he'd been unable to manage earlier. Her ability to shut him out, to deny her feelings for him, rankled. He should show her just how much she was missing, kiss her until she melted in his embrace, until she begged him to continue and quit fighting their love, until she gave in to it with every part of her.

Instead, he unsnapped his chinos, then lowered the zipper and carefully eased them and his undershorts down a couple of inches, his backside to her, the pulse at his temple throbbing in sync to the melodic thrum of his heart. Again, he felt the tweezers grabbing and plucking, then the stinging daubs of peroxide, followed by her sweet fingertips smoothing cream into the wounds.

Blood pooled hot and heavy in his groin. He fought against the slamming passion that threatened to really embarrass him.

"Nick." He'd swear her voice was breathy, raspy.

"You're going to have to pull your pants lower…so I can cleanse all the wounds."

Swallowing with difficulty, he inched them lower.

"More."

He did as she asked, peeling the wet, sticky cotton to the top of his thighs, his backside completely bared now, along with his need for her. He grabbed a towel from the top of the shower curtain and held it over himself, hoping she wouldn't realize he was fully erect, knowing if her gaze wandered there, it would be only too obvious.

Her fingers grazed his skin as she pulled slivers free. He swallowed over a moan that was both pleasure and pain. Keeping his eyes shut, he wrestled with the heat that raced through his blood, the scramble of emotions swirling through his brain.

He had to get his mind elsewhere. "Are you done…packing?"

"Yes." Her breath fanned his bare buttocks and he felt himself losing the battle to keep from grabbing her, making love to her. But she said, "All done."

He breathed a sigh of relief, realizing that though he was still tender in all the places she had cleansed, the wounds no longer ached. Except there was definitely a tender area near his lower belly. "Is there any more of that cream left, D?"

"Why?"

"I think the coffee may have burned me."

"Where?"

"Never mind, D. You don't want to know."

"Tell me something, Rossetti." Her tone had sharpened and rang with anger, though he wasn't sure what had snapped her into a disapproving mood. "Why do you always call me 'D'? Are you afraid you'll accidentally call me Dare? Has your problem always been that you wanted us both?''

Stunned, he dropped the towel and pivoted to face her all in one swift movement. He grabbed her and hauled her to him, all embarrassment gone in the flash of holding her against his throbbing need for her. ''Does this feel to you like I want Dare?''

She struggled against his hold, her face a mask of fury. ''Why don't you ever call me by my given name?''

''Because,'' he said between clenched teeth, ''your name suits you too perfectly, and every time I even *think* it, this is what happens to me. I want you, D. I want you so damn bad I can't stand it.'' He buried his nose in her neck, inhaling deep and long, nibbled kisses there, then higher until his mouth found hers. She moaned and his blood burned hotter. Pressing her against the bathroom counter, he drove his hands into her thick silky hair and delved the depths of her mouth with his tongue, tasting her, letting her taste him. He felt the tension leaving her body and the aching need increase in his own. God, how he'd longed for this moment, how he'd yearned to feel her compliance, but he'd forced this on her, and in the heat of the moment she hadn't been able to deny the physical passion they shared.

But he knew having her this way would only be getting half of her. And he didn't want half. He wanted all of her. For always. He pulled back, breathless, all but panting. ''I have never felt this way about any other woman. Don't ever make that mistake again, D.''

Her aqua eyes looked glazed, her lips bee-stung and swollen, her body trembling, her chest rising and falling as she struggled to catch her breath, to slow her pulse, to find words. ''Then...why did you stop?''

''When you come to me because you want me, then

and only then will I make you mine completely. Until then, this isn't going to happen. Until then, I'll keep calling you 'D'."

He held out his hand. "I'll take that cream now."

She put it in his hand and left the room. He shut the bathroom door, examined himself and discovered a reddish spot near the inside top of his right thigh. He swabbed cream onto the area, stepped out of his pants and shorts and shook both to be sure no slivers hid between their folds, then dressed. When he came out of the bathroom, his composure intact, he discovered she'd hauled the boxes to the front door. He had dampened the towel; the front seat of this car needed to be dried off. "I'll be right back."

She nodded. She was still a bit breathless and pink-cheeked and more damn desirable than a woman had a right to be. His passion for her reawoke, but before he fell prisoner to her again, he hurried outside. He strode to the edge of the sidewalk and stood watching the neighborhood as his jets cooled and his self-restraint returned. "Damn that woman."

He cleaned the driver's seat, retrieved the food and returned from his car. "I'm afraid the coffee all spilled, but the burgers and fries are still edible."

She gave him a grateful nod. "There's bottled water in the refrigerator."

They ate ravenously, and in a charged silence, then carried the boxes to her car. Their goodbye was brief. Nick knew he should go home—to change clothes, if nothing else—but the slashed tire was back on his mind, worrying him. He really shouldn't follow her all the way to Santa Beverly, not on the temporary tire, but he found himself doing exactly that. Maybe if Michael Pride had listened to his instincts and not to Dr. Falls, Dare would still be alive.

AS DESIRE NEARED her home, she thought how strange it was that she was glad to be here. Only this morning she'd felt the walls were closing in on her. Now it seemed a sanctuary that she could retreat into and lock out all the madness and ugliness of the world.

She'd leave the boxes in her car until tomorrow. In fact, like Scarlet O'Hara, she'd think about it all tomorrow.

She pulled onto her street and slowed. It was a well-lighted area of small ramblers built in the eighties boom. Her own sat near the middle. She knew most of the vehicles that were usually parked on the street. But tonight she spotted a white pickup outside her neighbor's house. Although the pickup was familiar, she was almost certain it didn't belong there.

She drove past, peering inside, trying to recall why she knew this truck. In the street light she saw a man sitting behind the wheel. He smiled at her. Ted Gunderson.

Her stomach lurched. She stepped on the gas and hit the automatic garage-door opener. She parked, lowering the door behind her car. Her heart hammered, and she dashed into her house, locking the inside door to the garage.

What the hell was Gunderson doing here? She left the lights off and, guided by instinct and familiarity she wove her way through the living room and pulled back the blinds. He was still sitting there staring at the house, at the window where she stood now. As though he could see her, he grinned again and tipped his hat, then lifted something—it appeared to be a cell phone—and drove away.

A second later her phone rang. Desire jumped. Then swore. Then found the phone in the darkness. "Hello?"

Heavy breathing filled her ear.

She hit the record button on her answering machine. "I'm recording this, Gunderson. Consider yourself warned and informed."

"Soon, my sweet Desire, soon." The voice was a distorted whisper.

She swore. If he thought he was going to pull these scare tactics on her, he was sorely mistaken. She'd have his ass hauled into court so fast his head would spin. Fuming, she left the phone off the hook, and flicking on lights as she went, retreated to the bathroom, stripped and stepped into the shower.

The hot water pounded her tense muscles, but it did little to drive off her fear, or her frustration. She emerged as tense as when she'd entered. Ted Gunderson wasn't at the bottom of her tenseness. Nick Rossetti owned that honor. Every time she closed her eyes, she relived his kiss, tasted his mouth, felt again his aroused body pressed to her, arousing her.

She buffed the towel against her skin until it hurt. If he'd been hers and not Dare's everything would be different. But it wasn't. And thinking it ever could or would be was foolhardy. She dried off, wrapping the towel around her wet hair and striding naked into her room. She went to the dresser for her pajamas. She opened the drawer. The scent of roses wafted up to her. She frowned, puzzled. There was no sachet in this drawer, or anything else that smelled of roses. Roses were Dare's favorite flower. Yellow roses, like the petals in her refrigerator.

She preferred gardenias.

She pulled out the pajamas, and yellow rose petals flew up and out with them, fluttering around her and on her like a net of freed butterflies. Desire recoiled in horror. "What the hell?"

Revulsion pumped through her. The whole drawer was filled with fresh yellow rose petals. Every drawer. The sense of violation seared her. She backed away from the chest, dropping the pajamas as though they were vile, once again feeling as though touching what *he* had touched in some way linked them. "Oh my God, oh my God, oh my God."

Chapter Seven

Desire's doorbell rang. Terror shot through her, freezing her brain for a solid second. She shook herself. She'd been in dangerous situations before, knew that panicking was not the way out of them. She counseled herself to calm down and think. The doorbell rang again. Was it Gunderson? She lifted the phone. No one was on the line.

He likely had pretended to leave her neighborhood, called her on his cell phone from down the street and had now come back. She started to punch 911, realized the phone in the other room was still off the hook then reconsidered as she set down the receiver. No matter how it terrified her, ringing her doorbell was not a crime. Calling in the law was an overreaction. Rumors spread quickly in this small community; her own colleagues were among the worst offenders. They would relish having something to hold over her head, something to laugh about behind her back.

That got her moving. She retrieved the robe from the hook on the bathroom door and the gun—given to her by her daddy the day she left Laredo for California— from its hiding place in a secret cubbyhole she'd had built into her headboard. She'd been shooting since she was old enough to hold a pistol, could hit a sidewinder smack in the head from fifteen feet while it was on the move. Judd Hamilton had also taught her never to point a gun at a human being unless she meant to use it, unless she *had* to use it.

She thumbed off the safety and, holding the barrel pointed to the ceiling so as not to accidentally shoot herself in the foot, she inched along the hallway and through the dark living room. She hit the porch-light switch and peered through the peephole. Expecting Ted Gunderson, she was not prepared for the sight that met her eyes.

Nick Rossetti.

A rush of emotions swept through her, the strongest of which was relief. Still wearing his tattered pants and T-shirt, his jaw blackened for need of a shave, his hair mussed, his eyes weary, he was a drop-dead-gorgeous sight.

What was he doing here?

She eased the door open a crack, the chain taut. "I thought you were going home, Rossetti."

He had the grace to look contrite. "I wanted to make sure you made it home okay."

She scowled at him, incredulous. "You followed me?"

His grin was lopsided, wry. "It seemed like the best way to accomplish the deed."

"What are you doing at my door? I mean, obviously, I'm here all safe and sound." She touched the towel still in a turban on her head. "Showered, even. Instead of sitting here for the last half hour, why didn't you just go home?"

"Well, yeah, that would have been the logical thing, but you see, now I'm too tired to drive back to L.A.

without possibly falling asleep at the wheel.'' He rammed his fingers through his dense ebony hair, causing it to stand on end. Conversely, it added to his charm. ''I thought maybe you'd fix me some coffee.''

''Are you serious?'' She shook her head at his presumption. Nick had never been here, never crossed her threshold, never been inside her house. Allowing him access seemed somehow too personal. Too intimate. Or was it that she felt too vulnerable at the moment? The notion sent a rush of heat to her cheeks. ''They sell coffee down the street—just watch for The Golden Arches.''

He glanced over his shoulder at her neighborhood, shrugged and leaned his shoulder into the door frame, his face inches above hers, his dark eyes imploring. ''I don't know my way around Santa Beverly.''

He made it sound as though this seaside town were as large and complex as Los Angeles, as though he'd be lost the second he left this block and his very life depended on *her* fixing him coffee. She didn't want to be swayed by him, lured by his disarming boyishness, but she was. Maybe the scare she'd had minutes ago had stripped her resistance, her common sense, her better judgment. At any rate, sleep was out of the question for a while.

''Oh, what the hell.'' She closed the door, undid the chain and reopened it. ''One cup and you're gone.''

''Thank you.'' As he entered the dark room, the light from the porch fell across her, and his gaze dropped to her ankles, slowly traveled up her bare legs to the hem of her thigh-high robe. She was suddenly too aware that all she wore was the tiny bit of soft terry.

His smile was all male and predatory. ''Nice look, but

you might want to redo the belt. There's a delicious gap developing.''

His voice had a husky, sensuous timbre that sent a shard of need through her belly, a hot electric shiver from her fingertips to her toes. The cool night air brushed her exposed skin, and she grabbed the edges of the robe, tugged them together, the gun making it difficult and awkward.

Nick stepped back from her, his eyebrows lifting, his gaze fixed on the pistol. ''Do you always answer the door packing heat?''

''My daddy taught me to be cautious.'' She eased the safety on and slipped the gun onto the coffee table, switching on the lamp. ''This seemed a good night to heed his advice.''

''I won't argue with that.'' Nick shut the door behind him and eyed the room, inspecting it, appraising it. Desire squirmed internally, wondering what it told him about her. That she was orderly, with a penchant for Danish simplicity and bold hues, eclectic blends of fabric and wood. That she owned one good painting, a small watercolor she'd bought years ago from a college roommate who was now making her mark in the art world.

This might be the first time he'd physically been in her home, but she'd envisioned him here, had figured he'd seem like matter out of place, or that his size would dwarf the room. Instead, he somehow complemented the space…like an accessory that had been missing until now. The thought caused her stomach to flip.

She didn't want Nick Rossetti fitting into her life as though he belonged, sliding into every aspect as though he was meant to be there. *Fix him coffee. Send him home.* ''The kitchen is this way.''

She turned on the kitchen lights. Nick gave a low,

approving whistle. "Hey, this is nice. My mother liked blue and white kitchens, too. I grew up in one like this."

Too much information, Desire thought, wincing inwardly with the knowledge that hereafter she would too often recall this tidbit when in this room. Dammit. Damn him. That settled it. She had six weeks off work. She'd repaint. Yellow. Pink. Green. Anything but blue and white.

"Hey, your phone's off the hook." He replaced it before she could protest. It rang almost immediately, a harsh jarring trill that seemed to scrape her spine. It rang again. And again.

Nick gave her a curious glance. "Aren't you going to answer that?"

She filled the coffeemaker with water, her back to him. "My machine will pick it up."

The phone stopped ringing and her message played. Heavy breathing followed the beep and then the same creepy voice said, "Soon, my sweet Desire, soon."

Desire glanced over her shoulder at Nick. He glared at the answering machine, then at her, then snatched the receiver. "Hey, buddy, guess what? That ain't gonna happen. You'll have to go through me first. So, take your sick mind games somewhere else."

He slammed down the phone. "How the hell long has that been going on?"

She scooped coffee into the filter. "I told you earlier that some heavy breather was making annoying calls."

"Annoying calls?" He caught her by the shoulders and spun her toward him. "That was a threat."

"I know that." She swallowed against the lump in her throat. He was furious, but not with her. She sighed, resigning herself to filling him in. He would badger her to death otherwise. "He called earlier."

Nick's fingers dug into her upper arms. "How much earlier, D?"

She wrenched from his grip and glanced at the wall clock. "About twenty minutes ago."

"Right when you got home?"

The sound of water bubbling into the glass pot punctuated the quiet. "Yes."

"As though he was waiting for you to come in?" He seemed to want to touch her again, but he held his hands at his sides, his fingers curling into his palms. "As though he might have followed you, too, or was watching for your arrival?"

"I suppose." She told him about spotting Ted Gunderson parked beside the house, how he'd smiled at her, tipped his hat as though he could see her looking out the window at him. "I'm sure he's the caller. He was holding a cell phone to his ear as he left."

Nick's neck was red. "What did he say the first time?"

"Same thing." She rewound her message tape and played it for him.

"I think you'd better tell me all about this Gunderson creep. Who is he?"

The coffee was ready. Desire filled two mugs. She considered adding a shot of whiskey to both, but decided against it. Whiskey had a way of blurring the edges that on a normal night would be welcome. There was nothing normal about this night. She needed a clear head.

With the table separating them, she curled her hands around her cup, letting the heat bite into her palms, the smarting pain keeping her focused, centered. She told him everything she knew about Ted Gunderson and Cindy Whiting. "He was acquitted this morning.

Walked free. I ran into him in the elevator and he called me sweet Desire.''

Nick's dark eyes shone with fury and determination. ''I think we need to pay this Gunderson a visit.''

''We?''

''Yes, *we*.'' He reached across the table and traced a fingertip over her knuckles. ''If you think I'm letting you out of my sight for one minute, you'd better think again. I'm not losing you to some weirdo, D.''

She stared at his large hands, heartened by his words and his touch. She wanted to remind him that she was not his to lose, but given his present mood, the point would be lost on him. She should never have let him in the house. She ought to toss him out before things went too far to turn back, but if she was honest, she'd have to admit that she was warming to the thought of not having to deal with whoever was making these calls alone, with whoever had come into her house and pawed through her lingerie.

The memory of this last dried the saliva in her mouth. She gripped her mug again and lifted her gaze to Nick's. ''I didn't tell you everything.''

His eyes narrowed and his expression clouded. ''What else?''

She decided it would be more effective to show him. ''Come here.''

She led him to her bedroom and pointed at the clothes spilled from the drawers in a heap on the floor. The scent of roses weighed heavy in the air.

''He…was in here today.'' She glanced at the chrome picture frame, the twin to the one in Dare's apartment, that belonged on the bedside table, but was now on the chest of drawers. ''He moved the photograph and…he spread yellow rose petals throughout the things in my bureau.''

Nick cursed, calling the intruder a slew of nasty names. ''How?''

She couldn't answer. Her bravado wilted like the petals among her clothing. Her knees wobbled. She reached out for something to grab hold of, but the only thing between her and the floor was Nick.

He caught her and gathered her to him. She buried her face against his chest, her hands reaching around him to the back where the cotton of his T-shirt was tattered. Careful not to touch his wounds, she held on, grateful for his support, grateful that she was not alone, alone the way Dare must have felt when the stalker came after her.

''I'm not afraid. I'm not a coward, Nick, but sometimes the world demands too much.'' Sometimes, like now, it felt wonderful to let someone else carry the burden. ''Just hold me, Nick, please?''

She thought she heard him moan, but wasn't sure. His arms tightened around her and she gave in to the comfort his embrace afforded. But soon, too soon, she yearned for more than comfort from this man, yearned for all that she'd rejected earlier that day, all that she had no right to want. At this moment, he was the only one who could make her forget, the only one who could return her sense of well-being.

She lifted her head and gazed into his eyes, eyes that smoldered with a need that echoed the one shimmering through her. She didn't fight his kiss, but welcomed it, ached for it. She felt the towel fall from her head, felt his long tapered fingers cool against her temples, stroking through her damp hair as his tongue feathered her lips, a touch so gentle and sweet it roused shivers of need in every intimate part of her.

His massaging fingertips set her pulse humming, and her breath came quicker, louder, a siren song inside her head, against her ears, drowning out all the reasons why this was wrong.

Silencing her guilt. Her thoughts of Dare.

Nick's hands moved out of her hair and down her shoulders, across her back, lower and lower, lifting the hem of her robe until his fingertips encountered her naked bottom. He moaned, pulled her roughly against his engorged need, then as though she'd smacked him, he straightened, breaking the kiss and pulling back from her, his breathing as ragged as a slowing runner, holding his hands up, palms out. "No. No. Not like this."

His withdrawal was sobering, as though he'd drenched her in ice water, or eclipsed the sun. She could barely catch her breath.

"It would be so damn easy to haul you to that bed, to take what we both need, but sooner or later you'd regret it…because you don't really *want* it." Nick struggled to regain his composure, looking as though he was mentally kicking himself for letting things go too far.

She'd like to kick him. She shoved her damp hair out of her face and tugged the belt of her robe so tightly it cut into her waist. "Why do you always assume you know what I want?"

They stared long and hard at one another, but Nick ignored her question. Soon he spun away, his gaze scanning the room, closing her out emotionally as she'd done to him many times. She supposed she deserved it, but was surprised at how it stung. Had he felt this hurt when she'd rebuffed him?

He squatted and gathered some of the rose petals and gazed up at her. "How did he get in here?"

"I don't know." She lifted her chin and batted her hair out of her eyes again. "You arrived before I could check."

They checked then. Every window and door was locked, none had been jimmied or otherwise tampered with that Nick or she could see.

Nick scowled. "Who has a key to your house?"

"No one who'd do this." Desire could not imagine anyone she knew stalking her sister...or her.

"Then how did *he* lay his hands on a key?"

"How should I know?"

"Did Dare have one?"

"No."

"Then who does?"

"My parents, me and...my neighbor, Mrs. Hagen."

Nick considered a moment. "Would your neighbor have let a stranger into your house?"

"I wouldn't have thought so."

"Then maybe this guy is someone you know?"

She frowned. "You mean, someone Mrs. Hagen would recognize?"

He nodded.

She tried to recall whether or not this was possible, but after a moment gave up. "I'm not sure."

"Call her and find out."

Desire shook her head. "She'll be in bed by now. She's pretty deaf and refuses to get a hearing aid. Vanity, I suspect. I won't be able to talk to her until morning."

"Then we'll call her in the morning. Meanwhile, since you don't appear to have a guest room, I'll crash on your couch."

As much as Desire liked the idea of not being alone

the rest of the night, she could not dismiss Michael Pride's words about the erotomaniac going after any person they perceived as an obstacle between them and the object of their affection. Nick had threatened the stalker, placed himself directly in the line of fire as it were. At the moment, he was probably in more jeopardy from this creep than she was.

That terrified her. "Nick, you need to go home."

He strode into the hall and opened the linen closet. He pulled out a pillow and blanket and hugged them to him. "I'm not going anywhere without you. You're not going anywhere without me."

She laughed, a terse, derisive chuckle in her throat. "Nick, that's ridiculous. We don't even know who this stalker is. Or when we'll find that out. We can't quit our jobs—"

"Who's quitting? You're on leave of absence and I'm, well, er, I have some time coming to me."

She planted her hands on her hips. "We are most certainly *not* moving in together until he is caught and dealt with."

Nick winked at her, then left her standing in the hallway. "See you in the morning."

She glared at his departing back. "This discussion is not over, Rossetti."

"'Night, D."

She groaned, but knew there was no arguing with him further tonight. She stalked back into the bedroom, faced again with the sickeningly sweet aroma of roses and the knowledge that some stranger had violated her, a stranger who was probably already plotting Nick's demise.

Chapter Eight

Desire spent a restless night, tossing and turning, unable to banish the scent of roses that pervaded her room, haunted her dreams. No. Not dreams, nightmares in which she chased after Dare on legs packed with concrete, trying to catch up to her, trying to apologize for her betrayal, trying to deny that she wanted Nick. She failed to reach Dare on all levels, failed to make her understand, failed to earn her forgiveness.

She awoke at dawn with a lingering sadness weighing on her heart, and her body feeling heavy, languid. *Coffee. Strong. Three sugars. That would get her blood moving. Her thoughts focused.* She padded toward the kitchen on bare feet, wearing an oversize cotton T-shirt and leggings she'd found in the dryer the night before, after dumping everything from the dresser into the hamper.

Sunlight filtered through the miniblinds and a gentle snoring echoed through the house like the throaty purr of a contented cat. Her gaze slipped across the man sleeping on the sofa, and a rush of emotion she didn't want to feel swelled inside her. He was on his back, one bare foot over the armrest, one leg propped on the floor, one arm over the pillow and one draped across his flat belly. The blanket, slewed sideways, half covered his naked chest.

A smile tugged at Desire's mouth, at her heart. He had to have spent a worse night than she, but he'd stayed, despite the discomfort to himself, stayed to keep her safe, despite the risk to himself. She'd always thought of Nick Rossetti as someone she was physically drawn to, but looking at him now, considering the whole man not merely his sensuous side, she discovered that she was more than attracted to him. She was developing a grudging respect for him and his dogged nature.

But since he wouldn't do what was best for himself, she would have to do it for him. She walked to the kitchen, mulling over what she could say that would send him packing and keep him from wanting anything more to do with her, no matter who was after her. Minutes later, the coffee was brewed and nothing clever or inspired had occurred to her. Cursing her sluggish mind, she gabbed a mug and began pouring.

"Make that two," Nick said, his sudden appearance almost giving her heart failure. She glanced over her shoulder, her gaze colliding with his. His chin was all black whiskers, his teeth gleaming white in the middle of all that ebony hair, his mouth curved upward in a sleepy, lopsided grin that curled her toes. He hadn't bothered with the tattered T-shirt, and her gaze fell to his well-defined chest. More black hair curled between his pecs and across that washboard belly down into the waistband of his jeans. She remembered the secret places adorned with denser hair and felt her cheeks redden.

She grappled for composure, concentrated on the purple bruise two inches below his left nipple. "Does that hurt as bad as it looks?"

"It's tender."

"How about the cuts on your back?"

"They're healing."

"Good. Good. Next time you sneak up on me, make some noise. I wouldn't want to hit you where you're already hurting." She handed him a mug, softening her expression. *Keep it friendly. Keep it light. Keep it professional.* "Aren't you expected in Los Angeles?"

His mug made it halfway to his mouth as though the question caused him more discomfort than his injuries. "I—I told you, I had some sick leave coming."

"I never took you for the type to be laid low by a bruise and some scratches." In fact, despite the damages, he looked too damn healthy by half. She cursed to herself. She'd counted on his going to work. If he'd decided against reporting in, she'd have an even tougher time getting rid of him.

He balanced his hip against the counter, standing close to her. "I don't suppose you'd have some spare male clothes anywhere in this charming house?"

"No." She reached for the box of sugar cubes in the cupboard above the sink, not looking at him, concentrating on sweetening her coffee.

"No men in your life, D?" Looking too pleased for her liking, he set his mug on the counter. "Well, that's okay, I've got some sweats in the trunk of my car."

"Sweats? Why don't you just go home and change? Sweats will be too hot for today."

"Too hot?" He lowered his voice and leaned toward her, so close his breath teased her ear. "Worried about me?"

"Damn straight, Rossetti." She turned toward him, found him too close and retreated a step, slamming right into the refrigerator. She wished her voice wouldn't wobble when he did things like that. "You're taking too big a risk being here."

His gaze seemed to stroke her cheek. "I'd risk anything for you, D."

"Don't say that." She poked her finger at him. "Even in jest."

"I'm not jesting." He took a step toward her, effectively cornering her.

She couldn't swallow. "Why don't you go home, clean up, shave, change clothes, do whatever else it is you have to do?"

He scowled at the suggestion and bent his head close to hers. "You've got someone calling and making threats and you want me to back off? This guy is nuts. He thinks you love him. He imagines that you're lovers. He's likely to show up here and prove that to you. Is that what you want—to be raped by a lunatic?"

Desire felt the heat drop from her cheeks. She'd wanted to shock him; instead, he'd shocked her. "Damn you, Rossetti. Don't try turning this around on me. You're the one in danger. You need to stay as far from me as you can."

Nick grabbed her upper arms and roughly pulled her to him. She swore she could feel his heart hammering against her own. "Nothing and no one can make me stay away from you. Get that through that thick, gorgeous head of yours, will you? We are in this together."

He gentled his hold on her and she closed her eyes, feeling his kiss at her temple, a soft nuzzle against her neck. *It would be so easy to give in to this pleasure, this passion he evoked, the way she had last night.* He lifted his head, released her and gathered his coffee. His gaze drifted over her, heat sizzling in the depths of his brown eyes. "As enticing as that outfit is, maybe you should get dressed."

Enticing? She glanced down at the old leggings and baggy T-shirt. Was he serious? The fire in his eyes seemed to blaze brighter, and her body started to respond.

"Unless you plan on us showering together," he said, his voice like roughened velvet, "I'd suggest you hurry."

"I'll be sure and use all the hot water, Rossetti. A cold shower is definitely on your agenda this morning."

"Oh, it would take more than a cold shower to make me stop wanting you, D."

Shaking her head, she skirted past him. As she did so, she swore she saw a shadow move through the backyard, away from her house.

RENEE HAGEN, Desire's neighbor, turned out to be a former silent-film star, a contract player at MGM named Renee Twilight, who had spent her twenties as a leading lady of B pictures. Near eighty now, she retained the good bones that showed she'd once been a beauty. "I retired when the lines around my eyes and mouth showed signs of developing into craters," she told Desire and Nick. "Plastic surgery was too expensive and ghastly painful, according to a couple of the big stars I was chummy with at the studio. And I wasn't about to settle for becoming a character actor. So, I decided to grow old gracefully.

"Besides, I had a current 'Mr. Renee Twilight,' my Bobby Hagen, who was making a decent salary. We bought this little house and moved in." She sat on her sofa, serving them tea. Two long-haired gray-and-white tabby cats crowded into her lap. Fur floated on the air and clumps of it clung to the furniture like furry little doilies.

Nick stifled the urge to sneeze. D had introduced him as her friend, but, despite the fact that his sweats bore the LAPD insignia, clearly identifying him as a cop, the elderly woman's eyes brightened as though with a secret smile. He suspected she thought there was more to the relationship than D had told her, than D would admit, even to herself. Nick decided she was a pretty observant old gal.

"Renee," D said, "did you let someone into my house yesterday?"

Renee grinned with delight. "Did you like the flowers, dear? They were so beautiful and fragrant."

She handed D a cup of steaming, weak brown liquid. A cat hair floated on the surface. D forced a pleasant acceptance of the tea, then slid cup and saucer onto the table beside her, looking distressed. "Yes, the flowers were lovely and…unexpected."

"Well, of course. He said they were a surprise." Renee held out a cup and saucer to Nick, but kept her attention on D. "Were you surprised, dear?"

"Oh, yes. Very." D's face paled and Nick's belly clenched.

He bent toward Renee. The house was too damn hot and sweat beaded his unshaven cheeks. "What did the man look like?"

Renee's silvery eyebrows lifted slightly, her expression puzzled. "Why is that important? *He* didn't send the flowers. He said they were from Ms. Hamilton's lov—ah, er—gentleman friend."

She gave Nick a knowing look, and he stifled the urge to tell her that she'd let a maniac into D's house. "Just the same, do you think you could describe him?"

"Well, I'm not sure." She scrunched her eyes and stared at the ceiling. "I remember the flowers very clearly. A hybrid tea rose. Peace, I believe it's called. Such a lovely specimen. So yellow. But the man, hmm, he was someone who'd be used in a crowd scene, wouldn't stand out, you know?" She glanced at Nick again. "I think he was shorter than you and stockier."

"Did you see his hair, perhaps, or his eye color?" Nick pressed.

"Well, let's see." Her gaze went to the ceiling again. "It was hot yesterday. I was in my garden working. I had on my gardening smock and my gardening hat and gloves."

"But what was *he* wearing?" Nick wrestled his patience.

She looked at him again. Her mouth turned up at the corners. "That's just it. I was hot in my gloves and hat and I remember thinking he had to be even warmer than I in those overalls and dark cap."

Nick felt a twitch of excitement. Finally, they might be getting somewhere. He pulled a palm-size notepad from the pocket of his sweatpants. "What color were the overalls?"

"Gray. I recall thinking that he looked more like a mechanic than a florist's deliveryman."

"A mechanic?" D said. "Did you notice whether his nails were dark with grime?"

Renee considered, then shook her head. "I can't recall."

Nick scribbled on the pad. "Was there any lettering on the overalls or cap?"

"Not that I noticed." She absently petted the cats, first one, then the other. Left, right, left, right. "Now that's strange, isn't it—that there was no insignia on his clothes? I wonder why I didn't think of that yesterday?''

''Did you notice if he wore a ruby stud in one of his ears.''

''Oh, no jewelry. That I would have noticed.''

D put three sugars into her teacup and began to stir. ''Did you see what he was driving, what florist he worked for?''

''Well, no, dear, but surely there was a card with the flowers…''

''No.'' D laid the spoon onto the saucer.

''Well, that's too bad. I imagined there was a love note attached.'' Her features collapsed in disappointment. She shook her head sadly, gazing first at D in sympathy, then at Nick pointedly, disapprovingly, stroking the cats harder, tsking her tongue. ''Men these days just aren't as romantic as they were in my day.''

Taking the reprimand personally, as he was sure it was meant, Nick grimaced and tapped his pencil on the tablet. ''Did the deliveryman stick around for any length of time?''

''Oh, no. I let him in the back door and he put the flowers on the kitchen table, and we left.''

And he came back, Nick thought, *having somehow managed to leave a window or door open.*

''You aren't drinking your tea, dear,'' Renee said to D. ''Is something wrong?''

''No,'' D said, standing. ''I'm sorry, Renee, I forgot about a meeting I have to get to. Please forgive us. I'll come back to visit when I can stay longer. Okay?''

''Well, certainly, dear.'' She tried wresting the cats from her lap.

Nick told her to stay put, they would see themselves out. ''Don't let anyone else in for any reason unless Ms.

Hamilton tells you specifically, okay?'' He handed Renee his card. ''If you see 'the florist' again, please call me immediately on my cell phone, okay?''

''My goodness, why?'' Renee read the card and frowned. ''Has that deliveryman done something wrong?''

''Not that we can prove. Yet.''

NICK PACED Desire's living room, easily making it from one end to the other in six of his long strides, his gaze steadied on the tablet. ''The kind of overalls a mechanic wears.'' He lifted his gaze to hers. There was excitement in his eyes, the kind she'd often seen in the eyes of policemen she knew when they had a lead that might pan out. ''Like Ted Gunderson wears? That's what you thought too, wasn't it?''

''It crossed my mind, but Gunderson is not a mechanic.'' She didn't know whether or not he wore or even owned overalls like the ones Renee had described. ''He works in a tire store.''

''He does?'' Nick's face lit up in a new way, and he smacked his hand on the tablet. ''Perfect. Since I need a new tire.''

A slow creeping smile stole over her. Ted may have been the one who'd destroyed Nick's tire, but by doing so he'd given them an excuse to confront him at work in a way that would not seem like harassment. ''If he slashed your tire in L.A., I imagine he'll be surprised you've come all the way to Santa Beverly to have the tire fixed.''

''Not fixed. Replaced.''

''Replaced, then.''

''Yes, but we need to know he's going to be there today.''

Would he be? she wondered. Or had Gunderson's been the shadow she thought she'd seen earlier in the backyard? Should she mention that to Nick, or would he just think she was so spooked she was seeing things?

He asked, "Where's your phone book?"

"In the kitchen, by the phone."

Nick returned with the book laid across his palm, flopped open to the Yellow Pages, her portable phone in the other hand. He was using the antenna to flip the pages as he searched. "Where exactly does Gunderson work?"

"Bayside Tires."

He found the number, dialed, and a moment later said, "May I speak to Ted Gunderson?"

Nick grinned and hung up, wiping his forehead with the sleeve of his sweatshirt. "He's there. Whoever answered called him to the phone." He returned the phone and book to the kitchen, then came back and reached for her hand. "Let's go."

She ignored his hand and rose from the sofa, giving his appearance a once-over. "Don't you want to shave first?"

This seemed to surprise him and he studied her long and hard, his eyes narrowing slowly, sexily. "Not unless *you* want to shave me?"

Desire felt a frisson of heat flash through the core of her. As a child she'd been fascinated watching her mother shave her father every Saturday morning. The intimate ritual was a playful experience that seemed fun for both her parents, bonding them, strengthening their love. Desire looked forward to sharing the same ritual with her own husband one day. But not with Nick. Never with Nick. The way he unsettled her, he'd be lucky if she didn't leave him a bloodied mess.

She squared her shoulders and forced steel into her tone, a ploy she'd used often in court. "Aren't you afraid I'd slit your throat, Rossetti?"

"I'd take my chances." His voice had deepened, going all rough and needy, and he reached for her face, stroking his knuckles along the curve of her cheek and laughing softly at her blush.

He stepped away from her, rubbed his jaw with his palm and studied himself in the mirror near the front door. "Kind of gives me an intimidating look, don't you think?"

"And that makes you feel what?" She blinked, wrestling for composure, angry at herself for her reaction to his every touch, his constant and always disconcerting glances. "Macho?"

"Dangerous. Ruthless." He grinned at her again and shook his head. "Mean."

She lifted her eyebrows and nodded. "I guess it might serve our purposes." Yes, it might just do that. She opened the door. "After you, scruffy."

As they started to his car, Nick said, "I'm not sure the outfit works though. Besides, I'm starting to feel like an overheated furnace. Does this town have a Smart-Mart or Bullseye, or some other kind of department store?"

"Of course."

Desire couldn't help herself from scanning the bushes at the edge of her house, then the road. Her pulse raced several beats too fast. But if someone was hiding nearby watching them, she discerned no one.

At the store, Nick bought acid-washed jeans and a Harley-Davidson T-shirt emblazoned with a crude sentiment. At the car, he reached under the hood and grimed up his hands then rubbed them on the pants to make them look worn. Desire felt overdressed in her clean khakis and striped camp shirt.

Bayside Tires was located nowhere near the bay, but rather on the main drag of Santa Beverly. It was a single-story stucco building, once pink, now faded to a dingy bisque. Cars were parked inside the three stalls, two lifted on jacks, one on a hoist. Tires were piled in stacks on the apron and inside the garage area, against the high walls and in the office near the windows.

Nick parked by the office door and left her waiting in the car with the windows down. The intermittent but loud whining whir of an impact wrench tightening lug nuts on wheels shrieked in the morning air.

As she watched the men working in the shop, she realized with disappointment that none of them wore overalls. In fact, one of them wore a muscle shirt. Ted Gunderson, she realized with a start, and he was striding toward her in that disjointed shuffle of his, a grin as cold as air-conditioning on his face.

Desire glanced at the ignition for the keys and swore. Nick had taken them with him; she could not raise the power windows.

A grimy hand landed on the window frame. "I thought that was you."

He stank of rubber and dust and body odor. She scooted as far from him as she could without giving away that his very nearness made her stomach churn. She ignored him.

He leaned closer, smacking gum, his dirty-brown hair as greasy as ever, the ruby stud as dull as a drop of blood on his earlobe. "In case you forgot, I was acquitted yesterday. This is harassment, lady. I'll sic my lawyer on you."

"Since when is buying a tire harassment?"

"The tire I want replaced is in the trunk, buddy," Nick's beefy hand landed on Gunderson's shoulder.

Gunderson jerked at the contact, the cocky glint in his eyes dispersing as he took in Nick's size and appearance. She had to admit he was a formidable adversary. She bit the inside corners of her mouth to keep from smiling, reminding herself that Gunderson might assume a meekness now, but he was dangerous. If she was right about him, he'd murdered Cindy Whiting, then Dare and had chosen Desire as his next target.

This small victory could very well backfire on them. He could come after Nick, using cowardly tactics to get rid of him.

Nick led Gunderson to the trunk and plunked the damaged tire into the tire jockey's arms. "See that gash?"

"Looks like you ran over some big sharp object," Gunderson said.

"Yeah, like a switchblade maybe."

Gunderson stepped back and frowned, his intimidation falling away like a dropped wrench. "What is this? You and your girlfriend trying to stick something new on me? Well, it ain't gonna work. I didn't do this."

Nick pinned him between the car and his large body. "What were you doing in her neighborhood last night?"

"Was I in her neighborhood? Huh, imagine that. Well, pal, it's a free country and I'm a free man. I can drive anywhere I like."

"Mr. Rossetti." Gunderson's boss approached with a handful of papers. "We'll take your car in stall two now. Ted, are you finished with the Martins' car?"

"Just about," Gunderson replied, shoving the tire at Nick, pushing him back a step. He circled around to where Desire sat in the car and whispered, "He your bodyguard…or your boyfriend? Either way, if I wanted to get to you, he couldn't stop me."

Chapter Nine

As they drove away from Bayside Tires, Desire pondered Gunderson and his threat. He was wiry with weight-lifter arms defined in a gym, as well as from his work as a tire jockey.

Nick, on the other hand...

She glanced at him—at the jeans stretched taut over his muscled thighs, the T-shirt strained over his strong upper arms—and felt a catch in her throat, a dart of heat in her belly. He was larger in every respect than Gunderson; she doubted Nick was in any danger of the smaller man coming after him in a physical confrontation.

Besides, she suspected Gunderson reserved his fists for women, or, perhaps, the occasional hapless soul less able to defend against such an attack.

She'd like to dismiss the man and his threats, but her job was prosecuting stalkers and other off-kilter individuals. She hadn't needed losing Dare, or even the fright last night, to instruct her on how vulnerable the average person was to the crazies in this world.

Gunderson, she feared, had something deadly in mind for Nick. A gun. A knife. A fatal accident. She felt suddenly cold, despite the sun beating in through the window, and hugged herself.

Nick glanced at her as he headed the sedan out of town. "Are you all right?"

"I'm fine," she lied, not wanting him worrying about her when she'd rather he stay alert. "I was just wondering what we were going to do next."

"We need to get the phone number of the *Celebrity Crier* and find out the real name and address of that Eager Eddie character. Meanwhile, we're going to visit the good Doctor Falls again."

"Why?"

He held what appeared to be a business card between his forefinger and thumb. "While the tire was being changed and Gunderson was finishing up the Martin job, I looked around his workstation and came up with this."

"What is it?"

"An appointment reminder card...for the Falls Clinic."

Shock tracked through her; she snatched the card from him. "Gunderson is seeing Dr. Falls?"

"Or one of the other doctors at the clinic—it doesn't specify who."

Her shock dissolved to curiosity. "What do you suppose he's being treated for?"

Nick changed lanes, tossing out suggestions. "Anger management, obsessive-compulsive disorder, schizophrenia, erotomania?"

"All of the above?" she said derisively.

Nick grunted in agreement. "I wonder if he'd tell us if he realized it would go a long way toward eliminating him as a suspect?"

She gave a scornful laugh. "Knowing what he's being treated for could also nail his hide to the wall. He might not be the brightest bulb in the four-pack, but he's not going to rat himself out.''

"Maybe one of his cohorts—one of those guys he works with—or his boss knows.''

She considered this, then shook her head. "I don't think so. He's too macho. He'd never admit to anyone he needed a shrink—and he'd rely on the confidentiality of the patient-doctor relationship to protect that secret.''

"There must be someone who knows,'' Nick persisted. "Someone always knows.''

"I can't even guess who that would be.''

"That's why we're going to the clinic.''

"Why? They won't tell us anything about him. So why bother?'' Her frustration was a tight knot in her chest. She handed the card back to Nick and he stuffed it into the visor.

"Because Dr. Falls owes us, D. That scumbag she wouldn't talk about yesterday, the one she *knew* was stalking Dare, got into your house, touched your things, made you feel violated and unsafe in your own home. The least she can do is explain the workings of the erotomaniacal mind to us.''

The fact that the man who had tricked her neighbor into letting him into her house might be Gunderson, and that the doctor, forced to be silent by her professional ethics, might be protecting him, filled Desire with an old helplessness. One of the most frustrating things about the law—which she respected and had sworn to uphold—was that it could also restrict her ability to gain the justice she daily sought for victims of crime.

Being *victimized* herself stripped her of her normal objectivity, made it almost impossible to see anyone else's side in this situation. Even Dr. Falls's. A ripple of surprise tripped through Desire. Until this moment, she'd never questioned her own black-and-white outlook on everything, every situation, never considered anything could fall into that supposedly gray area that Nick claimed existed, that Nick based his life decisions on.

But all the edges seemed fuzzy now—nothing clear, nothing within the usual guidelines that showed her how to proceed. Nick's life was at risk. She had to do something, even if that something went against everything she'd ever believed, even if it meant bending some of the rules she had sworn to uphold. Even if it involved exposing her own vulnerabilities. "Maybe we can reach Dr. Falls on a human level, touch that part of her that makes her care about all people, and get her to color outside the lines in a couple of places."

Nick's eyebrows lifted at this. He grabbed his cell phone. "Do you recall the number of the clinic?"

"No." Desire caught his hand, the one with the phone. Did he also feel the tremor that seemed to start in her heart and culminate in her hand on his? "I'm not sure we should call first. If she's not expecting us, it might give us an advantage."

He gazed at her, measuring her in some secret way, some purely male way. His beard had grown denser, increasing his unkempt appearance. There was something raw and sexual about the look that sent tiny electrons of anticipation through Desire every time she glanced at him. He seemed dangerous, and she supposed he could be, though he'd never shown that side to her.

She forced her mind from these intimate thoughts of Nick, but couldn't help wondering if Dr. Falls would think him dangerous, too. If she did, would that make her more cooperative or less? Probably less, Desire decided. "Are you sure you want to use the intimidating biker getup on the doctor?"

"Huh?" His eyebrows lifted, then he made the connection, and groped his chin whiskers, gazed at his shirt and grungy jeans. "Guess we should make a quick stop at my place."

HIS PLACE WAS SOUTH of the city, in Hawthorne, on a street lined with aged single-story, two-bedroom stucco houses, neatly trimmed hedges and manicured stamp-size lawns. Old trees grew throughout the block, and campers and boats were parked at nearly every other residence.

Nick pulled into his driveway, feeling suddenly, strangely, self-conscious. He'd dreamed of D coming here, but this was the first time she'd actually been here. He glanced at the bilious-green house with its asphalt-shingle roof and chain-link fence, the fence of choice on his block, and found himself struggling for something good to say about it. "It's not much, but the mortgage is affordable, the upkeep negligible."

D glanced at him, amusement rife on her lovely face. "Are you apologizing for this perfectly charming little house, Rossetti?"

"No," he lied, knowing he was doing just that. *Perfectly charming,* to his way of thinking, described a thatched cottage somewhere, or a dump that some high-pressure Realtor was trying to sell. This house was neither. What it was, was small, about half the size of hers, in a lower-middle-class neighborhood, the best he could afford given his salary.

She obviously made more money than he. Until this minute, the differences in their income had never occurred to him, never mattered. They seemed momentous now. He was a good cop, but it was really all he aspired to, whereas he suspected D would like to be more than a deputy district attorney one day. If ever they managed to get past the issue of Dare, this lack of ambition in him and abundance of it in her might be something to stop them cold. And as long as Dare stood in their way, he could not discuss the other with her.

Heavy-hearted, he shut off the engine. "You want to wait in the car? I won't be long."

She smiled, seeming to recognize and enjoy his discomfort. "And pass up a chance to see how the 'intimidating' bachelor lives?"

"Emphasis on bachelor. Don't expect much. It's suits me." Nick swore. He was still apologizing, couldn't seem to help himself. What was the matter with him? He unlocked the front door, trying to dredge up a memory of the condition in which he'd left the house, recalling at the last second that he'd been on suspension for a week now, most of which time he'd spent cleaning up, inside and out.

She entered first and Nick shut the door behind them. D was eyeing the room, inspecting it, appraising it. He squirmed internally, wondering what it told her about him. That he liked mission furniture, in saddle-brown leather, liked the way it fit a man's frame, pleased a man's eye, that he favored the rough-hewn wood that went with it—even if it better suited a ranch in Laredo than this two-bedroom rambler. That he had a fondness for Indian blankets and fake animal skins, preferred bear and moose sculptures and antique rifles to paintings. That he owned and played an old guitar—which leaned against the fireplace—instead of a stereo and a stack of CDs.

Not one time that he'd envisioned her here had he thought she'd seem anything other than at home...with him. Instead, she seemed out of place, too elegant, too

L.A., as though she'd stamped the red clay of Texas from her high-heel pumps and out of her system for good.

Did this mean that she would never share his life? Never fit into it the way he'd always felt she would? The possibility tore straight through his heart and stomach like a hollow-point bullet. He started to say, "Make yourself at home," but it seemed a cruel joke…on him. "I'll just be a minute."

"You mean you don't want me to shave you, Rossetti?"

A teasing glint danced in her aqua eyes, while sass issued from her like steam heat in every line of her hands-on-hips stance. *Such luscious hips.* Damn, but this woman was in his blood, in his heart. Why couldn't she also be in his life? Hell, he couldn't deal with this now. Nor should he. *Keep it light, Rossetti. Keep her mind focused on something besides the stalker who's turning her world inside out.*

He shifted his neck, as though the collar of his T-shirt was choking him, and grinned wryly. "Next time, D…when we aren't in such a hurry."

He returned within five minutes, shaved, his hair combed, wearing clean gray chinos and a red polo shirt, all traces of the biker gone. "How's this?"

D glanced up from the magazine she was perusing, drew a sharp breath at the sight of him, and yearning flashed through her eyes. His body reacted with a surge of need, hot through his veins.

Despite his growing misgivings about any hope of a future relationship with this woman, he chuckled. "I take it you approve."

She blushed sexily, but shook her head in denial, and a mocking laugh sounded in her throat as she stood, dropped the magazine on the coffee table and started for the door. "Let's put it this way, Rossetti. You'll do."

Nick couldn't stop the grin that spread across his face. He liked her wit, her sense of irony. This was a woman a man would never tire of. He followed her out to his car, pleased, too, that he'd gotten her mind on something other than Gunderson for a while. Even if it was himself. Especially if it was himself.

He spotted something on the windshield, trapped by the driver's-side wiper—a flyer of some sort.

He frowned, snatched it free and read it quickly, his skin going cold with outrage. Swearing, he glanced up and down the street, but whoever had left this was long gone.

"What is it?" D asked, the color drained from her face, the teasing atmosphere between them destroyed.

Nick wanted to break something, preferably the fingers of the creep who'd put this on his car. "It's from *him*. Warning me to stay away from you or I'll be sorry."

She blew out a noisy breath, as though she'd been holding it in until it hurt. "I told you that you were the one in danger. Nick, you have to listen to me. You have to stay away from me."

"So you can end up like Dare?" He caught her gently but firmly by the shoulders. "No. I'm not leaving you, D. This guy doesn't scare me. He pisses me off."

"Well—" she laughed shakily "—at least we agree on something. Tear that damn thing up."

"No, D. It's evidence, proof that we aren't imagining a stalker." He knew the only reason she'd suggested they destroy the threatening note was that she was shaken. Silently cursing the stalker, he released her and went to his trunk for a plastic bag. "And it might help convince Dr. Falls to be more cooperative."

NICK AND DESIRE started up the steps of the Falls Clinic. The doors opened and to her surprise a man she recognized, but hadn't thought to see here, emerged. She froze, grasped Nick's arm, wanted to disappear behind him, but could only stand and await the inevitable.

Ron Whiting spoke first. "A.D.A. Hamilton?"

Trying to swallow her nerves, Desire met his gaze. After Gunderson's acquittal yesterday, she'd dreaded coming face-to-face with Whiting, had hoped not to have to deal with him until she'd gotten through her own problems. Life was never that easy. As though she, and not the jury, had found Gunderson innocent, she also felt the intense and inexplicable need to apologize to this man. She resisted the urge. "Hello, Officer Whiting."

She introduced Nick and the men shook hands, but Whiting returned his focus to her.

"Please, call me Ron," he said with insistence. He was beautiful in an ethereal way; his flyaway white-blond hair seemed to float around his head like a halo. He looked anything but a police officer. "You seeing the doctor, too?"

"Yes, I—" She stopped herself, grappling with her composure. She'd expected him to be belligerent. He seemed anything but, angelic in manner as well as appearance. "Not professionally, if that's what you mean."

"Oh. I thought maybe—" He broke off. His fair complexion gained a pinkish hue, emphasizing his cherubic cheeks, his sad green eyes. "I'm doing grief counseling. I just thought maybe with your sister and all, that you were here for the same reason...."

His Only Desire

"A logical assumption." She recalled how upset he'd been yesterday. "How are you doing?"

"Maintaining." He took a step down and nodded toward the building. "Coming here helps."

"I'm glad. Yesterday's verdict was a farce."

He flattened his bow-shaped lips, glanced away and then back at her again. "Yeah. Catch you around City Hall."

She'd thought he might blame her, or her office, but all he exuded was a resigned sadness. "I'll see you."

He started toward the parking lot again. Nick's gaze was full of questions. She started to explain then stopped as it struck her that Whiting could help them, if he would. "Wait a minute, Nick, I'll be right back."

She darted down the steps after Whiting. "Ron, I need a really big favor, if you wouldn't mind."

"Name it." He sounded, surprisingly, as if he owed her something, instead of the other way around, which was what she felt. "You tried to put Gunderson away for doing Cindy and even though it didn't happen, you gave it a hell of a shot, *and* you were one of the few who didn't think I—" His soft voice caught. "What do you need?"

She touched his arm, a gesture of tenderness to this man who, like she, was grieving the loss of someone precious and dear to him. "I heard a rumor that you have a relative who works for the *Celebrity Crier,* is it true?"

"Oh, God, that awful rag." He grimaced, then nodded. "My cousin, Lois. It's the family shame according to my mother. You'd think Lo was writing the stories instead of running the advertising department."

Desire smiled sympathetically. "Could you call her and ask if she would give you the name and address of the photographer who sold the *Crier* those last photographs of Dare?''

His white-blond eyebrows dipped low, and she could see he was curious as to why she wanted the information. ''Sure. I'll get back to you as soon as I have it.''

She handed him her card. ''My cell-phone number is on this.''

She hurried back to Nick. He pinned her between his massive frame and the entrance door, a possessive and worried glint in his brown eyes. ''Who was that guy?''

''Ron Whiting. He's agreed to help us locate the photographer who sold the *Crier* those last photos of Dare.'' But it was Nick who had her knees weak as she gazed into his handsome face. Why did he have to have this effect on her? ''Ron's a Santa Beverly cop.''

Nick dipped his head, his eyebrows lifting, his breath warm and minty. ''The *ex*-husband of that murdered kindergarten teacher, Cindy Whiting, the one you tried Gunderson for?''

''Yes. Ron and Cindy were getting back together. It was what drove Gunderson nuts.''

Nick moved away from her and she felt as though a body shield had been removed, leaving her vulnerable, needy. For him.

Gathering her composure, she squinted up at him, and could almost see his mental wheels churning as he mulled something over. The glare of the sun, hidden behind the brownish haze that trapped humidity between the smog and the ground, was giving her a headache. Exhaust fumes from the constant traffic made it worse.

She felt overly warm, in need of shade. *Are you sure it's the weather and not Nick that's making you extra warm?* asked a small voice inside her head. She brushed aside the unwelcome question and gave way to her impatience. "What are you thinking, Rossetti?"

He planted his intense gaze on her and her internal heat register fluttered higher. "If Gunderson was stalking Cindy Whiting, when did he get fixated on Dare? And why? And not only that, if he *is* an erotomaniac, why didn't he just get rid of Ron Whiting instead of Cindy?"

The question set her aback. "This is the second time in the past hour that you've suggested the man who was stalking Dare and is now stalking me might be someone other than Gunderson."

"We don't know enough to convict him and we ought to keep our options open, just in case there's a snake out there who knows how to lay low until he's ready to strike."

Her insides gave a sickening quiver. She'd prefer Gunderson be the stalker—a known entity who they might be able to stay one step ahead of. But if it was someone Nick and she had not even suspected yet, the danger could, as Nick suggested, spring from anywhere.

They entered the black pyramid tower that was the Falls Clinic, and Desire felt again that sensation of stepping from a rank-smelling sauna into a four-story-high cooler etched from marble and glass where the air was filtered and sweet. Again, she was glad Nick was with her, waiting just outside. Something about this place gave her the creeps.

Maybe it was knowing there were so many disturbed minds all under one roof.

Nick said, "I've got to find a men's room. I'll be right back."

"Okay." Desire strode up to the receptionist, Tina, according to the pin on her blouse. She was in her early twenties, wore her streaked hair in the latest movie-star copycat do and had the childlike expression of a true airhead. Desire watched a ready smile part the young woman's thick lips, then surprise and confusion curve them into a perfect O. Her wide-set eyes gaped. It was obvious she thought she was looking at Dare—returned from the dead.

"I'm her sister," Desire told the confused, frightened young woman. "Her twin."

"Oh, man, wow, I never knew she had a twin sister. Whew, for a minute there, I thought—" She giggled, self-conscious, her cheeks glowing red. "May I help you?"

Desire smiled. "I wonder if it would be possible to see Dr. Falls?"

"Do you have an appointment?"

"No. But it's extremely important and I only need a couple of minutes."

"Gee, I dunno…without an appointment…" She seemed to consider, then said, "Is this about your sister?"

"Yes," Desire said, not really lying. Indirectly, it *was* about Dare.

"Dr. Falls is in group right now and can't be interrupted. But if you'd like to wait I'll ask as soon as she's free." She pointed to a line of leather chairs against one of the window walls.

Desire checked her watch. It was almost one o'clock. "How long until the session ends?"

But Tina didn't answer. She was staring at something behind Desire. Desire turned and saw Nick approaching. He was so eye-catchingly handsome, she lost her train of thought. So had Tina. As though Desire had dropped off the face of the earth, the receptionist said, "May I help you, sir?"

"Hi." Nick beamed at Tina, and Desire clenched her teeth. Did he have to turn up the light wattage so high? And why was he ignoring *her?* What was he up to? To her surprise, he produced the appointment card he'd stolen from Gunderson's work station, and said, "I'm not going to be able to keep this appointment and I need to reschedule—if that's not too much trouble."

"Oh, no, no trouble at all," Tina gushed, gazing at him as though he were Brad Pitt and had just told her he loved her. "What's the name?"

"Ted Gunderson."

Desire clamped her mouth tight. She wasn't sure exactly what he hoped to gain, but was willing to play along...for a while.

Tina sighed breathily as though this was the sexiest name she'd ever heard and tugged the card slowly from Nick's grasp, managing to rub her fingers against his, making the gesture irritatingly sensual. Desire felt an almost uncontrollable urge to smack this young woman.

Surely she wasn't jealous...not of Nick Rossetti?

Tina consulted her appointment book, flipping to the page in question, oblivious to the fact that Nick and Desire could and were both reading it upside down. *Very clever, Rossetti.* "Hmm, that's odd," Tina said after a minute, intermittently studying her book and the card. "I don't have you in the schedule. But this *is* Dr. Falls's writing."

"Maybe you should check in your computer?" Nick suggested innocently.

Tina giggled as though she should have thought of that. "Do you know your patient number, Mr. Gunderson?"

"No. I'm sorry. I don't. Is that a problem?"

"No. I can look up your name."

She typed G into the computer. Desire clasped her hands tightly, praying she remained invisible to the young woman, her own eyes glued to what they could see of the monitor. Tina was scrolling through a list of patients whose last names started with G. Why hadn't she simply typed in the name Gunderson? Did it have something to do with the clinic's filing system? *Perhaps Tina's filing system?*

A name flashed onto the screen and every other thought fled from Desire's mind. Connor Gregg. Her boss. Santa Beverly's D.A. What the hell did this mean? Had Connor been a patient here in the past? Or was he one now? She glanced at Nick. He was grinning at Tina. Had he, also, seen Connor's name?

"That's funny," Tina said. "There is no Ted Gunderson in the computer."

"How about T. Gunderson?" Nick suggested. "Or Theodore?"

"Nope. No Gunderson, period."

"Tina?" A woman's voice startled them all. Dr. Breena Falls stood in the doorway of her office, scowling. "What are you doing?"

Chapter Ten

"Oh, Doctor." Tina giggled. "Why, I was just looking for Mr.—"

"I was trying," Nick said, cutting Tina off before she gave him away, "to get an appointment to see you." He hadn't actually said *he* was Gunderson, but what he'd been doing was still illegal, unethical. He'd risked it for D, a risk that could land him in hotter water than he was in now, a risk that could finish his career as a cop, but one he'd take again. For D.

Breena Falls studied him, her gaze unnerving. How long had she been standing there? "Did you want an appointment for a professional consultation, Detective Rossetti, or does this have something else to do with Dare Hamilton?"

"Detective…?" Tina murmured.

Nick didn't know how much Dr. Falls had overheard, but just in case it was less than he feared, he cut Tina off for a second time and caught D by the hand. "Maybe we could speak in your office?"

"I, er, suppose we should." The doctor stepped aside and Nick and D entered. She closed the door behind her. Nick couldn't rid from his mind the visions of his career flushing down a toilet. How much *had* she overhead?

Dr. Falls's smile was taut, giving nothing away. "What might I do for you today?"

Neither Nick nor D spoke until they were all inside the office and the door was closed. Dr. Falls pointed to her desk and the chairs facing it. No one moved in that direction.

"We appreciate your seeing us without an appointment," Nick said, striving to keep the stress he felt from his voice. "We realize you're busy and we'll try not to take up much of your time. We wondered if you would explain an erotomaniac to us."

"An erotomaniac?" The doctor's auburn eyebrows lifted slightly. "Where did you learn that term?"

Nick shrugged, lifting his palms outward. "You do specialize in treating this type of obsession, don't you?"

"Yes, but it's not something I advertise. How did you learn of it?"

"From Michael Pride," Nick supplied.

She tensed. "I see."

D added, "He told us last night that you knew for certain a stalker was after Dare."

"Mr. Pride is free to tell you anything he likes," Breena said. "But, as you both know, I have no such freedom. I cannot discuss or expose anything from your sister's—or Mr. Pride's—sessions with me. Surely you understand, Ms. Hamilton, that my hands are tied?"

D looked as though she was wondering why the doctor was still so uncooperative, but Nick urged her to continue. She licked her lips as though they were dry. "The same stalker who came after Dare was in my house yesterday."

The doctor's eyes widened, and she seemed to choose her words with care. "As far as I know, Dare never actually saw or spoke with this alleged stalker—didn't know if it was a man or woman.''

"Alleged?" Nick said. "Are you saying you didn't believe Dare about there being a stalker?"

"I'm saying how can you know the *same* person was in your house?"

D said, "He brought me yellow roses. They were Dare's favorite. Not mine."

"He brought you flowers?" The doctor was studying D, trying to understand something.

"It wasn't as pretty as Ms. Hamilton makes it sound." Nick scowled at the memory. "The jerk scattered yellow rose petals in her bureau drawers, in all of them, mostly throughout her underwear."

Breena Falls showed no surprise, as though she'd expected this or something like it. "And you have no idea who this person is?"

"No." The slightest glint of fear slipped through D's eyes and sparked Nick's frustration. He cautioned himself to stay calm. But for the first time in his life, he appreciated D's black-and-white outlook. There were no gray areas in this situation, only sharp, clear-cut edges that were poking the hell out of him.

"But you're sure it's a man?" the doctor asked.

"Yes. My neighbor let him into my house. Unfortunately, her description could fit several men."

Including some who are your patients, Doctor, Nick thought, feeling his hold on his temper giving way, despite his best efforts to the contrary. Struggling to rein himself in, he produced the threatening note they'd discovered on his windshield a short time ago. He held the plastic evidence bag out for the doctor to read. "This was left on my car a few minutes ago. Not only is Ms.

Hamilton being scared by this scumbag, but now he's making threats to me."

For the first time, the doctor's enmity dropped away. "It's classic erotomaniacal behavior," she said, her face grave. She switched her gaze between them. "I can tell you that you should be on your guard. That his need to get to Ms. Hamilton and consummate the relationship he thinks he has with her will escalate. At first, anyone close to Ms. Hamilton may be perceived as an annoyance, but soon they will be seen as keeping her from the erotomaniac. This message is not just an idle threat. You need to take it seriously."

She inhaled noisily. "You should warn your family and friends about the stalker, Ms. Hamilton, for their sakes. You may even want to move as far as you can from here, but I must caution you that a determined erotomaniac will follow you anywhere."

"So basically," D said, her voiced edged with a mixture of frustration and fury, "you're telling me there is nothing I can do to catch and prosecute this stalker?"

"Nothing to stop him?" Nick was dumbfounded, his belly awash in anger.

The doctor shook her head. "Sadly, no. Not unless you figure out who he is. My best suggestion, Detective, is that you stay away from Ms. Hamilton. He is likely watching you."

Nick exploded. "That's the same advice you gave Pride and Dare and it led to Dare's death."

"Your captain, Detective—" Breena folded her hands together, a mannerism that seemed affected, as though she employed it in times of stress to remind herself to stay calm "—assures me that Dare Hamilton's death was an accident."

Nick flinched inwardly at the news that Breena Falls

had spoken to his chief. Damn. "That *accident* could have been avoided if Dare had been living with Pride."

The doctor eyed Nick with sympathy. "I thought you wanted my experienced opinion on erotomaniacs, Detective."

"We do. But nothing you've told us so far will lead us to figuring out who this person is or how to neutralize his actions."

She considered a long moment, then said, "Perhaps if you laid a trap for him, you'd find out who it is and you could go from there."

"You want D to set herself up as bait for this scumball? What kind of medicine are you practicing, lady?"

"I'm not your doctor. This is hardly professional advice, just a suggestion that might help you figure out who your adversary is—so that you don't accuse some innocent—"

"Do you know who the stalker is?" Nick interrupted.

"No. I told you that."

Nick curled and uncurled his hands at his sides. "Why do I think you wouldn't tell us if you did?"

Her chest rose with indignation.

Nick took a step toward Breena. "Do you know a Ted Gunderson?"

"Nick," D protested.

The doctor blanched. "No."

Nick would swear she was lying, and even knowing he couldn't get her to admit it, he couldn't seem to stop himself. He shoved the appointment card he'd lifted from Gunderson's work area under the doctor's nose. "He's seeing someone at this clinic. Who?"

Breena blew out an exasperated breath and shook her head. "Really, Detective."

"What about Connor Gregg?" Nick blurted out.

"Oh my God, Nick, stop this!" D pleaded.

"This interview is over." The doctor strode to the door and swung it open. "I'm sorry that I can't help you, Ms. Hamilton."

Nick felt like a runaway train, all the brakes in place, none of them holding, the wheels screeching, the shriek harrowing inside his mind, catastrophe straight ahead. "Please, at least tell us whether Gunderson or Gregg are being treated for erotomania."

Breena went stiff, her face tight with disbelief and outrage. "If you don't leave, Detective, I'll be forced to call security, after which you can rest assured that I will put in a call to your superiors."

"Nick, come on. Let's go." D's voice penetrated his anger, but did not restrain him.

"If it's not Gunderson or Gregg, who is it?" Nick persisted, leaning down and getting in Breena's face. "You know, don't you?"

The doctor backed away from him. "Tina, call security!"

"That won't be necessary, Tina. We're leaving." D clutched his hand and tugged him through the doorway.

He turned once more toward the doctor. "If I find out you're protecting this slimeball, I'll have your license yanked."

"Be careful who you threaten, Detective." Breena Falls had hold of her door as though getting ready to slam it. "Don't think I can't see to it that this suspension you're on is made permanent."

DESIRE WAITED until they were back in Nick's car, then she turned toward him, still shaking with disbelief. "My God, Rossetti, what were you trying to pull in there?"

"She was lying," Nick offered in defense. "Gunderson is not a patient at the clinic, but he has an appointment card. And according to Tina, the date and time are written in Dr. Falls's handwriting. The doctor knows him. She said otherwise, but she really blew up when I mentioned his name.''

''*She* blew up?'' Desire was incredulous. ''Your tactics made it nearly impossible for her *not* to blow up. You were way across the line, Rossetti.''

''I know, D.'' His voice softened, his expression too. Her heart skipped. ''I just can't help myself when the threat is to you. You don't deserve the crap that's happening.''

She wanted to yell at him, smack some sense into him, but the fight went out of her. When he looked at her like this, apologetic and genuinely meaning it, like an innocent little boy, she couldn't stay angry. ''Will you quit acting like some knight in shining armor?''

He reached across the seat and stroked the side of her face. ''God, D, I can't help it. I love you.''

''No.'' She closed her eyes, reveling in the touch of his hand, nuzzling it.

''Yes,'' he whispered. ''It's true.''

She glanced at him. ''Don't say that. Don't even think it.'' But her resistance was gone, lost in his smoldering liquid gaze. He moved into her and she lifted her face to meet his kiss, unable to combat the searing ache, the melting need that was turning her body to molding clay in Nick's hands.

He tasted so good, so right, made her feel incredible, made her see possibilities that she'd never dared dream, that she had no right to dream, dreams built on her sister's heartache. Nick deepened the kiss, and his hands skimmed sensuously across her arms, her back, her neck, his hands shoving into her hair.

Her own hands pressed Nick's chest, felt his heart beating strong, fast, so alive. A sudden wracking chill shivered through her. *He is probably watching you.* Lord. What were they thinking? She pushed away from Nick.

How could she have allowed herself to be swept into kissing him, especially in the parking lot of the Falls Clinic—where *anyone* could see them? The hair on the nape of her neck prickled with the sensation that that was exactly what had happened—that someone *was* watching.

As she pushed at Nick, her gaze fled outside, scanning the parking lot. Her heart skipped. Had she seen someone duck down behind a nearby car? "Nick, stop. I think I saw *him*. Over there."

Nick disentangled himself from her and glanced to where she pointed. He reached for the door handle, meaning to scramble out after whoever she'd seen. Terror shot through her. "No. Don't. Just start the car. Drive us out of here."

"Like hell I will." He jumped from the car and raced through the parking lot before she could stop him. His quick, hot-blooded pursuit turned up no one.

Had anyone been there? Or was her imagination, her growing fear, casting shadows where there were none— like the one she'd seen in her backyard this morning?

"He got away." Nick slammed back into the car and started the engine.

Her nerves burned. "If you do something like that again, Rossetti, I swear I'll shoot you."

He gave her a smart-ass smile. "You're going to shoot me for kissing you? Or did you mean for trying to catch the jerk who's terrorizing you?"

"Don't joke about this. If you won't think about your safety, then dammit, Rossetti, I'll have to do it for you."

"How would your shooting me keep me safe?"

She blew out a heavy breath. "Why are you always so reckless?"

"Me, reckless?" He merged with the traffic on the busy avenue. "Never."

"Reckless and a liar."

"I don't lie."

"Sick leave, you said." A sarcastic laugh spilled out of her, and her anger branched out in another direction. "Why didn't you tell me that you're on suspension?"

"I was going to." He shrugged, but didn't look her way.

"When?" She pressed. "When were you going to tell me?"

"When the timing was better."

"Why were you put on suspension? What the hell did you do?"

"I beat the crap out of a…a suspect. He's filed harassment charges against me." Nick's eyes darkened, but before he could expand further on the incident, Desire's cell phone rang. She jumped. Nick pulled to the side of the road. She read the number registering in the tiny readout window. "It's not a number I recognize."

"You want me to answer it?" Nick offered, sounding, she thought, relieved to have a change of subject. He was also scanning the street on either side, ahead and behind them, looking, she realized with a sickening chill, for someone who might be following them. "If it's our *friend* I'd like to tell him what a coward I think he is."

Desire glared at him. Had he heard nothing she'd said about watching out for his own safety? Damn his sorry hide. "It could be Ron Whiting, or even Connor with news about the valentine." *But he was right, it also could be the stalker.*

Grappling with her nerves, she put the phone to her ear. "Hello?"

"That you, Ms. Hamilton?"

"Yes, it is." Desire felt relief loosen the knots between her shoulder blades.

"This here's Lorelei Collins."

"I recognize your voice."

"He was here again."

He, who? Desire sat straighter, her heart beginning to hammer. "The stalker?"

"I ain't sure if he's no stalker, but I knows he's a pest. It's that popper-ratzy scuzzer who wouldn't leave yer sister 'lone."

"Eager Eddie?"

"Yes. Thas him. Keray and me got him locked in the storage shed, but he ain't gonna stay in there long from the sound of the racket he's makin'. You oughta get on over here afore he bangs his way outta there."

"We'll be right there." Desire broke the connection and relayed the message to Nick.

He slapped a portable flasher on the roof of the car and wove through traffic like an ambulance chaser, taking corners on two wheels. Desire clung to the armrest and the back of her seat, hanging on for dear life, praying no one had slashed any of the sedan's tires today and that they wouldn't end up in an emergency room somewhere.

She had not given another second to Nick's suspension; her every thought zeroed in on what the man they were going to see could tell them about Dare, about the man who had been stalking Dare.

They reached the Pacific Palms within minutes. Nick

was out of the car before it stopped moving completely. She scrambled after him, running up the cracked sidewalk on his heels. Before she reached the door to Dare's bungalow, she heard the racket: muffled male cries punctuated by metallic clangs.

Lorelei stood to one side of Keray, who was leaning against the door of a storage shed, one of those portable jobs used to house garden tools. The small building was rocking back and forth.

"Finally." Keray stepped away from the door and held out a set of keys. "I think that fool's taken to breaking my tools. Don't he know I could snap him like a pretzel?"

Nick accepted the keys and approached the shed. "Hey, you in there. Eddie, or whatever your name is, I'm Detective Rossetti with the Los Angeles Police."

"The police?" came a reply from within the shed, the voice containing a slight East Indian lilt. "I am doing nothing wrong."

"I know that." Nick assured him.

"You are letting me out, yes?"

"Yes. I will need to ask you a couple of questions."

"Questions?" The voice sounded leery.

"I'm going to let you out now, but you must promise you aren't going to take off." Nick took a spread-legged stance before the door and slid the key into the lock.

"Go slow, Nick," Desire cautioned. "He's likely to agree to anything you ask just to get out of there."

"Use your gun on him, man." Keray stood nearby, flexing his beefy arms. "Show him you mean business."

Nick glanced over his shoulder at Keray. "I don't have my gun at the moment."

"No gun?" Keray gave a disgusted grunt. "What kinda cop are you, anyways?"

Rolling his eyes, Nick spun back to the task at hand. The second the lock was off, the door bumped against him, the prisoner shoving to gain his freedom. Nick leaned his shoulder against the bucking door. "I said easy, partner, and that's what I meant. I'll let you out. But you're going to talk to me no matter what. Understood?"

"I am understanding."

Nick straightened but kept alert, in case the man was lying.

He came out of the shed squinting. Like Sikhs she'd encountered in this country driving cabs, he wore a turban that hid his hair and had a fuzzy, chest-length black beard. He was about five-ten, Desire guessed, with black eyes in a face as brown as dirt. Cameras hung from his neck. The cameras were expensive, and given his worn and unwashed clothing, she'd like to know how he managed to keep himself in film, let alone costly photo equipment.

Eddie implored of Nick, "I do no harm. I am taking my pictures only. That is legal, yes?"

"Yes." Desire stepped into his line of vision. There was something odd about his broken English, something false.

Eddie retreated a step. "You are not died."

She eyed him suspiciously. "I am Dare Hamilton's twin sister."

He considered this a moment, then straightened, his slender hands going to his cameras. "Are you, too, famous?"

A gleam lit from the depths of his bottomless eyes, and his tongue slid out to lick his lips in anticipation. She could see why Dare had tagged him "eager."

"No," she said. "No one would pay you for photographs of me."

His face fell. "That is a shame, no?"

"Yes," Nick said.

Desire scowled at Nick, then turned back to Eddie. "*I* will pay you for photographs of Dare. I want everything you have that you haven't sold to the tabloids."

The gleam in those black eyes deepened, along with a smile that seemed vaguely familiar somehow. "You would pay me much monies?"

Nick caught the guy by the arm. "She will pay you something much less than the *Crier*."

"I am not thinking I can sell the pictures then."

Keray moved before Nick. "Take this fool to jail. Toss his sorry ass in a cell and throw away the key."

Eddie's eyes rounded and he shook his head. "You are not listening to this one, yes? No? I am do nothing wrong."

Keray narrowed his eyes at Eddie. "I'm sure this cop can come up with something to charge you with, fool…like trashin' my gardenin' tools."

Eddie looked ready to run. Nick glared at Keray. "Don't you and your wife have something better to do?"

Keray shrugged and took Lorelei by the arm. "Come on, woman. There's crumbs 'neath the toaster more interestin' than this."

Nick put a restraining hand on Eddie, his voice a low threatening growl. "Now, pal, about those photographs."

Eddie swallowed hard, his beard wobbling. "I am thinking there may not be pictures for the selling."

Desire had had enough. This kind of creep only understood one thing. She dug some twenties out of her wallet and held them out to him. "I want everything that you haven't sold the tabloids and the negatives of what you have sold them."

Eddie reached a grimy hand out for the cash. Nick slapped it away. "First you give the lady the photographs and the negatives, then you'll get the dough."

"They are being at my studio."

"Which is where?" Nick asked.

The question made Eddie jumpy.

"What's your name?" Desire asked. If he decided to cut and run, she wanted to know who they were looking for, where to find him.

Eddie's gaze scanned right, then left, as he obviously calculated escape routes. But suddenly he shrugged and his stance changed, grew straighter. "Hell, I might as well—"

He broke off. Something in his eyes altered as it settled on a point somewhere over her shoulder. Terror claimed his face. "Nooo."

Nick and Desire spun toward where he looked, but there was nothing and no one to see. Keray and Lorelei had disappeared. A flash of light from somewhere near Dare's apartment caught her eye. It was followed by a loud pop. Nick tackled Desire, sending her crashing to the ground.

As she fell, her gaze went to Eager Eddie. A bright red stain had appeared on his grungy shirtfront, his horrified expression had slipped into a mask of surprise, as though he'd just been told the answer to the mystery of life and found it startling.

As she hit the ground, Nick landed on her, knocking the wind from her. She felt the skin scrape on her right arm and leg and cried out in pain. Nick covered her with his body. "Stay down. I think it was a gunshot."

"Eddie," she gasped, trying to pull in a breath, feeling crushed by Nick's weight and the memory of the red stain spreading on Eddie's shirt. "He's hit."

"I thought you said you didn't have no gun?" Keray's voice broke through the shock. He stood in his open doorway, pointing to Eddie. "So, hows come you shot this fool?"

"Get back inside!" Nick cried. "Call the police."

Lorelei's eyes were huge. She nodded and stepped back. "And a amblance."

Nick leaped off Desire, ordering her to stay down. Hunched over like a cat, he darted to Eddie's side. His gaze flipped between from where the shot had been fired and Eddie as he checked the man's wound, his vital signs. Nick swore, and still keeping low, ran toward Dare's apartment.

"No. Nick, don't. You're unarmed." Fear brought Desire up off the ground and running after him.

"D, dammit, get back."

She wouldn't listen. The sound of tires squealing off, set them both running toward the street. They arrived in time to see a white pickup pulling around the corner. The license plate was obscured by parked cars. Nick swore long and hard.

Only then did Desire notice the slashing black mark that tracked Nick's upper right arm just below the cuff of his polo shirt. She moved closer to him, thinking he'd scratched himself when he knocked her to the ground, but she caught the stench of spent cordite and burned flesh as she drew near and knew she'd jumped to the wrong conclusion.

The bullet had only grazed him. The wound was bleeding slightly. He seemed not to have noticed it yet.

She relived in her mind the seconds before the shot,

saw again Eddie's terrified gaze that had brought Nick spinning around a blink before the gun had been fired. If he hadn't turned, Nick would have been hit in the upper back, straight through his heart.

Her mouth went dry. Her stalker had meant to kill Nick. She nearly collapsed at the realization, but relief and fury chased the weakness from her, held her upright. Another accident. Another innocent dead. And a madman out there somewhere…watching…waiting…free to strike again.

The distant sound of approaching sirens cut through her dark thoughts. Her heart was coated with fear. The only way to ensure Nick would stop being a target was to stay away from him.

"Come on." Nick caught her hand. She tried to pull free, but he was stronger and held on to her as though his very life depended on it, while the exact opposite was true.

He hurried her back to Eddie, stopping as Keray reappeared in his doorway and pointed to the fallen man. "Hey, lookit that."

The strange Sikh lay sprawled on the uneven concrete, blood pooled on his chest. His turban had flipped off, revealing a shock of carrot-red hair.

"Now, that just ain't right." Keray pursed his lips and emitted a low whistle.

Nick squatted and tugged at the Sikh's beard. It came free in his hands. "A fake."

Keray clicked his tongue. "What he wanna go dressin' up like that for. It ain't Halloween."

Nick ran his finger down Eddie's cheek, sniffed his fingertip, then scowled. "Makeup."

"That fool sure ain't no East Indian." Keray stated

the obvious, then folded his beefy arms against his chest
and glanced at Desire. "I bet his eyes ain't even black."

"Welcome to Hollywood." Lorelei moved up behind
Keray and glared down at Eddie's lifeless form. "Where
ever'body's a actor."

Desire studied Eddie's face, that feeling of something
familiar striking her again. *His eyes ain't even black?*
Were they blue, maybe? Recall swept her like a wildfire,
and Desire's hand flew to her mouth. Dear God, she
knew this man. And so had Dare.

Chapter Eleven

Desire stood riveted, her feet frozen to the cracked sidewalk as she stared down at the lifeless, luridly disguised face of Dare's high-school sweetheart, Eddie Wollinski. "Eager Eddie." If the situation weren't so awful, she might have been amused at the inconceivability of Dare giving her paparazzi pest the same nickname she'd given her old boyfriend. Or was it so unbelievable? Had Dare recognized Eddie, despite his ludicrous costume?

If so, why hadn't she told Michael Pride?

"Nick, I—" She broke off. Footsteps approached at a run. Fear screamed through Desire's terrified mind and jerked her around with a startled cry. She bit back another as she spotted two EMTs rushing toward them over the broken walkway, past the dreary apartment units, the browned flower beds, their fresh uniforms like streaks of blue sky winking through a cloud-dulled day.

Nick flashed his badge, then nodded toward Eddie. "No need to hurry for his sake."

Desire moved to Nick's side, capturing the attention of the paramedics. "Would one of you check out Detective Rossetti's arm? He's wounded, though I'm not sure he realizes it yet."

Nick's dark eyebrows notched upward, and he groped

at his right arm, shifting his shoulder forward, craning
for a look. He winced as though the pain that had to be
radiating around the burned skin was finally making itself felt. "What the hell?"

"I think the bullet grazed you." Desire tugged his
fingers away from the wound and showed the paramedic.

The taller of the two EMTs confirmed Desire's diag-
nosis, examined the wound, asked Nick if he'd had a
recent tetanus shot and cleaned and bandaged the injured
arm. Then he checked the scrapes on Desire's arm and
applied antiseptic. The shorter, stouter EMT knelt over
Eddie's body while the Collinses watched from their
doorway.

More sirens sounded nearby and within minutes police
investigators arrived en masse, sending Lorelei and
Keray scurrying into their apartment, silently closing the
door.

Nick greeted uniforms and plainclothes by name. Desire stepped back, out of the way, knowing she'd be
questioned soon enough, but for now Nick would handle
the initial recounting of the murder. He had clicked into
"homicide cop" mode, his face losing some of its ani-
mation, going somber, seemingly cold and uncaring.
Sentimentality wasn't an emotion one could afford in
dire situations. She'd never seen this side of Nick, and
was surprised that he worked much the same way she
did. Shut off. Do the job. Get through the grisly business
of collecting the evidence, building the case, solving the
crime.

She could use a dose of that professional indifference
now. Every nerve felt exposed, raw, leaving her edgy,
jumpy, unable to think clearly. Her thoughts were a
snarled ball of yarn so tightly jumbled she could see no
center. She needed to sort it out, talk it out, disentangle

facts and clues from questions and conjectures until the mess started making sense.

To accomplish that, she needed to get away from this ordered chaos. She stole to Nick's side, snagged his attention. "I'll wait in the car until they need my statement."

"No." He caught hold of her, shaking his head. "I'm not leaving you alone."

Damn this man, this wonderful, reckless man. Didn't he realize the danger he was in every time he was with her? Didn't he care? *Well, she cared.* "Just stay away from me, Rossetti. I keep telling you I don't need you, but you don't listen."

He grasped her upper arms firmly, his handsome face fierce, a dangerous hum in his voice. "Don't pull this crap on me, D. I know what you're doing and it's not going to work."

Desire felt her face fill with heat, felt the curious and amused glances of all the law enforcement personnel around them.

"If you know anything about me, Rossetti," she said between clenched teeth, "you know I hate being stared at, laughed at. Let loose of me or spend the rest of your life riding sidesaddle."

Either he recalled her kneeing him the other day in Dare's apartment, or he realized she was furious. Nick released her as though her arms were fire beneath his fingers. She spun on her heel and stalked away, ignoring the catcalls of her cohorts.

He fell into step beside her. She blew out a frustrated breath. For all her bravado, she scanned the street up and down, searching for *him,* terrified she'd find him, terrified Nick would leave her alone, terrified he wouldn't. "Nick, I'll be fine. Look, the street is full of cops. No one is going to try anything. I'll even lock the car doors, if it will make you feel better.''

"The only thing that's going to make me feel better is catching and throwing that scumbag in jail.'' He crossed with her to the car, and as though thinking out loud, he added, ''Let's just hope *Eddie's* fingerprints are on file, or your friend Ron comes up with a name and address for him. It's the quickest way to track down the photos we're after.''

Desire rubbed at her aching temples. ''I know who Eddie is.''

Nick's surprise was palpable. ''What? How? Who?''

Desire glanced up and down the street again, her skin itchy, as though someone was watching them. Unable to trust the sensation, unable to ignore it, she opened the door to his car and scampered inside. Unreasonably, she felt less exposed perched on the front seat, partially hidden by the blackened windows.

Nick landed on the driver's seat. Shutting the door behind him, he started the engine and set the air-conditioning to cool. She didn't wait for him to ask her again. She explained that Eddie Wollinski had been Dare's high-school boyfriend. ''Eddie never reconciled Dare's breaking up with him.''

Nick steepled his hands on the steering wheel. ''Sounds like Dare attracted more than her share of stalkers.''

''Eddie wasn't creepy, just annoying. He never made threats or mistook Dare's feelings for him. She used to laugh about him, at him, even to his face.''

''Even if a guy doesn't show it, D, having the woman he cares about laugh at him is like cutting his guts to ribbons.'' Nick narrowed his eyes on the crowded street. ''I suppose that explains Eddie disguising himself *and* his choice of Dare for the photos he sold to the tabloids. Great revenge. The satisfaction of humiliating her while getting paid for it.''

Desire knew he was probably right. She frowned. ''I can't help wondering if Dare knew it was Eddie despite the disguise. I mean, the nickname. She must have known.''

''Then why didn't she tell Pride?''

Desire shrugged. ''I wondered the same. Maybe she did. Maybe they just didn't know where to find him. Maybe they didn't care to find him.''

Nick shoved his hair back from his forehead and shifted in his seat. ''You mean, maybe Dare felt the tabloid items were helping her career?''

Desire tucked her hair behind one ear. ''Since she was about to give up that career and disappear in order to try and shake the stalker, I was thinking those tabloid stories were probably convincing *him* that Dare wasn't leaving Tinseltown anytime soon.''

''Another diversion tactic.'' Nick's voice had gone flat, cold.

''Exactly.''

''None of which worked, D. And that's why I'm not leaving your side, no matter what you threaten to do to me.''

''You have to.'' She touched his bandaged arm. ''That bullet in Eddie Wollinski was meant for you.''

''No—'' But his denial held no bite and they both knew it.

''You have to stay away from me.''

His eyes darkened and his breath rushed out. He reached his hand to cup the side of her face. ''First you push me away because of Dare, now it's this creep. I won't have it, D. I won't.''

She couldn't shake the sensation that someone was watching them, spying on them, growing more and more distraught, more deadly. She pulled back from Nick. "Dr. Falls warned us. It's the only way. He missed this time. You might not be so lucky next time."

He swore, made a face, looked away from her. She reached for his shoulder, his face, but she dropped her hand short of touching him. *I couldn't bear it if he killed you, Nick.* She supposed it might have been unfair to him all these years, pushing him away, denying her feelings for him, burying them, but she'd had no choice. And, she'd had the comfort of knowing he was alive in the world, which had eased the pain of not being with him.

She wasn't sure she could breathe if he were gone. If he were dead. But if she told him that, he'd dig his heels in deeper, would stick to her as though they were handcuffed together.

A tapping on the window of her car door scattered Desire's thoughts and kicked her pulse beat higher. She gazed sharply up at the man standing on the sidewalk outside. Connor. "What's he doing here?"

"Who is it?" Nick asked, leaning across her and peering up at the man, his whole body so tense she could feel it without touching him.

"It's my boss."

"D.A. Gregg?" He looked as puzzled as she felt, and repeated her question. "What's he doing here?"

"I don't know." She rolled down her window. "Connor?"

He squatted, putting his face eye level with hers, peering around her quizzically at Nick, then back at her. The hot breeze hadn't disturbed a hair on his head. His monochromatic, pearl-gray suit looked as though it had just been pressed, and even his expression was cool. "Small world, Hamilton. I was nearby. Listening to my scanner."

"You're always listening to your scanner, Connor. What made you come to this call?"

"I recalled the Pacific Palms was where your sister lived. I swung by to see what was going on. To make sure you weren't somehow involved in this mess."

"I didn't know I'd told you where Dare lived."

"Didn't you? Huh? Well, maybe I read it in the tabloids." He brushed at the air as though brushing the subject aside. "They tell me you witnessed this murder. Are you all right?"

"Yes."

"You want to tell me what happened?"

"It's a long story." *That might even involve you, Connor.* But did it involve him? Such a thought would never have crossed her mind last week. Now, however, she wondered if his put-together appearance was something inbred in his nature, or an obsessive-compulsive disorder. No, that was ludicrous. Whatever reason Connor had for seeing Breena Falls, it was not because he was an erotomaniac. She would know—in that way women just *knew* when something was off-kilter in a man.

"I need to talk to you, Hamilton. Outside." Connor rose and took two steps back.

Desire turned to Nick, and he reassured her, "It's okay. The area is secure. Our gunman is long gone."

Desire wished she was as sure of that as Nick was. The gunman could be anywhere in this crowd. If he was crazy enough, he might even try another shot, despite the slew of police everywhere.

Nick turned off the car. She climbed out, trying to look in every direction at once. Nick slipped up behind her, giving her the feeling again that he was a body shield. She could smell the scent that was his alone, her senses recognizing it even as she tried to squelch the sensations it roused. His nearness made her too aware of him as a man, too aware that he was vulnerable, flesh and blood, that someone wanted him dead.

Maybe Ted Gunderson.

Maybe someone else.

Nick stuck a hand out to Connor. "Detective Nick Rossetti."

Connor glanced at Desire, a knowing look in his ice-blue eyes. "*That* Rossetti?"

She winced inwardly as Nick's eyebrows lifted and his gaze warmed with curiosity. She knew he was reading into Connor's comment exactly what she'd feared he might. Her fault for breaking her cardinal rule of keeping her own counsel. Almost from the start, she'd considered Connor more than her boss, a good friend, an older brother. They'd fought in the trenches. He'd respected her, treated her like an equal, and once, she'd opened up to him, told him things she'd never shared with anyone.

A year or so ago, after winning a huge case, they had gone out to celebrate. They'd talked into the wee hours, expensive whiskey loosening her tongue, and in bits and pieces she'd spilled out her guilt over the breakup of her sister's marriage.

"Yes, Connor, Detective Rossetti was once married to my sister." Had she also told Connor that long-ago night how she felt about Nick? Heat filled her cheeks.

"Detective Rossetti." Connor shook his hand, giving Nick an assessing look, but whatever he thought was anyone's guess, his cool eyes gave nothing away. Connor had long ago mastered the art of misdirection.

As he sized up Nick, Nick was returning the favor, his expression as unreadable, but his eyes were full of fire.

The two men seemed about to circle her, each moving closer, more protectively, around her, the testosterone so ripe in the air she expected any minute they might start a spitting contest. Nick, ever the knight in shining armor. Connor, ever the older brother. Both smothering her, annoying her, scaring her. If Nick was a threat to the stalker, so was Connor.

Dear God, no man she cared about was safe near her. She exhaled as though she'd been gut-punched. "Connor, you said you needed to speak to me…?"

He tugged his gaze from Nick and his expression grew serious. He reached into his jacket and pulled out a large manila envelope. "This came to the office for you. It's from a law firm in Los Angeles."

She glanced at the return address. "I'm not familiar with the firm."

"Neither was I. So I called and tried to find out who had sent it. The receptionist said it was sent by one Arnold Lawson."

She shook her head. "Never heard of him."

"Neither had I. Lawson was in court this morning and the receptionist had no idea what he'd sent you. I didn't want to stick the envelope in the mail since it might have contained something to do with one of our pending cases. I came by your house this morning to give it to you, but you weren't there."

She eyed the envelope curiously. "Nick and I have been…busy."

Connor tapped the envelope against his palm. "Anyway, when you weren't home, I decided to drive down here and see Lawson myself. That's why I was nearby when I heard the call on my scanner.''

Her gaze lifted to his. ''What's in the envelope?''

He placed a gentle hand on her arm, his angular face softening uncharacteristically. ''Lawson was Dare's attorney. Apparently, she named you executor of her estate. These are copies of papers he held for her, along with a copy of her will.''

Desire stumbled back, bumping against Nick. He caught her by the elbows, his solid body offering her support. Her heart was beating too fast. ''Me? Dare named me executor? But she wasn't speaking to me.''

Nick's voice came soft against her ear. ''It's a sign, honey. Despite everything, she still trusted you.''

Desire let that sink in, and in accepting it, she felt as though her sister were reaching across an ethereal plane to her, touching her in a way that only she could feel and understand, letting her know she'd forgiven her, that she hadn't stopped loving her.

Tears filled Desire's eyes. *Never let them see you cry.* She sucked in a hard breath, bit back the impulse to sob her heart out, and straightening, stepped away from Nick. Despite her best efforts to sound composed, her words came out shaky. ''Thank you, Connor.''

She took the envelope, holding it against her thudding heart, still reeling from Dare's gesture, still fighting the swell of grief that threatened to dissolve the shredded vestiges of her equanimity. ''So, what about that valentine? Were any prints found on it?''

Connor adjusted his steel-gray tie and lowered his voice in deference to the crowd gathered on the street. The medical examiner had arrived right after Connor and was now accompanying the bagged body to a waiting ambulance. Connor glanced in that direction, then back at Desire. "There was a thumbprint on the upper inside corner. It's not Gunderson's, though. You want me to check out this dead guy against it?"

"No." She shook her head. "He didn't send the valentine."

"Check it out anyway, Gregg," Nick ordered. "It doesn't hurt to eliminate suspects."

Connor seemed to bristle at Nick's demand. "Is this *your* case, Detective?"

Nick started to answer but was interrupted by an irate male voice. "What in hell is going on here?"

Michael Pride, wearing the Hawaiian shirt and khaki pants that constituted his Flamingo restaurant "uniform," wove between the melee of police cars that blocked the street, his attention flashing from the M.E. back to Nick and Desire. The proverbial cigar poked from between two of his fingers like a fat pencil and designer sunglasses showcased his intense eyes.

"What brings you here, Pride?" Nick asked, once again moving to protect Desire.

Pride glanced at the ambulance again, then questioningly at Nick. "Who's that in the bag?"

Nick glared at him. "I asked you a question, Pride."

He pointed the cigar at Nick. "Not that it's any of your business, Rossetti, but Dare's landlady called me."

"What for?" Nick scowled.

Pride shifted his head toward Desire. What she could see of his face looked pained. "She said you were done packing up Dare's things and I was welcome to take a look, see if you'd left behind anything that I might care to have."

Desire nodded.

"So, will you, at least, tell me what's going on?"

Pride asked her. "What happened to the person in...
they're taking away?"

"He was murdered." Desire hugged the envelope, address side, to her body, conscious that *she* and not Pride
had been named executor of her sister's estate. Did Pride
know? "It was the photographer Dare nicknamed Eager
Eddie."

Above the sunglasses, Pride's eyebrows lifted. He
sucked on his unlit cigar. The anxious bubble in Desire's
stomach seemed to be growing. She wanted away from
here, away from these men, off this street, out of plain
sight. She especially wanted Nick somewhere else. But
her curiosity about Eddie needed sating.

She took a step closer to her sister's fiancé. "Dare
and you knew Eager Eddie's true identity, didn't you?"

Pride tilted his blond head to one side. "What if we
did? You don't think *I* killed him?"

"No," Nick interjected. "We think you were using
him to keep Dare's stalker off guard, right?"

He ignored Nick. He glanced toward Connor as
though wondering who he was. Desire introduced them,
but her anger rose again at the games these men seemed
intent on playing at her expense. She'd had enough. She
spun toward Michael. "You should have told us the
other night that you knew who Eddie was. Maybe he'd
still be alive."

Michael shook his distasteful cigar at her. "Hey, he
was a jerk, always lurking nearby, shooting off those
flashbulbs in our faces, disrespecting our privacy. You
want me to say I'm sorry that he's dead? Well, I'm not."

Nick stepped threateningly close to Pride. "That *jerk*
may have inadvertently caught the stalker on film. If
we'd known who he was, we'd have those photos by
now, have our hands on the stalker."

"Dare's stalker?" Beneath his tan, Michael Pride paled. He rolled the cigar through his fingers, his eyes narrowing. "You think Eddie has pictures of him?"

"It's damn likely." Nick looked as though he'd like to hit Pride, knock some brains into him, make him use what little sense God had given him.

From inside the car, a cell phone rang. Nick and Desire exchanged a glance. He said, "Yours or mine?"

"Sounds like mine." She moved toward the car. "It might be Ron Whiting with Eddie's address," she said, clambering into the car, her window still open. She tucked the envelope onto the floorboards behind her seat, to be read later, when she was alone.

Nick got in on the driver's side. Connor hunkered down near her again, Michael Pride squatted next to him.

She dug the ringing phone from her purse and answered, "Hamilton."

It *was* Ron Whiting. His soft, angelic voice gentle against her ear.

She told him she'd already discovered Eager Eddie's real name, but still needed his address, if Ron had managed to get it. He had. As he read it to her, she relayed it to Nick, who wrote it into his palm-size tablet.

She said, "Thanks, Ron. I owe you one."

"Let's call us even," he said solicitously. "Say, you want me to check out his place with you?"

"No. That's not necessary." She thanked him again and hung up.

"This address is in Malibu," Nick told her. "We could be there in about—"

"Whoa, Rossetti. What are you doing, Hamilton?" Connor demanded. "Surely you're not thinking of looking into this murder. It's not your jurisdiction."

"I know, Connor. I won't do anything to embarrass our office. You know that."

"I'm not worried about any blemish you might put on our office. Santa Beverly politics were notorious long before you or I came along. Just don't do anything to get yourself in the sights of this crazy gunman," he said with passion. "It's bad enough some nut is sending you love notes. I'll keep on top of that. You keep her safe, Rossetti."

Connor turned and left. Michael Pride, she realized, was already gone.

Desire watched Connor walk away, praying that the stalker hadn't seen him with her, wouldn't focus his bile on him. Suddenly weary, she asked, "Nick, how soon can I make my statement?"

"Let's get it over with now."

She told the investigating officers all that she'd observed, then promised she'd come by to sign a statement the next day.

Back in the car, Nick started the engine. Desire scanned the street, her anxiety back with a vengeance now that the cops were leaving, the traffic snarl easing. "I want to go home, then I want you to go home."

"Really?" There was an "are you sure?" note in his voice that triggered her internal alarm bells, made her wonder what he was up to now. He pulled the sedan in amongst the other moving cars. "Wouldn't you rather check out Eddie's studio?"

"We can't do that," she protested.

"You want the LAPD investigators there before us, tearing it apart, maybe confiscating the very shots we're after?"

"No, of course not." She blew out a frustrated breath, torn between what was right and what was wrong, between what she believed in and what she needed to stay alive, what she needed to set her world back on its axis. Did the end justify the means? Could she go on being a prosecutor if she began breaking laws to suit her own purposes? "Hell, you heard Connor. We don't have jurisdiction."

"True." Nick was holding a small, shiny object and grinning slyly, that wonderful delicious grin of his that signaled danger and trouble and was totally irresistible. "But I searched Eddie's pockets before the other police officers arrived, and slipped what looks to be his house key off the ring."

Chapter Twelve

Eager Eddie's Malibu address was an incredible dwelling that sat at the edge of a jagged rock cliff—the beach a short climb below. The house, at least twenty years old, appeared to have been constructed from raw materials that might have washed ashore—sun-bleached timbers for the walls, crushed shells on the roof.

Nick studied the rearview mirror for the hundredth time, then pulled up to the eight-foot-high, wrought-iron gate that was set in natural stone walls that all but obscured and protected the house from anyone traveling this road. He gave a low whistle of surprise. "I'd say spying on celebrities pays a hell of a lot better than being a cop."

"You thinking of switching professions if you can't get off suspension, Rossetti?" she joked, trying to break the tension that had laced their conversation on the way here. It hadn't helped that Nick constantly checked to see if they were being followed, causing her to crane around in the seat and scan the road behind them.

"It's a thought." Nick grinned and killed the engine.

She glanced out the rear window once more. If *he* had followed them, neither had spotted him. Even now, no vehicles slowed or pulled to the road ahead of or behind them.

Nick's hands landed on her shoulders, startling her. "Hush, D. It's okay. No one knows we're here."

Desire leaned back against him, letting him knead the tension from her neck, a taut breath slipping from between her pursed lips, along with a moan of pleasure. *God, this felt great.* "Rossetti, your hands should be against the law."

His low, husky chuckle was warm against her ear. "They aren't lethal, D."

"Well, magic, then." She released another pleasured breath, almost a purr.

He chuckled again. "If I could, I'd wave my wand and make this all disappear."

But he couldn't. Magician's tricks were not going to vaporize a stalker turned deadly. Only they could do that. She straightened and glanced toward the house at the imposing eight-foot gate. "How do you plan to get through that?"

"Good question. There's no lock or keyhole, so this key won't work on it, and Wollinski's car is probably sitting somewhere near the Palms with the push button opener inside." His hands slipped from her shoulders. "Plus there's a security camera and some kind of wiring that might be an alarm system. We don't want to set off anything that brings armed guards."

"Then I guess that's that." Despite the fact that she'd agreed to do this, against everything she believed in, she was disappointed that they were bested so quickly.

Nick smirked confidently. "We're not defeated yet. There's still the beach side to investigate."

They got back in the car and Nick pulled a U-turn.

He parked four blocks away, on the opposite side of the road.

Clasping her hand, he tugged her across the street and down the low embankment. The tide was out, the sand wet and hard, their footfalls lost in the roar of the surf. They passed two other residences without encountering anyone or drawing any attention that they were aware of, before reaching the steps that led up to Eddie's house. Here, too, there was a gate, this one only waist high.

Nick inspected it, then smiled at her and unlatched the gate hook. "No camera, no wires and no security."

"After you, Detective." Desire stepped close to Nick, glancing over her shoulder as they began the climb. The breeze was warm, but she felt cold shivers moving over her, imagined someone—beachcombers or neighbors on an after-dinner walk—spotting them, calling after them, or calling the police.

But they arrived at the landing uninterrupted. The stairs ended at a private deck that ran the length of the house across the beach side and was wide enough to accommodate several cushioned loungers and a cluster of potted flowers.

"See any security, or possible alarms?"

"No. Nothing." Still Nick proceeded with caution.

Desire had never lived on the ocean, never noticed before how noisily disturbing was the constant boom of the surf. She spun back toward Nick, studying the house from this angle. Floor-to-ceiling windows were covered with full-length drapes. Nick walked to the center of the glass door and slid the key into the lock. "Bingo."

A twinge of excitement she wasn't sure she approved of tripped through Desire. This was wrong. Necessary, but not right. She'd promised Connor…

Moving the drapes, Nick stepped inside, checked

along the wall for an alarm system, but finding none, beckoned Desire in. The room was cast in shadows but not entirely dark. The drapes filtered the light and had been designed to keep prying eyes from seeing in, while allowing those in the house to see outside.

"Wait here, D. I'll make sure we're alone." Nick left her standing just inside the door.

Desire released an anxious breath as her eyes adjusted to the shift in lighting. The living room was spacious, furnished for comfort by someone with a creative streak and deep pockets. Her gaze snagged on a portrait-size photograph above the fireplace, and her hands flew to her mouth, cutting off a startled cry.

Dare. As though something dank had skimmed her flesh, goose bumps lifted on her legs and arms. Her sister had been captured in an unposed moment, the sun glinting off her long hair, giving it the appearance of spun gold. Her expression was serene, unguarded, beautiful.

"Oh, Dare." The grief that had nearly undone her earlier came back with a vengeance, tamping down the uneasy thrill she'd been feeling. She couldn't move, could barely inhale.

She wasn't aware that Nick had returned or that he had seen what held her riveted until he said, "Wow. I'll give Eddie one thing—he knew how to use a camera."

His words were like winter wind, icy, startling, shattering her trance, and as she moved, her gaze swept the room. There were photographs of her sister everywhere—on tables, on shelves, on the baby grand piano. "My God, Nick, Eddie was just as obsessed with Dare as the stalker."

Nick glanced where she pointed, then at her, shaking his head. "So it seems."

Disbelief overshadowed the spookiness she felt.

"How could he have continued to care about Dare when she treated him as she did?"

"Beats me," Nick said. "But do you suppose we could figure this out another time? We have to hurry, D. Investigators could show up any minute. Let's search the studio and get out of here, okay?"

"The studio?" She moved toward Nick. "Where is it?"

"One level down. This way." He clasped her hand again, his large, warm fingers reviving that sensation that they were kids doing something naughty, a sensation she preferred to the grief and distress that kept attacking her. In fact, she liked this feeling too damn much.

They descended a spiral staircase to a windowless room that seemed to have been carved from the rocky cliff on which the house was built. It was half the size of the living room.

Nick pointed to the end wall. "Darkroom's over there, through that door. It looks newly remodeled, like it might have been an oversize bathroom in a former life."

Desire surveyed the surroundings. There were portable lamps and backdrops, settees and camera stands, built-in shelves that held every manner of camera equipment, lenses and boxes of film and built-in drawers beneath, full of photographs and negatives. Everything was orderly, labeled and filed alphabetically.

"This ought to make our task easier." Nick began digging through a file drawer marked F through K, his eyebrows serious slashes above his brown eyes as he concentrated. "Wollinski has quite a catalog here and Dare wasn't his only subject."

She wasn't surprised. Paparazzi were definitely star-struck voyeurs. "Other celebrities, huh?"

"No, actually."

"No?" No other celebrities? She frowned. "Who are the pictures of?"

"Not who, but what. Landscapes, buildings, food, things. Believe it or not, he was running a legitimate business, selling to magazines and other publications."

She tilted her head and moved her hair back from her face. "That would explain the house, I suppose."

"Yeah, but you know what I can't figure out is what he was doing at Dare's again today. He knew she was dead. What did he hope to get going back there? Did Lorelei Collins say?"

"No. I didn't think to ask where they caught him. But I will."

Nick lifted out a file folder and held negatives up to the light. "This file has Dare's name on it, but there's not much in it."

She squinted, gazing at the negatives he held to the light, trying to see what was there. "Are these what we're after?"

"I don't think so. Dare's alone. No one lurking in the shadows. There aren't even any with Pride."

"None?"

"Nope." Nick considered a moment, then blew out a breath. "Hell, given his obsession with Dare, he probably destroyed any negatives with her fiancé as soon as he sold them to the tabloids."

Until Dare's death, Desire had never even glanced at the tabloids. But she thought now about the photo over the fireplace upstairs, Dare caught in an unposed moment. Her surroundings had been trimmed or otherwise cut. *Cut.* "If there were others in the photos he took of Dare, maybe Eddie cut those people out of the frame."

Nick shrugged. "I guess that's possible."

He stopped digging through the negatives, lifting them

to the light and studying them, to turn and study her. She felt as though he thought she were a piece of crystal that had a crack running through it, as though the crack was growing as he watched.

But she was strong at the core, too solid at the root of herself to crack from the stress of this situation. The only thing that could bring her down was the tenderness in Nick's eyes.

But would being with Nick mean that she'd forever be compromising everything she'd always believed in? That she would bend or break the law, as they were doing now, whenever it suited their purposes? Would her world be permanently colored in gray, all the sharp edges gone, no more solid black and white to trust? Would that be good for her, or would it destroy her?

"Nick, I—" She broke off at the creak of the floorboards overhead. Her eyes widened and fear exploded through her. She whispered, "Someone's upstairs."

Nick nodded. He'd heard it too. Silent and quick, he tucked the folder back into the drawer, eased it shut and hauled her into the darkroom. It stank of chemicals she couldn't identify, and as Nick pulled her to the end of the room, she glimpsed strips of negatives clipped on wire strands above the long, cluttered counter. There was nowhere to hide. "Nick, this won't do. They'll find us right away."

She went back into the studio room. Beneath the spiral staircase, she spied another door. "Look."

They rushed to it as the footfalls overhead sounded closer. She hated that she felt conflicted about being discovered by the police. She ought to be appalled that she wasn't giving herself up, instead of looking for somewhere to hide.

The door opened into a walk-in closet with clothes

poles running full length on both sides. Robes, shawls, sheets and feather boas draped hangers. Nick glanced up the stairwell. Desire tugged him into the compact space. He hit a light switch, erasing the darkness. "This level must've been guest quarters at sometime or other."

"Shh," she warned, silently easing the door shut. "They'll hear you."

He grimaced, the realization that his career hung by a thread at the moment written on his handsome face. She reached up to touch him, then pulled back at a sound beyond the closet. A loud metal clank. Followed by another, then another. Footsteps on the staircase.

Nick shut off the light, groped for her and scooted them both to the end wall, then sideways behind something silky, probably the robes she'd spied a second ago. He huddled protectively against her, his front to her back, his arms encircling her neck and shoulders like one of the feather boas, his cheek pressing hers, his aftershave mingling with her fear, lifting her senses to dizzying heights.

Terrified, exhilarated, conflicted on every level, she was learning things about herself that she'd never known. Or had always known but never admitted. Like the fact that she'd thought Judd Hamilton had misnamed his twin daughters. Dare, she'd long ago decided, was the passionate one, the desirable one, the one who could have any man she wanted. She, on the other hand, was the brave twin, the strong twin, the daring twin.

But now, she realized, as though some curtain had just lifted in her brain, that she had interpreted everything wrong, even herself. Especially herself. She played according to the rules, expected others to do the same, was stringent about that, self-righteous, even. Yes, she was brave, yes, she was strong, but what she'd considered risk taking before today was nothing. She had been as daring as an ant running from an anteater.

Dare *had* been the risk taker, the one to act on spontaneity. That was how she'd ended up married to Nick, a man she hardly knew, a man with the same kind of impulsive nature as her own.

But it took more than one correlating trait to make a happy couple, a loving pair, lifelong mates.

Here in the darkness, a light dawned for Desire. She prided herself on controlling every situation, on keeping her Crayola inside the coloring-book lines, on facing her mistakes, being accountable. No wonder she'd felt so ashamed and guilt-ridden for falling in love with her sister's husband.

There had been no accounting for that, no making amends, no apology in the world that could make it right. Or make it go away. No way she could have avoided hurting Dare. It had just happened…completely outside her life plan.

A series of bangs beyond the door halted her self-exploration. Drawers being opened and shut? She strained above the pulse roaring in her ears, trying to tell how many policemen were there. But no one spoke, no partner shouting to another.

She whispered, "Is he alone?"

"Not likely." Nick's jaw moved against her cheek— a sensuous stroke as enticing as his arms about her neck that wiped away wisdom and logic, leaving only raw sensation.

The press of Nick's body against hers, the sense of protection he gave her, the danger of this moment, the insanity of it ignited something feral inside Desire, a wild, hot need for Nick. That same frantic need that had hit her the first time she'd laid eyes on him, that same wanton need that had swept her during that first startling kiss. Incontrovertible. Intoxicating. Irresistible.

Always before, she'd tried to deny it, bury it. Today, another Desire had emerged, freed by the tumbling walls of her convictions, by the graying edges of her beliefs. Not only did she want Nick, she wanted him here and now, in this place where the stalker could not find them, could not know to look for them.

She nuzzled Nick's cheek, loosening his hold on her, then turned toward him, feeling him rather than seeing him in the darkness. She folded herself against him, pressing her hips to his, and whispered, "Make love to me, Nick."

"God, woman," he groaned in a husky whisper. "Could you have picked a more inappropriate time to finally admit we belong together?"

"Not interested?" she teased, since she could feel just how interested he was. Shamelessly, the need denied too long, she snuggled closer, making him even more interested.

"They'll hear us," Nick warned without conviction.

"Not if we're very, very quiet." She lifted her face, pulling his down, finding his mouth in the dark, running her thumb over the firm arc of his upper lip, then across his full lower lip. She lifted on tiptoe and grazed her tongue along the same path, then dipped it into his eager mouth.

His arms came around her in a sweeping embrace, pulling her roughly, fully against him, both of them aware of the danger outside this closet, the danger within it. His voice sang in her ear, "D, D, you're making me crazy."

She felt the exact sensation of being slowly driven mad...by the tiny kisses he nibbled along her neck, up her cheek, by his hands on her back, her bottom. Her every nerve tingled with need, with want, with impatience. Clothes fell from them with a speed and silence Desire had not thought possible, the urgency to be naked guiding their fingers and hands, giving them unusual grace.

Her only regret was that she could not see him, only feel him. But, oh, he felt incredible, every inch of him male. She explored with eager fingers the warm, taut flesh of his small tight buttocks, moved gently over the wounds on his wide muscled back, stroked his lightly furred chest, his hard flat belly, and lower, taking him in both hands, hearing his sharp indrawn breath.

A moan of pleasure climbed her throat. Terrified it would escape, she buried her face against Nick's chest, and felt then heard his heart thrumming like the building beat of a Celtic tune played on an ancient lyre.

Her own heart sang a sweet, sweeping response, her body going liquid with his touch, hot and pulsing, ardent, urgent. Her chest rose and fell, her breath puffing in fast spurts. In the outer room, the bangs and bumps continued, but her fear of discovery vanished as Nick's mouth captured her breast, one then the other, sending delicious tingles spiraling through her. "Now, Nick, now."

Catching her mouth in a crushing kiss, he inched down the wall to the floor, pulling her with him. She straddled his narrow hips and with slow, slippery movements, she lowered herself onto him, swallowing a gasp at the pure sweet joy she felt with him sliding hot and hard and huge into her. For a long savoring moment, she couldn't move for the sheer pleasure of it, but then the urgency of her need would not be denied.

Up, down, with every lift of her hips, every descending thrust, Desire swore stars exploded in the closet, bursting over her head and dazzling her with their brilliance.

She bit her lip, squelching the scream that wanted to blast free as her body clenched with shudder after shudder of ecstasy, his body tensing too, trembling with release in unison with hers as he buried his head in her neck, presumably to stifle his own outcry of delight.

Seconds later, on a breathy moan, he murmured, ''Oh, D.''

He said it too loud. They knew it instantly. The floor creaked near the door. She pressed against Nick, snatching at something, maybe her blouse, or his shirt, gathering it to her nude body. Her gaze riveted where she thought the door was. She could not see the doorknob, but even above the thunder-beat of her heart, she heard the slight metallic clink of it being twisted in someone's hand.

She held her breath. To her surprise, the thought of being found naked in a closet with Nick didn't bother her. But Nick was on suspension. He had no business in this house, let alone in a compromising situation that could increase his career problems tenfold.

She counted to five, once, twice, three times. The door remained shut. Why?

The knob rattled hard, as though it had been released, startling her. A second later she heard footsteps ascending the stairs. ''Nick, why didn't that cop open the door?''

''Damned if I know, but maybe we shouldn't look a gift horse in the mouth, huh?''

''I guess,'' she said uncertainly. She couldn't deny she was grateful not to be explaining to the police what she was doing at the moment naked in a closet with her sister's ex-husband.

Nick kissed her temple, then disentangled himself from her, stood and pulled her into his arms. "Regrets?"

"No," Desire answered. "Yes. One. I couldn't see your eyes."

"Next time, D." He switched on the light, his gaze caressing her from head to toe as though he touched her, lovingly, sweetly, stirring in her a fresh need for him. She tamped down the urge, grabbed her underclothes, watching him dress, amazed at the beauty of his naked body, amazed that she felt none of the self-consciousness that she'd felt after making love with other men.

Nick pulled on his slacks. "We need to get the hell out of here."

She managed the buttons on her blouse with less grace and speed than she'd had undoing them, aware of his gaze locked on her every movement. "I've never...done anything like this...before."

"Really?" He smiled wryly, zipping his fly. "You were very good at it."

She smiled at the compliment, but lowered her head so he wouldn't notice and tucked the hem of her blouse into her pants. "Ready?"

He pulled his polo shirt over his head and finger-combed his hair. "Sure."

She inched open the door, both of them straining to hear if someone remained in the house. But it was eerily quiet, the only sound the distant roaring of the surf. Nick checked the drawer with Dare's file. "Dammit, D. They took the file."

"What about those negatives in the darkroom?" She crossed to it and looked in. "Gone."

Nick swore again.

She said, "Isn't there some way you can see the ones from the darkroom? Aren't homicide detectives allowed to look at evidence, even if it's not your case?"

"I'll find a way." He gestured her up the stairs ahead of him. "Call in a couple of favors."

To her untrained eye, the upper level seemed undisturbed. Nick stopped at a sound outside the front door. "Stay here."

He went to the entry and peered out. He returned at a run, catching her by the arm. "Let's get out of here."

She didn't ask why, just caught his anxiety. As they reached the glass door, she saw it was still wide open, the way they'd left it. "Nick, why didn't the investigators close and lock this door?"

Nick hastened her over the threshold and out onto the deck, then slid the door shut, thrusting the key into the lock. He hurried her toward the stairs that led to the beach, warning her to descend as quickly and quietly as possible.

"Nick? You're scaring me. Who was at the front door?"

Without missing a beat, he said, "The LAPD investigators."

They were halfway to the beach. She glanced over her shoulder at him, fear nipping at her muscles. "Then who was in the studio with us?"

He shook his head. "I don't know, D. But you can bet it wasn't any cop."

Chapter Thirteen

"Nick, who do you think that was in the studio while we were in that closet?"

Desire and he were in his car, racing away from Eddie's house and the team of LAPD investigators who'd arrived at the front door as they tore out the back. But what lay behind them didn't interest Nick. With every ounce of his being, he wanted to discuss what lay *between* them, to explore further the intimacy they had shared moments ago.

Night had fallen, but he could see her clearly in the dashboard lights and the lights from the steady line of oncoming traffic. He reached over, traced the angle of Desire's jaw with his fingertip and drew a sharp breath. Just thinking her name heated his blood, but touching her brought a need he'd never felt before they'd made love. This new need for her was ten times more fierce, and ached for fulfillment, but it wasn't just sexual. It was more a sharing of souls.

He strove for something clever, something romantic, poetic to say to her, something that conveyed the depth of his feelings, but all that came out was, "Your place or mine?"

"What?" She arched a querulous eyebrow, but a second later, as she realized what he was suggesting, her cheeks glowed a fetching shade of pink. She narrowed her eyes. "What I want is to know who you think might have the negatives."

"No, no, no, no." He shook a finger at her, resisting the urge to pull to the side of the road and shake *her* instead. "Don't dismiss what happened in that closet. It was important. It was wonderful and you are not going to start holding me at arm's length again."

"Dismiss it?" Her chin shot up defensively, denial sharp in the set of her shoulders. "I'm not dismissing it."

"Damn straight."

She was silent a long moment. "Nick, I don't know what happened in that closet. I—"

"Don't try to explain it away. Don't say you're sorry. Don't—" He broke off, his emotions as volatile as live wires in a hurricane.

"I'm not apologizing or expressing regret." She stared at her fingernails, and despite everything, he wanted to feel those long nails against his back, sharp on his naked flesh as he had earlier. She sighed. "I just don't usually behave that...rashly."

He eyed her for a full five seconds, grappling with his emotions. Was she saying that she didn't let go with other men, as she had with him? The idea made him smile. He touched her cheek once more. "We really should cultivate that wild impetuous side of you. The sooner the better."

Her blush returned, and his grin broadened.

She said, "Will you be serious?"

"I *am* serious. I want to take you back to my house, to my bed, and make love to you with all the lights on.

I want to see your body, D. I want to hold you and kiss you and rouse every inch of you until you—''

''Nick—'' Her voice held a warning. Her face was crimson, her eyes dark pools of determination that gave him an uneasy feeling. ''I am not going back to your place, Rossetti, not now, maybe not ever.''

Anger threatened again. He raked his hand through his hair, stared ahead, then back at her. ''What the hell does that mean?''

''I should have expected this from you, should have fought my—'' She clamped her lips together, her face flaring red again. ''It means what happened between us shouldn't have. Not now. Not with an erotomaniac out there who thinks he and I have a relationship. He's already tried killing you once. I won't risk your life, Nick.''

Nick swore silently as resignation settled over him. He knew from experience how stubborn D was, that no amount of persuasion would change her mind once it was set. He might as well save his breath, distract her for now, then push his case later, because contrary to what she thought, there would be a later.

He blew out a long breath, his gaze steadied on the traffic, his hands tight on the steering wheel. ''I'm not sure who might have been in the studio. We know three people who had the address besides us—Connor Gregg, Michael Pride and Ron Whiting.''

''God, that's right. Connor and Pride were both there when Ron called with Eddie's address. But why would any of them have taken the negatives?'' The connection of one thing to the other seemed to have eluded her.

On purpose?

He said carefully, ''One of them might be the stalker.''

"That's crazy." She laughed with derision and shook her head. "Connor is not only my boss but my friend. He is not stalking me."

"What about Pride?"

"Dare's fiancé? Even if I believed he was stalking me, why would he have stalked Dare? They were getting married."

"Okay." He hadn't really liked that idea himself. "But he might have taken the negatives in hopes of finding the stalker on his own."

"Oh, God, you're right." She shifted toward Nick. "He might have. Remember he said he hired a private eye to try and find out who was stalking Dare?"

"Yeah, and when that failed, and she died, he came to me."

"Nick, he had to have known who you were before contacting you."

Nick swore under his breath. Before this moment, he supposed he'd felt sorry for Pride, for the grief he was going through, and that probably explained why he'd cut him some slack for the bad manners he'd shown, for his rudeness to D. But Nick hated being used and being lied to. Pride had done both. His words held his anger. "He had to have known that no one else at the department would have given Dare's death a second thought."

"If he was the one who took the negatives, how will we get him to admit it?"

Nick tightened his grip on the steering wheel, wishing it were Pride's neck. "I know what I'd like to do to him."

"Brute force won't work on Michael Pride."

"No, but maybe the threat of arrest or a search warrant will." Neither said anything for another few miles, then Nick returned to the subject. "What if Ron Whiting took the negatives? Could he be the stalker?"

"Ron?" She sounded incredulous. "That doesn't make sense either. I can't imagine why or how he could have become fixated on Dare, but I'm sure he didn't kill Cindy."

Nick glanced at her again. "Why are you so sure?"

She gestured with her hands. "He and Cindy were getting back together. He had no reason to follow her around, watch her, scare her."

Nick rubbed his jaw, feeling the roughness that meant he'd soon need another shave. "Who told you they were getting back together? Cindy? Or Ron?"

"Well, Ron..." She grew thoughtful. "Anyway, Cindy made a complaint against Gunderson."

Nick considered this. "Are you sure? Did you speak to the officer who wrote up the complaint, ascertain for a fact that Cindy actually made the complaint in person?"

"In person?" Her voice wobbled. "What are you suggesting?"

"Maybe Ron filed a complaint, doctored it to appear to have been filed by his ex-wife, framed Gunderson, created evidence that his ex-wife was having a problem with her former boyfriend."

Her eyes widened. "That's what Gunderson claimed."

Nick wasn't surprised. Gunderson was the kind of guy who would protest his innocence if he were caught red-handed and videotaped. "Maybe the man in the studio was Gunderson."

"Gunderson had no way of knowing where to look for Eager Eddie's studio."

"Didn't he? He might have followed us from the Palms."

She released a shudder and hugged herself.

Nick forced his gaze to the road, curbing another wave of need. Along with the physical need for her, he wanted to talk to her, to share with her, plan with her, make a future with her. But if they couldn't find the stalker and put an end to his reign of terror on D, there would be no future for them.

He knew better than to underestimate her determination to protect him. It was as strong as the urge he felt to keep her safe from this madman. She would chase Nick away. Make him stay clear or find some way to elude him.

The only solution was to apprehend the stalker. Nick frowned, thinking out loud now. "One way or another, all four of those men are connected to the Falls Clinic." He glanced at her again, as another thought occurred to him. "Where did Gunderson meet Cindy Whiting?"

She looked genuinely surprised at the question. "What difference does that make?"

"Does he have a kindergarten-age child?"

"No. No children."

"Then he didn't meet Cindy Whiting at school."

"No, I guess not." She considered a moment. "Maybe she had tires put on her car at Bayside."

"Yeah, I guess that's the most likely." Still, Nick had a funny feeling that this detail was somehow important, but couldn't pinpoint why. "Maybe we should check it out all the same."

"Sure." She seemed to notice they were in downtown L.A. "Where are we going now?"

"We're going to get a hotel room."

Her heard her breath grab. "Didn't you hear anything I said?"

"Yes. You said you won't feel safe at my house or yours, so we're getting an anonymous hotel room."

"Nick, we can't—"

"D, we need to eat and sleep and start again tomorrow with renewed energy."

Her expression asked how either would sleep while sharing a hotel room. Nick wondered the same.

He looked away from her and realized they were passing the Falls Clinic. Nick noticed lights on inside. He scanned the parking lot. Two vehicles occupied the spots nearest the entrance. He assumed the sleek gray Jaguar belonged to Breena Falls, the other was a familiar white pickup truck. "D, look!"

She jerked to where he pointed, but they'd driven past and she couldn't tell what he'd meant for her to see. "What is it?"

"Gunderson's pickup truck in the clinic lot." He pulled onto the next side road, circled the block, tires squealing, and headed back to the clinic.

"You think he's keeping that appointment that Tina couldn't find listed in her book?"

"Maybe. But I want a better look at that truck, see if I can tell whether or not it was the one at the Palms."

"Nick, it's dark. How much do you think you can see?"

"Those vapor lights overhead put out a lot of light and I've got a flashlight in the trunk." He pulled into the slot next to the truck, scrambled out and touched the hood of the pickup. "Still warm. Just got here."

He retrieved his flashlight, and a second later was panning it around the taillights, his forehead furrowed in a thoughtful frown. "If I'm not mistaken, this is the model and year of the pickup we spotted speeding from the scene of Wollinski's murder.''

She huddled near him as though it was cold, but the night was warm and he suspected she was anxious not chilled. ''But thinking it's the same pickup and proving it are not the same thing.''

''True.'' He proceeded to the cab and gripped the door handle, then glanced over his shoulder, grinning like a Cheshire cat. ''Unlocked.''

She stood to one side, her head tipped, her voice low, stilted. ''Rossetti, do I have to remind you that what you're about to do would be considered unlawful search and seizure?''

''I'm not planning on seizing anything.''

''All the same, evidence you find this way will be inadmissible in court.''

''Only if I remove it from the truck.''

''And how would you explain your fingerprints being found inside Gunderson's truck?''

''Why would anyone think to look for my fingerprints in Gunderson's truck? You're not planning on ratting me out, are you, D?'' He walked back to the trunk of his car and grabbed a pair of rubber gloves, snapping them on. ''How's this? Feel better now?''

She blew out a noisy breath. ''Is this the kind of rash act that landed you on suspension, Rossetti?''

He shrugged. ''Sort of.''

She sighed. ''Figures.''

''Keep an eye out for Gunderson, okay?'' He eased open the driver's door, the inside light blaring on and startling him. He reached up, popped the plastic frame free and unscrewed the bulb. His adrenaline was pumping; the thought of being caught at any second giving him a rush, reminding him time was not on his side. He had to hurry.

He located the registration and assured himself the truck did indeed belong to Ted Gunderson, before squatting and checking under the bench seat with the flashlight, then one gloved hand. Nothing. He yanked the back of the seat forward and scanned the light behind, the beam landing on a contractor-size measuring tape, a couple of bungee cords, a coiled yellow towing rope and jumper cables.

"Find anything?" D asked, her voice as full of nerves as his belly.

"Not yet." He leaned across the seat and flipped open the glove box. It was crammed with papers. He poked a finger at the stack, lifting maps, a truck manual, tire brochures, and beneath them all, a gun. "Bott-a-bing."

"What did you find?" D stood in the open door.

Before he could answer, a loud "pop" sounded from inside the clinic. She jerked toward the building. "Nick, that was a gunshot."

"Are you sure?" He forgot his discovery, hustling out of the truck, leaving the overhead light unscrewed, the plastic cover off, the glove box open.

"I've gone hunting with my dad from the time I could hold and aim a pistol. I know gunfire when I hear it."

"Get down, dammit." He grabbed her, pulling her into a squat, covering her instinctively, protectively, with his larger body. His gaze poked the shadows beyond the lot. "Where did the shot come from?"

"Not out here." She pushed against his hold. "Inside the building."

He swore again, leaped up, slammed the truck door and set out at a run for the entrance steps. "Stay there, D. Call 911."

"No." She kept up with him pace for pace, digging her gun from her purse. "You're unarmed. I'm not. Besides, we don't know that there is any kind of an emergency in there. Or whether or not we can even get inside through this door."

He considered arguing with her, taking the gun from her, but she was too stubborn to listen and probably a much better shot than he. They proceeded cautiously up the stairs, approaching the double glass doors warily. A dim light showed them that the entrance hall was empty. The door was unlocked.

Nick stepped into the cool interior, cautioning D to keep directly behind him. They crept toward the receptionist's desk, their footfalls silent on the hard tile flooring.

Dr. Falls's office door was wide open, the subdued lighting within giving the sense of peace and calm, as though all was right with Breena Falls and her manufactured world. But his nerves buzzed, a sure sign something was very wrong. He gestured for D to get behind Tina's desk as he inched forward, pressing his body to one side of the doorjamb.

To his horror and fury, she ignored him, stealing to the other side of the door, her gun poised and ready as though she'd gone through the police academy.

He gave her a furious glare, and the sharp retort on his tongue was silenced by a low moan, like the groan of a wounded animal. He peered around the door frame and his chest tightened.

Dr. Breena Falls lay on the floor on her back, thick, dark liquid spreading from beneath her in an ever-enlarging pool. Ted Gunderson knelt beside her, a gun in his bloody grasp.

"Drop the gun, Gunderson." D trained the pistol on

his bent back. "Put it down and step away from the doctor."

Gunderson dropped the gun, then to Nick's surprise, reached down and gathered Breena Falls into his arms and sobbed, "Bree, Bree, Bree."

Chapter Fourteen

Desire glanced across at Nick, who was once again behind the wheel of his car driving them away from the city. It was nearly dawn. Homicide investigators had just finished questioning them. Nick's jaw was bristled with ebony whiskers. The tiny creases around his eyes were deep, pronounced. "You look like your captain chewed you up and spit you out."

"Yeah, Cap hates being bothered in the middle of the night." Nick shook his head as though trying to clear it or to shake himself awake. "Thinks it's damn inconsiderate of our prominent citizens to get themselves murdered after he's left for the day."

"I'm sure it wasn't convenient for Dr. Falls, either." Desire buried a yawn in her palm.

"It didn't help that Cap had no idea, until he got to his office, that this was the second homicide within ten hours that I was personally involved in—as he put it—'up to my suspended ass.'"

A flash of alarm swept Desire. "He doesn't suspect you of anything, does he?"

Nick gave her a wry smile. "He suspects me of everything, D, most of which I'm guilty of, but he'll never be able to prove it."

"I mean about the two murders."

Nick yawned and shook his head again. "No, and after I explained the possible connection between Wollinski and Falls, and that we had the suspect cooling his heels in one of our cells, he was moderately mollified."

Desire breathed easier and leaned wearily back against her seat. Gunderson was indeed in jail. He'd seemed a broken man, refusing to speak to anyone after Dr. Falls was pronounced dead of the single gunshot wound that had entered her back and pierced her heart.

As bad as she felt about Breena Falls's death, Desire was relieved. Ted Gunderson was finally where he belonged: locked in a cell. Caught red-handed this time. No question of his guilt.

Connor had been elated. Being rousted at the late hour hadn't upset his mood. He'd shown up to vouch for her and to confirm that his office was pursuing a quiet investigation into the possibility that Ted Gunderson was an erotomaniac who had stalked Dare Hamilton, and was now obsessed with Desire.

She shoved her hair away from her cheek, realizing she probably looked a mess and not caring at the moment. "Connor extracted a promise from your captain to share information regarding whatever evidence they recover that might confirm Gunderson is our stalker."

Nick gave a short whistle. "Cap isn't usually so generous to other counties."

They rode in silence for another block, Desire noticing that as the sun rose it drenched buildings and rooftops with an ugly reddish hue, reminding her of the blood on Gunderson's hands. Dr. Breena Falls's blood. How ironically sad that the doctor's professional ethics, her insistence on keeping her patients' confidences might have been the death of her. "Do you think he shot her because she was going to tell us that he's an erotomaniac?"

"That's the way I've got it figured." Nick yawned and shook his head harder than before. "But Gunderson seems intent on keeping his lips zipped...at least until his attorney shows."

She made a scoffing noise. "His lawyer will probably advise him not to talk at all."

"No matter. They'll get a search warrant for his house and truck. They'll find the negatives he stole from Eddie's studio and proof that he sent those valentines. His phone records should be helpful and interesting, too."

Her eyes felt gritty, her mind fuzzy. Something about his reasoning hit a sour note, but she couldn't figure out what at the moment. "I want to see his files from the Falls Clinic."

"Yeah." Nick yawned again, stretching until his hand rested on her shoulder.

There was something reassuring about his touch. She reached up and laid her hand on his, giving him a grateful smile. "Do you think it's too early to call Ron Whiting? I can't wait to tell him that Gunderson is finally going to pay for Cindy."

"Do it. It's never too early for good news. Call Michael Pride, too. Both of them should know."

Ron Whiting sounded as though he, also, had been up all night. Or maybe it was that sadness she'd seen in his eyes yesterday now conveyed in his voice. Her news about Gunderson seemed to give him a bit of a lift, but she understood that it didn't assuage his grief, and she empathized. Successfully prosecuting Gunderson wouldn't bring back Cindy, or Dare.

She caught Michael Pride's answering machine, and

left the message. As she hung up, she said, "I imagine he'll feel some closure now, too."

"Don't worry, D." Nick moved his hand to her thigh, his touch tender and intimate, rousing memories of their tryst in the closet. "The case against him is airtight. A jury will make sure Gunderson stays behind bars for life."

For life. She had thought her life with Nick would have to be put on hold indefinitely. Gunderson's arrest had changed that. She was free to love Nick...and that was exactly what she intended to do. She stared, mesmerized by his handsome profile for the beat of several sensuous seconds, arrested by the realization that this gorgeous man was hers, hers for the taking. She reached over and touched his face, claiming her right.

He looked at her, his gaze warm, melting, molten. It heated her from the inside out, bred need in wildfire proportions that she knew shone in her expression. She caressed his whiskers. "How about that shave I promised you, Rossetti?"

"Sure." The word came out on a raspy sigh.

"Your place or mine?" she asked, unable to resist teasing him with his own words.

They chose his place; it was closest.

They meant to make love slowly, languidly, taking the time to explore and pleasure, but fueled by a desperate passion, they'd come together once again with a speed and explosion of feelings that had stolen what little remained of their energy. Afterward, laughing and sated, they'd collapsed into each other's arms and slept.

Desire woke ravenous, but with a sense of fulfillment that she'd never known, a mending of the wounds in her tattered heart. She glanced down at Nick, who still needed that shave. His whiskers were denser than a few hours ago, her cheeks still tender from the encounter.

A smile climbed from the depths of her and spread across her face, warming her as this man warmed her. She left him snoring softly, donned a clean T-shirt she found in his dresser drawer and took her rumpled clothing to the washer.

She found her way to the kitchen. It was mostly oak and chrome, obviously recently remodeled. She stood at the sink, gazing out at the yard, lost in happy thoughts, amused at Nick's gardening skills. The grass was green, but the flowers were as dead as those at the Palms. The thought reminded her that she hadn't called Lorelei to ask if she knew what Eddie had been doing there yesterday.

Keray answered on the third ring. She identified herself. "Mr. Collins, where was the photographer when you captured him yesterday?"

"The faker, you mean?"

His accent left her wondering if he meant fakir or faker. Either way, she supposed, in Eddie's case it applied. "Yes."

"He was inside yer sister's 'partment. He'd tore off the rest of the boards and climbed on in that broken window."

"Taking interior photos of the place." Desire wasn't surprised. Given Eddie's obsession with her sister, she supposed in some sick way he just couldn't stop himself even though she was dead.

"He wasn't takin' no pictures." Keray belched. "Still had the lens caps on his cameras. He was just sittin' on her bed. Lookin' round the room. Sad as a umpire without a game to referee."

Sad. Sicker still, Desire thought.

A movement caught in the periphery of her sight. Something man-size. Outside. She jerked toward the window. What had she seen? A shadow—like someone ducking out of sight, like the shadow she'd seen in her own backyard?

With her pulse leaping and her stomach clenching, she thanked Keray and hung up. She darted to the larger window beside the oak dinette table and scanned the yard, the corners of the house. Nothing. No one lurking anywhere. Her breath shuddered out.

God, what was she doing? *Looking for stalkers where there were none.*

If that wasn't so pathetic, she'd laugh. Gunderson was behind bars. She was safe. Happy even. Why did she have to have doubts? She had been handed back her life. Had everything to look forward to. She forced herself to take several calming breaths, glancing at the clock as she did so.

It was nearly three in the afternoon. Knowing the time seemed to make her even more hungry. Deciding food would take the edge off, she padded to the refrigerator and was surprised to find it fully stocked. Most of the bachelors she knew kept a half case of beer and cold pizza in their fridges. Did this mean Nick could cook?

It would be a bonus if he could.

She had spent her formative years learning everything Judd Hamilton could teach her about surviving in a man's world. The only cooking she'd ever done was over a campfire; the only meal she'd mastered was breakfast. She began fixing bacon, eggs, hash browns, toast, coffee and orange juice.

Soon the kitchen was alive with mouthwatering aromas.

"Now, that is a sight I could grow used to every morning," Nick said from behind her.

"It's afternoon." She glanced at him over her shoulder. He was barefoot, naked, it appeared, beneath the thigh-length robe belted at his narrow waist. He approached from behind, wrapped his arms around her and nuzzled her neck. She leaned back against him, welcoming him with a throaty groan. Even the whiskers against her temple felt wonderful. "I think this is what I could never grow tired of."

He moaned with pleasure. "I could be persuaded to accommodate you…starting right now."

She realized he was aroused, and spun playfully in his arms, bumping the spatula against his chest. "Oh no you don't, Rossetti…not until we've eaten. I don't want you passing out on me from hunger."

He laughed heartily, kissed her cheek, then set the table. As they ate, she told him about her conversation with Keray, how the landlord had discovered Eddie in Dare's apartment sitting on the bed, not taking pictures as he'd claimed.

Nick frowned as though something about that bothered him, something beyond what had bothered her. "Feeling guilty, maybe?"

She considered this and shrugged. "We may never know."

"I guess." He seemed to continue to mull over the information, as though now, after hours of revitalizing, mind-clearing sleep, he was rethinking earlier conclusions, questioning something important.

She recalled her own niggling doubts today, the shadow she *thought* she'd seen. Should she tell Nick? No, no. The shadows were figments of her imagination, just an unsettling jumpiness from being scared for too long. She didn't want anything to spoil this day, didn't want to know what bothered him, didn't want to think about anything at the moment except them, didn't want anything else on his mind either.

She stood, crossed to his side of the table, then gently massaged his furrowed forehead with her fingertips. "I need a shower. How about you, Rossetti? Want to save on your water bill?"

He relaxed his brow, his eyes clearing, then heating with the speed of a gas jet catching a flame. His hands moved to her calves, eliciting a gasp from her as they climbed her thighs, burrowed beneath the T-shirt she wore and skimmed past her waist and higher. "You are a distraction, D."

"Is that a bad thing?" she murmured, moving between his legs.

"How would I know? I can't reason when you're this close."

He rolled the hem of the T-shirt up her stomach and kissed her naked flesh as it was revealed to him. He nibbled his way to her breasts, his mouth capturing her nipples, teasing them until they ached with pleasure, his whiskered jaw prickling the sensitive skin. He lifted his head, his eyes dark with passion, and a tiny frown creased his forehead. He touched the rash his beard had caused on her pale skin. He glanced up at her, an apology in his expression as he rubbed his jaw. "How about that shave you promised me, D? Do you think you could manage it without drawing blood?"

She was trembling with need, unsure of herself in a whole new way. "Are you sure you trust me that much, Nick?"

"That much and more, love." He rose, hooked an arm around her, caught hold of the chair and hauled it with them into his bedroom, past the rumpled bed, into the bathroom, setting it down on the blue bath mat that covered most of the tile floor. He gathered a disposable razor and shaving gel, then sat on the chair.

Desire swallowed with difficulty. She'd never shaved a man before, but had watched the ritual for years. How hard could it be? She found a towel and placed it around Nick's shoulders, then stood between his spread legs, his short robe hiked high, leaving little to her imagination, a glorious sight she was fighting to ignore. She squeezed a portion of shaving gel into her palm. Nick offered no guidance, just looked at her with fascination, the hint of a smile in his eyes. *He ought to be terrified,* she thought. *Foolish man didn't know better.*

She daubed her fingers into the gel and starting at one sideburn began smearing it across his jaw, under and over his mouth, to the other sideburn until the lower half of his face was lathered in white. The slick soapy slide of her fingers against the stiff, short whiskers had tingles of excitement and anticipation rippling through her.

Nick's eyes darkened with want. She fought to ignore the power of that look, but her body had a mind of its own where this man was concerned. Her breathing was deepening, quickening. She wiped her soapy hands on the towel at his neck and grasped the razor. Nick still said nothing, just looked at her with that distracting gaze.

His hands, she realized, gripped the seat of his chair, and she grinned. "Scared, Rossetti?"

"Not of you, D."

"Really? Then why are you clutching that chair so tightly?"

"You don't want to find out."

"Oh?" The heat in his eyes leaped inside her. She

decided to give it back to him. "Maybe I should distract you? Take off my shirt?"

He made a husky noise deep in his throat. "Just get it over with, woman."

"My, such impatience." She chuckled sweetly and brought the razor to his cheek and firmly, smoothly tugged it downward from the left sideburn to the curve of his jaw as she'd watched her mother do to her father since she'd been a child. "So far, so good."

Nick was breathing faster, noisier, a heavy push and pull of air between them, across their faces, electrifying the minuscule space separating them. Her hands felt slick. She wiped them against the towel again and stroked the razor across his face a second time, a third time, a fourth, leaning close, her body and mind undermining her concentration, making her too aware of the aroused man, too aware of her own arousal.

Nick turned his face, offering her the other cheek. His breath was coming faster still, the rise and fall of his chest causing his robe to separate, exposing the patch of crisp raven hair on his chest, impossible to ignore.

An anguished purr slipped from her. It seemed to snap the restraints Nick had been holding on his need. His hands unlocked from the seat of his chair, catching her, startling her as he pulled her onto his lap, his lips finding hers in a fierce, whisker-burning, soapy-tasting, mind-blazing kiss.

Moments later, Nick lifted his head. He gazed at her and laughed, a low, sensuous lover's laugh, caught the towel at his shoulders and daubed the shaving gel from her nose and chin, her mouth. "Such sexy lips, D."

He lifted her off his lap and stepped to the mirror. In rapid strokes, he finished shaving, and used the towel to wipe the remaining lather as he wrenched on the faucets in the shower. He gave her *that* look again, causing the quick rush of her heart to match the flux of the water.

Sun poured in through the skylight, drenching him in a golden glow that gave his raven hair a blue-black tint. His hand went to the belt of his robe; her gaze did the same. He unwound the knot and eased the robe from his shoulders, letting it drop to the floor. She drew a sharp breath. She doubted she'd ever tire of looking at him like this. He was fully erect, a dazzling sight, a beautiful man, made more glorious by the wounds he'd suffered trying to protect her.

She stared at him for five whole seconds, both of them breathing hard, her blood feeling heavy and thick in her veins, her need coiled and demanding in the core of her. She removed her T-shirt, dropping it atop his robe, shaking her hair as she closed the gap between them.

His gaze grazed the length of her, from her toes upward, and the smile breaking across his face held pure appreciation. "You are one incredible-looking woman."

"I'm glad you approve." She held his gaze, tested the water, finding the temperature satisfying, and stepped beneath the spray, wetting her hair, aware of Nick's gaze locked on her, devouring her.

"Let me," Nick said, reaching for the shampoo. "I've always wanted to do this."

"Have you?" The notion pleased her.

She poured a handful of the greenish liquid into Nick's palm. The scent of ripe apples and sheer male wired her senses. He lathered it into her hair, his hands large and strong, but his fingers against her scalp were as tender and sensuous as feather strokes, moving over her ears, down her neck, across her shoulders, spreading the lather there, then onto her aching nipples, down her flat belly to the dense blond curls below. He was a master, his massage hypnotic, intoxicating.

She poured more green-apple shampoo into her hand, this time slathering it into Nick's wet hair, her long fingernails combing, cleansing his thick ebony locks. Then she smoothed the lather down his shoulders, careful of his wounded arm, across his chest, easy on the yellowing bruise, scrubbing, kneading, glorying in the sharp moans of need her touch elicited from him.

She gently raked her fingernails across his belly, then into the dense nest of black hair beneath, and soon her eager fingers curled around the sleek, swollen, pulsing length at its apex. He groaned her name as she crouched and took him into her mouth, licking, sucking, then scraping her teeth over the sensitive tip.

On a deep sigh, Nick gently, firmly clasped both sides of her face, calling her name, urging her to stand, dragging her up his body and kissing her deep and long, his tongue twisting with hers as he pulled her arms around his neck and lifted her hips high, higher, then brought her down, his own hips thrusting upward.

He was barely inside her when the first explosion rocked through her, her body clenching him, increasing his urgency. She kissed his neck, his mouth, his forehead, frantic, frenzied, fired by her need for him, the coil inside her so tight and sweet it was tossing her into the clouds, tugging her breath from her, pushing her over some delirious, delicious edge she couldn't define.

"Oh, Desire, my Desire," Nick cried, climaxing as he found the edge with her.

For several minutes, he held her to him, leaning against the wall of the shower, the spray falling warm over them as they panted, clinging to each other, grinning at each other with joy and delirium.

THE AFTERGLOW LASTED until Connor called around seven and asked them to meet him in his office. "I've got news, Hamilton, and you're not going to like it."

"Then tell me now."

"Not over the phone. I want Rossetti to hear it at the same time."

They promised they'd be right there. Nick was introspective on the drive over, unwilling to share his thoughts, obviously not wanting to cause her more stress than she was giving herself. But she could tell he wasn't surprised that there was bad news. Something, she knew, had been bothering him since he'd awakened.

They arrived in Santa Beverly within the hour, and parked in the city hall lot. They hurried to the back entrance. Nick had her by the arm, as usual acting like her bodyguard. Three feet from the door, a sharp popping sound stopped her in her tracks.

Nick shoved her to the ground.

At least, that was what Desire thought, until she felt something warm and sticky beneath her palm and realized it was Nick's blood.

Chapter Fifteen

"Nick! Nick!" Desire struggled out from under the dead weight of him. *Dead weight? Dead?* She gasped. "No, Nick, answer me."

She rolled him onto his back. His blood was on her hand. On the sidewalk. Pumping from a groove that sliced along the back of his head to his left sideburn. *God, don't let this wound be fatal.* Panic slammed her heart against her ribs. "Oh, Nick! Oh my God!"

He didn't answer. *Unconscious.* There was a pulse, not strong but there. He was losing too much blood. Fear attacked from every direction. Was Nick going to die? Was the shooter still out there in the parking lot waiting to try again? *No.* She flopped over Nick, covering him with her body, shaking so hard her teeth chattered.

"Help! Help us!" But no one came. Evening. Santa Beverly's *finest* reduced to a skeletal crew. Office workers gone too. Desire was the only one who could help Nick now. She forced herself to move from him and, keeping low, she scrambled to the door, tugged it open and shouted, "Help us! Somebody! Quick! Get an ambulance!"

Running footsteps responded immediately. She raced

back to Nick. The blood kept pumping. She tore off her blouse and pressed it to the wound to stem the flow.

Someone came through the door and knelt beside her. ''What happened, D.A. Hamilton?'' She knew this officer, Linda something or other.

''Shot.'' Words stuck in her throat. ''Get an ambulance.''

''One's coming.'' Linda, gun in hand, scanned the parking lot. ''Where's the shooter?''

''Out there.'' Desire pointed, unable to look away from Nick's beloved face, fearing that if she did, even for an instant, he would slip away from her.

Linda shouted to someone inside the building, then was back at her side, touching her shoulder. ''Maybe we should move you both inside.''

The suggestion increased her panic. ''He's too heavy. We might hurt him worse.''

''Okay, but keep low.''

Someone joined Linda, another officer, a man, and, with guns drawn, the two moved quickly, stealthily through the parking lot. Desire crouched over Nick, holding her blouse pressed to his head. Where was the damn ambulance? Fear screamed through her mind, and she pleaded, ''Damn you, Rossetti, wake up!''

She caught the sound of sirens. *At last.* She pulled in air like someone long denied. ''It's coming, Nick. Do you hear? Hang on, my love, hang on.''

The siren stopped, and tires screeched.

''Desire?'' Someone touched her shoulder again. She flinched hard, pouring her body protectively over Nick.

The person squatted beside her, forcing his way into her line of vision. He wore black sweatpants, a hooded black sweatshirt with a T-shirt beneath, all emblazoned with the Santa Beverly Police logo. *White-blond hair*

like angel wings above a cherubic face. Detective Ron
Whiting, she realized. His cheeks were pink and his sad
green eyes brimmed with tenderness and sympathy.
"Desire, are you all right?"

He began pulling her away from Nick.

She wrested from his grasp. "No, I have to keep pressure on his wound."

"The medics will take care of that now." His voice
was almost a melodic whisper.

She glanced up. EMTs were scrambling toward them.
She gave herself a mental shake and stopped fighting
Ron. He removed his sweatshirt and draped it over her
shoulders, lifting her as he did so.

She allowed herself to be pulled to one side, near the
door. Her gaze was riveted on Nick, but her brain was
jammed with panic, her body numb with fear. Ron
forced her arms through the sleeves of the sweatshirt and
zipped it. "Wouldn't want you to catch a cold."

"What?" She had no idea what he was talking about,
her state of dress of no concern. She felt as though her
whole world was collapsing, that she was collapsing. If
Nick died… The possibility nearly dropped her to her
knees. No, no. She couldn't lose Nick. Not when she'd
finally found her way to him. Finally let him into her
life.

Linda and her cohort ran up, breathless, shaking their
heads. Linda said, "No one out there, Ron. You think
she saw whoever it was?"

"De—D.A. Hamilton?" Ron asked softly. "Did you
see the shooter?"

"See?" Desire wrenched her gaze from Nick, letting
the question sink in, running the whole incident through
her mind again, feeling the panic threaten to overtake
her again. The professional detachment she relied on in

such situations had vanished with Nick's consciousness. "No, we were facing the door, coming to meet with D.A. Gregg."

As though the mention of his name had summoned him, Connor came storming through the back door of the city hall building. Taking in the scene, he swore, his gaze going to Desire. For once his icy eyes were hot...with concern. "What the hell happened here? Hamilton, are you all right?"

"I'm okay. But Nick...?" Her pulse was thudding against her temples. "Is he...?"

The EMTs were moving with speed, strapping him to a gurney and hustling him into the ambulance. One of them said, "The bullet creased his skull. He's concussed, but his vitals are strong."

"Where are you taking him?" Connor demanded.

"Santa Beverly General." The ambulance sped away.

His vitals are strong. Desire clung to the heartening news as tightly as she clung to her boss, her mind beginning to unfreeze, to melt the awful panic, to fill with anger. "Who, Connor? Who would want to shoot Nick?"

"Come on, kiddo." His expression was sympathetic, but he seemed reluctant to look her squarely in the eye. She felt an uneasy tightness in her belly that had nothing to do with Nick's wound. What did Connor know that she didn't? He caught her arm. "Let's get to the hospital. My car's right over here."

They arrived at the hospital within five minutes.

The emergency room receptionist assured Connor and Desire that Nick was being attended to and directed them to the waiting area, a twelve-by-twenty space crowded with uncomfortable vinyl chairs and strain-faced people, several of whom glanced up expectantly as they entered.

Desire made her way to one of the few remaining seats, comforting herself with the knowledge that as serious as his injury and concussion were, Nick was not dead or physically disabled. His chances of a rapid and full recovery were good. Great even. But she didn't understand who could have shot him.

As a homicide cop with a great solve record, he undoubtedly had enemies, but how many would have known he'd be at the back door of the Santa Beverly City Hall tonight? It had to be that someone had followed them from his house. God, they'd paid no attention, had let their guards down, had seen no reason to be on the alert for anyone tailing them with Gunderson in lockup.

But who knew where Nick lived?

She thought of the note that had been left on his windshield the other day and felt a chill in her belly. Gunderson had left that note. He was the stalker. He was in jail.

Then who shot Nick? And why?

The possibility that Gunderson was not the stalker crept into the edges of her mind. She pushed the idea back, refusing to consider it. If Gunderson was not the stalker, she and Nick were finished…though they'd barely begun. Erotomaniacs never gave up. She and Nick had no future.

She clasped the sides of her head, pain throbbing at her temples as though she was the one who'd been shot.

NICK WOKE with the worst headache of his life. Eyes shut, he felt for the source of the pain, but someone clasped his wrist. "Don't touch the wound, Nick."

"Wound?" He pried his eyes open. The room wanted to spin. Where the hell was he? Hushed voices nearby, an occasional cry of pain, a green curtain hung on large metal loops, a hospital, he realized. What "wound" had brought him to a hospital? The last thing he recalled was walking with D toward the back entrance of the Santa Beverly City Hall. He'd felt a sudden sharp heat at the back of his head, then nothing.

"D!" Fear slammed through his mind, setting it on fire. He jerked straight up on the hospital bed, dizzying pain banging from temple to temple like a swatted racket ball.

"Nick, don't." It was D holding his wrist. She was sitting on the edge of his bed, her other hand pressed to his chest. She wore a pinched smile, her aqua eyes full of concern. "I'm right here."

She urged him to lay back. He complied, his heart slowing as he took in the knowledge that she was safe. Unharmed. Her face seemed shades paler than usual with the green privacy curtain behind her. Her hair was tousled, her makeup smeared, her nose and eyes swollen and red. She looked like an angel to him.

He traced his knuckles along the silken curve of her precious cheek. "Don't look so sad, love. I'm going to live. Or is that what has you so sullen?"

That pulled a smile from her, weak but sweet. "It's good to know you're feeling well enough to joke about this, Rossetti."

She tried for an angry look, but he could see she was relieved and it warmed his heart. He clasped her hands and brought them to his lips. "Now tell me what happened."

She reached up as though to touch his head, but he flinched and she dropped her hand back to cover his own. "You were shot."

Shot? His eyebrows arched upward, the pain instant.

Wincing, he blinked. Who the hell would have shot at him? Nick didn't understand. The only one who'd want him dead was behind bars. Wasn't he? "Who shot me?"

The curtains moved back and Connor Gregg strode toward the bed. "Maybe I can answer that."

A sudden dread filled Nick's belly, and in that instant he feared he knew who'd shot him, but hoped against hope he was wrong, even strove for another possibility. "A drive-by?"

"I doubt it." As usual, Connor's appearance was impeccable, as though disorder was something he never had to deal with. His clear eyes, which usually gave away nothing he was feeling, showed discomfort.

Nick knew he wasn't going to like whatever D's boss had to tell him. The fire in his brain went out, going as cold as long-dead ashes, bringing with it resignation. "What was the news you had to tell us in person, Gregg? Have you already told D?"

"No. She hasn't thought about anything but you. I figured it could wait until you were conscious."

"I'm conscious now." Nick still clasped D's hands. He felt her flinch and gave her a gentle, reassuring squeeze, letting her know that whatever it was, they would face it together. "So, tell us what's going on."

"The LAPD searched Gunderson's house." He glanced from one to the other of them.

"And his pickup truck?" Nick asked.

Connor nodded.

"What did they come up with?" D asked. "Other valentines?"

"No." Connor unnecessarily straightened his tie. "None. I told you his thumbprint wasn't a match with the one found on the card left under your door."

"What about the negatives?" Nick frowned, the effort

costing him a jab of pain. A memory flitted in and out of his grasp. If his head would quit aching maybe he could recall whatever it was that had been bothering him about Gunderson.

"What negatives?" Connor asked.

Looking decidedly discomfited, D explained about their visit to Eddie's studio. Connor scowled, causing her to falter in her narrative for a second, but she rushed ahead, omitting the personal details and recounting for him the unexpected visitor they'd thought was a policeman and later realized wasn't. "It had to have been Gunderson."

"I don't think so." Connor pressed his lips together, his expression solemn. "They didn't find any negatives at his house."

"Well, of course not. He hadn't had time to go elsewhere after leaving Wollinski's beach house. The hood of his pickup was warm. He'd arrived at the clinic just before us. The negatives would have been in his truck."

"But they weren't, D," Nick said, realizing, at last, what had been bothering him since the previous night.

"If Gunderson had taken the negatives from Wollinski's house, as we'd thought, they would have been in his truck. They weren't."

She drew a hard breath, her eyes blazing. "Okay, then he had them on his person."

"He didn't," Connor insisted. "There were no negatives of any kind found."

D looked more pale than she had minutes ago. She shook her head at both men. "That doesn't matter. We caught him with Dr. Falls. He killed her. You know that, Nick. His records at the clinic will prove his motive."

Connor wiped his face with his hand. "No, Hamilton, they won't."

"What do you mean?" D raised her voice. "Of course they will."

"Ted Gunderson," Connor said, lowering his voice, reminding her by example that they were in a hospital with other patients to consider, "was not Dr. Falls's patient."

D's expression went incredulous, as though she couldn't figure out why Connor wouldn't listen to reason. Nick tightened his hold on her hand. She tugged it free. "Well, then he was the patient of one of the other doctors there."

"No." Connor leveled his cool eyes on her. "Never."

"But...the appointment card..." She looked confused. "Nick, tell him about the appointment card in Dr. Falls's handwriting."

"Hamilton." Connor touched her arm and she went silent, giving him her full attention. "Breena Falls was Ted Gunderson's sister."

Desire drew a sharp breath. Nick thought he'd heard wrong. But Connor was stoic. He let them absorb this bomb, then dropped another. "The gun that killed Breena Falls wasn't Gunderson's. His fingerprints were on the barrel. He did, after all, pick it up. But he wasn't wearing gloves and there are no fingerprints on either the trigger or the bullets inside the gun."

Nick felt as though a light had gone on inside his head. *That damn gun in Gunderson's glove box. It was one of those loose ends that could screw up an airtight case.* He swore, then caught D's hands in his again. Her gaze lifted, the denial was finally gone; a resignation, not unlike the one he felt, had taken its place. "We'll get through this, D."

She nodded, as though mentally surrendering in some way or other, but Nick could almost feel the wheels churning inside her gorgeous head. This was not a woman who gave up on anything without a fight. It was a quality he both respected and feared in her. What was she thinking? Deciding?

She cut her gaze to Connor. "Has he made bail?"

"Yes."

"Does Ron Whiting know?"

Connor shrugged. "Depends if he made it his business to know. I didn't tell him."

Nick studied her, gauging her. That trace of fear that had finally dissolved with Gunderson's arrest was back in her eyes. Whoever had been stalking her sister was still out there. Stalking her. Shooting at him.

God knew the depths she would plumb in order to protect him.

"If it's any consolation," Connor said, "Gunderson did start talking once his lawyer arrived."

D arched an eyebrow with disbelief. "He kept mum when he was on trial for murdering Cindy Whiting. Why would he talk this time?"

"Because this time his sister was killed. It seems to have undone him."

She appeared unconvinced, in need of tying up loose ends. "If he was really Dr. Falls's brother, why didn't her receptionist, Tina, know that?" She shifted her gaze from Connor to Nick. "Why didn't Tina know immediately that you weren't Gunderson?"

Connor said, "Gunderson claims Dr. Falls didn't want anyone to know they were related. She gave him a generous monthly allowance to keep that fact hidden. Apparently, she didn't trust him not to give away family secrets to the tabloids and was paying for his silence. He almost blew that though, he admitted, when he walked in on Breena and Cindy Whiting one evening."

"Is that where he met Cindy?" D asked.

"That's what he claims," Connor said. "He said she was taking one of those divorce-survivor sessions his sister gave in the evenings and had apparently stayed behind for some reason or other."

A nurse yanked back the green curtain and bustled into the confined space. "We're moving Detective Rossetti to a private room."

"Just bring me my clothes," Nick protested, trying to rise again, groaning and falling back with the effort. "I'm leaving."

"Oh, no," the nurse insisted with happy authority. "Doctor wants you kept overnight for observation. Your pupils are still uneven."

"I don't care if my pupils are pink. I'm not staying here."

"Nick, please listen to reason," D pleaded.

"I'm being as reasonable as this new development allows me."

"I'll be fine. But not if I'm worried about you every moment."

He reached up and touched her hair. She nuzzled her head against his hand, so tense he could feel it, and the fight went out of him. The last thing he wanted was to make her stress worse, but on the other hand he had to ensure her safety. "The only way I'll stay here is if you promise me that you'll stick to Connor like you're glued to him."

"I promise." She kissed him and whispered, "I love you, Rossetti. Behave yourself."

"Same to you, D." He kissed her again. "And remember, what's happened—this news about Gunderson—it changes nothing between us."

She nodded. Tears he knew she would never shed in

public shone in her eyes. He wanted to hold her to him and never let go. He half rose, but pain and dizziness brought his back against the pillow with a grimace. Frustrated at his weakened condition, he turned to Connor and demanded, "Keep her safe or so help me God you'll answer to me."

"I will." Connor put his arm around her. "Count on it."

"I am."

"Connor has arranged for round-the-clock guards on your room, Nick," D said. "It was the only way I would agree to leave."

Connor nodded. "Anyone wanting access to you will be monitored and identified beforehand."

As the nurse began moving his wheeled bed from the cubicle, he said, "Stay away from your house, D."

"Absolutely." She blew him a kiss.

"The minute I can get up," Nick groused at the nurse, "I'm outta here."

DESIRE WOULD HAVE REMAINED at the hospital with Nick, but as long as the stalker was still after her, the only way she could protect the man she loved was to stay far away from him. She paced the length of the guest room in Connor's condo, feeling as restless as a caged lynx.

The residential community Connor lived in was as secure as they came. But she didn't feel safe. She would never feel safe as long as her stalker was still out there. Whoever it was, he would not stop trying to kill Nick until he succeeded.

Despite her promises to Nick, she knew hiding from the stalker would not lessen his zeal to be with her. Connor could even be next on the man's hit list. She hugged herself and stopped in front of the floor-length mirror on the closet door. The face that stared back at her held resignation. Grim determination. Only she could end his rein of terror.

She knew what she had to do.

Chapter Sixteen

He liked small, dark places. Liked the way the tightness sheathed him—the way he wanted her body to sheathe him. He sank onto his haunches, invincible in this space that smelled of her. Of his sweet Desire. Of that mind-teasing scent she favored: gardenias, like the petals in the plastic bag beside him, the petals he would soon spread over her bed, that they would make love on. That same fragrance that lingered on her creamy skin. On her clothes. And in his mind. Forever.

His nuzzled his nose against the hem of her dresses, drawing the scent into him as he wanted to draw her into him.

Soon now, he would.

A smile crooked his mouth at both corners and his insides heated with anticipation, picturing her expression as she discovered the gardenias on her bed. He'd made a mistake with the yellow roses. Assumed twins would like the same scent. But now he knew. Knew her. His need for her stirred, filling his mind with her image. Her cascading blond hair had waved around her perfect oval face, her wide aqua eyes beckoning him. A siren call of promises.

Desire. His sweet Desire. His only Desire.

Straight off a ranch in Laredo, Texas. As wholesome as an angel. Innocent and pure. But career success was fraught with pitfalls. Even now, her sensuality threatened her virtue with evil temptations. Resolve swept through him. He would save her as he had not been able to save her sister. His love would save her.

Thank God, she was finally free to accept their destiny.

His smile widened as he saw again Desire's eyes looking directly at him from the photograph he'd taken from her twin's apartment. She'd spoken to him through that picture, her lush lips telling him, "We can be together now. You and I. Today. Come to my home. To my bedroom. Wait in my closet."

And so he waited.

Chapter Seventeen

Morning dawned as clear as Desire's resolution. The fretful night had reinforced her determination to catch the bastard who had tried to kill Nick, cemented her conviction that there was only one sure way to draw him out of the shadows. She was amazed that what she was going to do didn't terrify her. It was as though by finally deciding to confront her stalker, she was no longer the main game piece he could maneuver at will in this sick diversion of his.

Control the situation and you'll always be a winner. Judd Hamilton's mantra. His young daughter had eaten it up like a favorite candy. And Daddy had been right. Control always gave her confidence. It had also, she understood now, shaped her life into the lonely mess it had become. It was amazing the erroneous advice well-meaning parents often gave their children. If she'd been willing to loosen the reins of control, to see past her own fierce guilt at hurting Dare, maybe she'd have discovered a way to mend the rift with her sister.

Maybe she wouldn't have snagged the attention of an erotomaniac.

God, what was she thinking? She hadn't asked for this. She had done nothing to deserve or bring this on

herself. The anger simmering inside her all night bub-
bled to the surface and she shrieked with fury. She knew
better. Lifelong experience through her parents's charity
work had taught her better. Women were so often
blamed for the crimes men perpetrated against them that
it was second nature to accept undeserved culpability.
Had Cindy Whiting felt shame or guilt or responsibility
for being the focus of a stalker? Had Dare?

The god-awful possibility curled Desire's hands into
fists. Striking back at her stalker would be like striking
a blow for other victims of stalkers. A small victory for
womenkind everywhere. But her motive was more self-
serving than that. She wanted a life with Nick. A life
she would never have as long as some pervert was obsessed with her.

"Hamilton?" Connor pounded on the bedroom door.
"Are you all right?"

"Fine."

"I heard you scream."

"Sorry. Just frustrated. Didn't mean to startle you."

"Coffee's ready."

"I'll be right down." She finished dressing in her
khaki pants and Ron Whiting's zip-up sweatshirt, noticing that it held an odd mix of her favorite scent—had
she had enough on her skin for the shirt to have absorbed
it?—and his minty aftershave, which added to the discomfort of wearing it. Silly, but she felt as though she
hadn't bathed in a week. Looked it too.

She found a clip in her purse and twisted her hair off
her neck, erased the dark circles under her eyes with
makeup and applied mascara and lipstick. She wanted a
long hot soak in a fragrance-filled tub, wanted to wipe
Ron Whiting's scent from her awareness, wanted some-

thing fresh and crisp from her own closet; in another hour or so, she was going to have exactly that.

She found Connor in the kitchen, gulped down toast and coffee, then poured herself a second cup, feeling body and brain begin to respond to the initial jolt of caffeine. "Have you spoken to Nick?"

"No. But you'd better call him." Connor pointed to his telephone answering machine. "He's left four messages since dawn, threatening on the last call to come here in person if we don't let him know you're okay."

"He would, too, the stubborn fool."

"I'm sorry the thing with Gunderson didn't prove out," Connor said.

"Well, like you told me the other day, you win some you lose some. However, his being Breena Falls's brother explains why that doctor seemed to hate me on sight. She knew who I was before we met, and it's a pretty good guess that she hated me. In her position, I'd have felt the same." She took another sip of coffee. "Connor, while Nick and I were investigating Gunderson, we came across your name in the clinic files."

His eyebrows shot up. "Perhaps I could use some psychoanalyzing, but I've never sought help amongst that particular profession. Must be some other poor guy with the same name. And all this time I've thought I was one of a kind."

"You are definitely unique." She laughed, glad to have that point cleared up. "I'd better phone Nick."

She spun to the phone, noting as she did that Connor's home was as pristine as the man himself, his coffee as strong as his presence. It explained why he didn't have a woman in his life. He was too rigid. Too controlled. Maybe a psychologist could help him.

The thought made her smile.

They were quite a pair, her boss and she. Perhaps that made them a good team professionally. It had also kept them both single. She ought to explain the pitfalls of that to him, she thought, dialing the hospital. Give him some pointers on the benefits of letting loose once in a while, but she doubted he'd listen. A week or so ago, she wouldn't have believed it either.

Nick answered on the first ring. "D? Is that you?"

"Nick, I'm fine. Connor's condo is as secure as Fort Knox." The relief of hearing his voice spread a pleasant warmth through her heart. She'd never realized how great it could feel to have a man care this much about her. But the glow chilled at the thought of what his devotion had cost him. "How are you this morning?"

"Damn. I've been imagining…"

"Please, stop fretting."

"My pupils are still not even and my head aches like gremlins are hammering rivets into my skull. In other words, they won't spring me for a while."

"Then quit fighting and get some rest."

"Rest?" He groaned. "How can a man rest when sadistic nurses keep waking him every hour on the hour to shine a flashlight in his eyes?"

"Oh, poor baby."

He made a disgruntled noise, and she stifled a laugh.

Behind her, she heard Connor jingle his car keys. He was due in court this morning, would be there all day if she was lucky, a fact that she'd persuaded him not to share with Nick. He'd agreed only after she'd convinced him that, in his absence, she'd be under the constant protection of Ron Whiting.

She told Nick, "We have to get to the office. I'll call you from there, okay?"

"Okay. I love you, D. Take care."

"Same to you, Rossetti." *That's why I'm doing what I must today, my love. For us.*

She hung up, feeling confident that Nick was safe by the mere fact that *she* wasn't with him. But what about Connor? As they drove past the uniformed guard at the gated entrance of his secured community, she scanned the road in all directions. Did *he* know where she was? Was he out here somewhere waiting for them—with his sights set on Connor?

A clammy flush layered her skin, and the coffee and toast felt like bricks in her stomach, reinforcing her urgency to get away and stay away from Connor. She had no illusions about this; as long as she was with him, his life was in danger.

But her nerves were for nothing. They arrived at city hall unmolested. Desire was relieved to see Nick's car still in the parking lot, but wished she'd thought last night to take the key from Nick's pants pocket. He might have a spare somewhere on the car, but she wasn't going to take the chance.

Connor insisted on accompanying her to her office and waiting for Detective Whiting. She phoned Nick as she'd promised, assuring him that she'd arrived without incident and would remain in her office until the doctor released him and he came for her. He sounded weary, in pain, and her hatred for the stalker tripled.

But she forced herself to keep her voice even, hiding the anger from both men. She smiled at Connor, who sat across the desk from her. Neither man could suspect what she had planned. "Nick, please try and rest. You have a concussion."

"Do you miss me, D?" he drawled in a low sexy tone.

"Of course."

"As much as I miss you?"

"Yes." More than he knew, more than she'd thought she would or could.

"In every way I miss you?"

Vivid images, sharp and sweet, rushed her. She felt a blush break across her skin, and she glanced at Connor feeling as self-conscious as if he could hear Nick's end of the conversation, could sense her reaction. "Yes... every way."

"Should I tell you what I'm going to do when I get my hands on you this afternoon?"

The blush deepened, flashing heat throughout her. She swallowed against the yearnings sweeping her body. "Nick..."

"I'm going to take you someplace where no one will interrupt us, then I'm going to strip off whatever you're wearing, get you as naked as the day you were born." His voice sounded rough, whiskey-toned. "I want to look at you, touch you, D, taste you, bury myself deep inside you, tease you until you make that needy little sound deep in your throat that drives me wild. Just thinking about it has me so hard I'm aching."

Longing rushed through her, curling her toes and quickening her pulse, her breathing. She lowered her gaze and her voice and turned away from Connor. "Rossetti...now is not a good time... Get some rest."

She rang off and gave Connor another self-conscious glance, then rose and strode around the desk, propping her hip against its edge.

"Where the hell is Whiting?" he asked, checking his watch, then the wall clock. He had to be in court in minutes.

"I'll call down. See what's holding him up." She spun away from Connor, cutting off his line of vision, and pretended to dial the Santa Beverly Police desk on the first floor and ask for Ron Whiting. "Ah, thanks."

She dropped the phone and pivoted toward her boss, smiling with assurance. "He's hitting the elevator even as we speak. So, get going. Judge Hopkins insists on promptness."

"Me, too." Connor growled. He started to the door then turned back to her, making a gun with his thumb and forefinger. "Keep your head down, Hamilton."

"Bad taste, Connor. But I promise I won't do anything you wouldn't do."

He shook his head, as though she was an incorrigible child. She watched him board one of the two elevators, then locked her door and hurried to the phone. Afterward, she waited five minutes more, her mind occupied with Nick's sexy promises, then slipped from her office and hastened down the stairs. Her mind kept tripping back to Nick. She gave herself a mental shake. *Damn you, Rossetti, you are a distraction.*

A distraction she could not afford at the moment. She reached the first level, skirted the lobby, then traveled the back hall to the parking lot without encountering anyone who spoke to her. But thanks to thoughts of Nick, she had no idea whether she'd passed Ron Whiting somewhere in the lobby, had no idea whether or not he'd seen her making for the parking lot.

The locksmith she'd secretly arranged to meet was already there.

Half an hour later, he handed her a key. She scanned her surroundings one last time. Her hands were unexpectedly damp, her pulse racing at the possibility someone would report to Connor that they'd seen her leaving by herself. She would calm down the second she was out of this parking lot.

She climbed into Nick's car and thoughts of him rushed her anew as she caught the slight whiff of his cologne. Damn, how she wished it was Nick she was going to meet. She ached for him the same way he ached for her, wanted to be with him in some secret hideaway, wanted his fingers, his flesh touching her where, even now, need pulsed for him. She swung her purse onto the passenger seat and froze, the sensuous reverie gone in a snap.

Beneath her purse was a wedge of white envelope. She freed it. Another valentine. Addressed to her in the same childlike printing as the first one.

Her mouth dried. How the hell had he gotten it into the locked car? She lifted it, too furious, too shaken to care that her fingerprints would obscure any the sender might had left on it. She tore the sealed flap. This valentine was similar to the other, which, according to Michael Pride, was like the ones sent to Dare—as though they'd all come from one of those variety boxes. It started, "My only Desire."

She shuddered with revulsion, then stiffened in anger. This guy was not going to get to her, not going to keep playing his mind games on her. She dropped both valentine and envelope on the floor behind the passenger seat and spied a large manila envelope. Her chest squeezed. Dare's papers. With all that had happened, she'd forgotten about them. She grabbed the manila envelope and shoved it under her purse, adjusted the driver's seat, then the mirrors and took off.

Her nerves calmed with every revolution of the tires against the pavement. She was home in eight minutes. For the first time in days, she didn't care if she was being followed. In fact, she hoped she was, hoped this fishing expedition of hers would net the big one. "Come and get me, you pervert, because I'm going to be ready for you.''

Her neighborhood looked much the same as it did on any other day of the week. Quiet. Normal. Nothing out of the ordinary happening. Most of the residents at work. Retirees enjoying the sunny morning, working in their gardens or on their flower beds.

She parked out front and approached the house with caution. Her gaze sought anything that seemed out of place, but found nothing. Renee Hagen's door slammed and the former silent-film star came bustling off her front porch and across the lawn that separated her house from Desire's.

She brushed at the gray and white cat fur that clung to her gardening smock. ''Good morning, dear. That flower delivery fellow has not been back. I've kept a lookout.''

''Thank you, Renee.'' A lookout. Damn. The last thing Desire wanted today was her neighbor spying on her, possibly using Nick's business card to contact him if she noticed someone around her house, and yet, she *had* to know whether or not Renee had seen someone other than the ''flower delivery fellow.'' She clutched the manila envelope to her chest. ''Did you happen to notice anyone else near my house?''

''Anyone else?'' Cunning gleamed in the retired actress's eyes, an expression reminiscent of one of her gray-and-white tabbies spotting a mouse within pouncing distance. ''What's going on, dear? An obsessive fan? Some nosy paparazzi? Don't think I haven't 'been there, done that,' as they say these days. I can give you some pointers, oh yes. That's why they invented pepper spray, don't you know. I'm sure I have a spare canister of it around here somewhere I can give you.'' She turned to make for her own house.

Desire stopped her. ''That's not necessary. I have my own tube of pepper spray right here in my purse.'' *Along with my gun.*

''Good. A gal can't be too careful these days. Would you like me to keep watch for someone else, dear?''

''No, you've gone above and beyond. Please, don't spare me another minute of thought. Oh, and I'd like some quiet time, so if anyone should ask—not that I expect them to, but just in case—you haven't seen me today, okay?''

Mischief danced in Renee's eyes. ''Not even that handsome police detective you were with the other day?''

''Especially not him.'' Nick's promises filled her mind again, triggering that sensuous need for him.

''Still haven't forgiven him about the flowers, have you, dear?'' A knowing look replaced the mischief. ''Can't say I blame you. They don't make gentlemen like they used to. Mum's the word.''

''Thanks.''

''But if you need me,'' Renee said over her shoulder as she headed toward her house, ''just shout.''

If I yelled my lungs out, Desire thought, striding to her own porch, *Renee would never hear. She's too deaf. My screams will be as silent as a Renee Twilight movie.*

At her door, Desire pulled the gun from her purse. She hoped Renee was right, that *he* hadn't been back. But she wouldn't risk her life on the elderly woman's word.

Desire unlocked and entered her house. Closing the door, locking it, she leaned against it, listening, alert for anything askew, letting the familiar sounds and scents surround her. Was she alone? She put the envelope and her purse on the coffee table, then made a quick search of the living room, looking behind furniture and assuring herself the windows were all locked.

She continued through the house, gun cocked and held at her side as she checked the back door, the kitchen windows, the garage, closets. All as she'd left them. All locked. She would unlock them only when she was ready, after her bath. He was no longer the one in control. Their meeting would be on her terms.

She stole into the hall. It was an old, large two-bedroom with only one bathroom. No one lurked in the smaller of the two rooms that she used as a home office. Nor was anyone crouched behind the shower curtain.

She went into her bedroom last, moving with the most caution here, recalling that the stalker had waited in Dare's bedroom. She looked behind the door, under the bed, then approached the closet, nudging the double doors open with the barrel of the gun. No one. Nothing disturbed that she could tell; even the hatch to the crawl space that was cut into the corner of the closet floor still had her old sneakers perched on it.

Blowing out a huge breath of relief, she eased the hammer off, flicked on the safety and retrieved the envelope from the living room. She went to the kitchen, laid envelope and gun on the table and poured herself a glass of lemonade. She sat and extracted the sheath of papers Dare's lawyer had put together for her.

The letter accompanying the papers stated that if Dare had not married by the time of her death her twin sister, Desire Hamilton, was assigned executor of her estate. If she had any questions, she was to contact the lawyer.

Heavy sadness fell over Desire as she scanned the papers, the death certificate, the will and a couple of deeds. She looked for a checkbook, a savings book, something that would give her an idea of where Dare's new contract money had been placed. They weren't among the papers. Did the lawyer have them? Or were they lost in the accident that had killed her sister?

The lawyer must have a clue as to where she banked, so records could be found if he didn't have them.

As she shuffled through the papers again, her hand came to rest once more on the two deeds, and she jerked straighter in her chair. Dare had purchased property. Not only had she purchased property, but the transactions seem to have been finalized weeks ago.

She studied the deeds. Both properties were local. Why had Dare purchased property in California? She was moving to Denver. She read the addresses and felt a shock. Could this be? My God, what did it mean?

She stood and crossed to the phone, noticing for the first time that her answering machine was flashing like a neon sign. She dialed Dare's lawyer. His receptionist said he was out of the office, but expected back within the hour. Desire left her number, asking that he call the moment he returned.

She longed for that soak in the hot, scented bath, for long minutes of letting her mind drift and clear so she could get a handle on things that made no sense at the moment. Instead, she pressed the play button on the answering machine. The first message was from her heavy breather. She deleted it.

The second was a chillingly intimate whisper that sent a shiver down her spine, also from *him*. The third was a vile threat against "the cop." Each call grew bolder, more disturbing, but Desire wasn't scared. She was livid; anger tensed the muscles in her face. She snatched the clip from her hair and tossed it atop the stack of papers on the table.

The fourth voice peeling from her machine was commanding, as recognizable as the sun in the morning: her father's husky drawl. "I hate these damn contraptions. Desire, where the hell are you? I've been calling you all damn day. Your mama's walking 'round this house wringing her hands. We don't need this worry, missy. Call, dammit."

She stopped the machine and phoned her parents. When she could finally get a word wedged sideways between her father's tirade—that she knew was more concern than ire—she said, "You didn't leave other messages, Daddy, and I called the minute I got this one."

He blustered a few more times, again muttering his hatred for answering machines, then gave it up. "Where have you been?"

"Nick and I have been looking into Dare's accident."

"Nick?" Suspicion slid into pique. "Not that son of a sidewinder Nick Rossetti?"

"Yes." The word came out weaker than she'd meant it to against her father's renewed fury.

"I don't want you anywhere near that man. He's caused this family enough heartache. If not for him, your sister would still be alive."

She gave an incredulous laugh. "How do you figure that?"

"She wouldn't have moved to Hollywood."

"She would have, Daddy. Dare was meant for fame." It was true, she realized. Her sister had found her destiny and claimed it with her whole heart. That she had lost it too soon was not Nick's doing. At least her sister had gone after her destiny. Desire had pushed hers away with both hands.

"Just promise me you'll stay away from that no-good peckerwood, honey. He's nothing but poison to this family."

That no-good peckerwood was almost killed protecting me, Daddy. But she couldn't say that. Couldn't worry her parents by telling them she had a stalker after her, the same stalker who had precipitated her sister's death.

"I promise." Her heart felt heavy with the lie. Her parents would never accept Nick as a son-in-law, not feeling about him as they did. "I've got to go, Daddy. Give Mama my love. I'll call again tomorrow."

She hung up, her soul feeling like scraps in a paper shredder, her hatred for the stalker so intense she was burning from the inside out. She restarted the answering machine where it had left off. The fifth message was also from *him*. "My sweet Desire, we can finally be together…without anyone keeping us apart. I'm coming, my love, to you."

She fought the natural revulsion at his words, hating that he could reach beyond her resolve and soil her with his sickness. She glared at the answering machine, lifting the gun from among the sheath of papers. "Then come on, you creep. I'm ready for you."

She strode down the hall to the bathroom and locked the door. She set the gun on the toilet tank, turned on the shower and stripped. Beneath the hot spray, she lathered her hair, scrubbing hard, feeling dirty, as though *his* hands and not his voice had stroked her, gotten inside her.

Swallowing hard, she grasped for something else to think about, something to erase the sick disquiet she felt, and there he was, Nick Rossetti, in all his male perfection, sensuous, mind-consuming, body-heating. Thoughts of how Nick had lathered her hair and her body brought his loving promises of this morning back to her and with them another rush of passionate need. She spread the soapy bubbles down her neck and over her breasts and belly, touching her skin as he had done, her intimate places as he had done, yearning for him, for the way he made her feel, her own hands poor substitutes for the man she loved.

But thoughts of Nick brought the realization that he would be furious if he knew she'd defied his command to stay away from her house. She shut off the water, dried and donned the terry-cloth robe hanging from the hook on the door.

She towel-dried her hair, then combed out the tangles and left it loose and damp and wavy around her face. She hefted the gun and unlocked the door, her mind on what she should wear, something Nick would have no trouble stripping from her. She started toward her room. The door was still ajar. Everything as she'd left it. She drew a deep breath, noticing the air was scented like a tropical garden, overly sweet, as cloying as spilt perfume.

She had spilled no perfume.

Every nerve in her body snapped awake. She kicked the door wide, her gun steadied in front of her. Gardenia petals blanketed the bed, browning, dying, the scent funereal. Desire's skin crawled and her steps faltered.

He was here. Somewhere in this room. Her flesh seemed to shrink on her skull. She glanced at the bedside phone. Too far away. The kitchen phone farther. Retreat was no longer an option.

She'd have to subdue him before she could call 911.

She eased the safety off, cocked the gun, stepped into the room. The hardwood planking was cool against her bare feet. She checked the far side of the bed. He wasn't there.

The closet. Like at Dare's. She spun to it. The double doors gaped. The crawl space. Dear God, he'd been there when she'd checked the house. Fear washed through her, but she threw it off. He didn't have her. *She* had him. She took a wide-legged stance, bracing herself, the gun barrel tipped forward. "Come out, *lover*. I've got a surprise for you."

A shadow from behind fell across her. *The door. He was behind the door.* She jolted. Started to wrench around. Too late. Something heavy crashed into the back of her head. Pain sliced her skull and stripped her motor responses. Her grip on the gun released. It clattered to the floor. As she sank in its wake, the last thing she heard was, "Don't fight it, my sweet Desire. You know you want my love."

Chapter Eighteen

"I'll catch a ride with you to the courthouse," Nick told the uniformed police officer who'd been guarding his hospital room. He couldn't wait to see D's face. To hold her. To touch her. To deliver all that he'd promised and more. To hear again that sexy little groan she made when he...

The visuals filling his mind brought blood pooling hot and thick in his groin. His head still ached like hell and sported an iodine-red racing stripe, but the rest of him was functioning just fine, thank God.

His hand strayed toward the wound that cut from his crown to his temple. The sorry piece of crap who'd done this to him would rue the day he'd missed killing Nick Rossetti. "I need to call Assistant D.A. Hamilton, then we can leave."

Nick dialed her office number. The phone rang four times, then transferred him to her voice mail. He tried her cell phone. Again he was switched to voice mail. Frustrated, he hung up. Where was she? He clasped the uniform by the upper arm and spun him toward the door. "Let's move."

As they drove the streets of Santa Beverley toward city hall, Nick's throat muscles tightened, cutting off his breath. He wanted to jam the uniform's foot to the floor, demand he use a siren, flashers, anything that would get them to city hall faster. The tension gripping him sent pain through his skull. *Calm down, Rossetti, or you'll land your conclusion-jumping fanny back in the hospital.* But calm wouldn't come and the remaining three minutes seemed like three hours.

As they pulled into the rear parking lot of city hall, Nick flashed back to the previous night, to his own vulnerability. To D's vulnerability. They were dealing with a madman. His palms felt clammy, his mouth dry. He shook himself and hauled himself out of the squad car.

He had the impression of something he expected to see not being there. He hustled for the building, then halted, pivoted. His car. It was gone. Nerves pricked his skin. He warned himself against rash deductions. His keys were still in his pocket. Maybe someone had had the car towed. Or maybe D or someone else had found the hide-a-key box and moved the car to some secure area.

That was it. That had to be it.

Nick hurried inside the building, down the back hall, past the police desk, through the foyer and beyond the block of courtrooms. He skipped the elevators and climbed the stairs two at a time. He reached the third-floor landing out of breath, his heart racing and his head pounding.

Her office door was closed. Locked. He knocked. Called her name. "D? You in there? It's me, Nick."

No answer.

This was wrong. Nausea pulled at his stomach. He bolted for the stairs, descending faster than he'd climbed. But the first floor was no longer all but deserted. Court-room doors hung open and clusters of people spilled out, blocking his passage. He pressed against a wall, scanning the crowd. In the crush, he spotted Connor. "Gregg."

Connor jerked around. His eyes narrowed. Nick moved closer. "You look awful. Are you sure the doctor should have released you?"

Nick blew out an impatient breath and repeated, "Where *is* she?"

There was a slight tensing in Connor's face. "Isn't she in her office?"

"No. Why didn't you know that?"

"Well, ah, I've been in court all morning."

"And she wasn't with you?"

"No."

Nick caught Connor by the lapel. "You promised to watch her."

"Get a grip on yourself, Detective." Connor hit his hand away. "I may not know where Hamilton is this second, but I know she's safe."

His words penetrated Nick's growing panic. "How do you know that?"

Connor led Nick through the crowd to a private corner. "She made me promise not to tell you that I had a case to preside over today." He kept his voice low, his gaze sliding over every person passing too near them. "She didn't want to worry you. I agreed only after she arranged for Ron Whiting to stand in as her bodyguard."

"Ron Whiting?" Nick's stomach clenched. "Why him? He has ties to the Falls Clinic. What if he's the stalker?"

"Detective Whiting?" Connor jerked back, his expression incredulous. "His wife was killed by a stalker."

"Ex-wife," Nick reminded him, wanting Connor to keep an open mind. "How well do you know Whiting?

Can you swear he's not the stalker who killed his ex-wife?''

"That's ludicrous."

"Is it?" Nick wished he were as certain. "You're risking D's life on that assumption."

"Well, I—" Connor glanced at someone over Nick's shoulder, then back at Nick. "Look, I'm sure they're around here somewhere."

"Somewhere isn't good enough." Nick's voice rose with every word, his temper escalating. He knew fear was driving his emotions, but no matter how hard he tried, he couldn't rein it in.

"Come on," Connor said. "We'll check with the desk sergeant."

The desk sergeant was a beefy Latino named Raul Estes.

Connor introduced Nick, then said, "We're looking for Ron Whiting. Have you seen him, or A.D.A. Hamilton?"

Estes curled his thick bottom lip. "It's Detective Whiting's day off. He hasn't been in."

"Sure he has." Connor's voice betrayed his own rising emotions, and Nick's worry hitched higher. Connor said, "Two hours ago Hamilton phoned down and spoke to you about Whiting. You told her he was on his way up."

"No, sir." Estes shook his head. "I have not spoken to A.D.A. Hamilton today."

Connor's face reddened. "Well, someone at this desk did. I was right there. I heard her end of the conversation."

Estes curled his lip again. "I haven't left my post since I got here at 0800. She did not call here."

Connor pointed to the telephone at Estes's elbow. "Get me Ron Whiting at home."

Estes dialed and listened. "No answer."

"I suppose Officer Linda what's-her-name is off today too?" Connor said.

"Officer Martinez?" Estes checked the schedule. "She's pulling the night shift this week. She's probably sleeping. You want I should wake her?"

"No." Connor's neck was red. He'd obviously been duped and it wasn't going down well.

Nick felt queasy. He grasped the D.A.'s arm. "My car. Did you have it moved, Gregg?"

"No." Connor stared at him, frowning. "It was in the parking lot where you left it last night when Hamilton and I came in this morning."

"It's not there now." Nick saw the same fear he was feeling dawn in Gregg's cool eyes. For the first time since he'd met this man, he looked disheveled, rattled.

Another uniformed officer strode up to the sergeant's desk.

Connor's gaze remained on Nick. "You think Hamilton took your car? Did you give her your keys?"

"Excuse me," the newly arrived officer interrupted. "Are you talking about a blue sedan?"

Nick lurched toward the man. "What do you know about it?"

"I saw Ms. Hamilton near a blue sedan. She was with a locksmith. I figured she'd locked her keys in her car."

"Why would she take your car?" Connor tugged at his tie. "Where was she going?"

Nick swore. He knew where she'd gone. What she planned to do. Terror tore through him. "Her house. She's setting herself up as bait. We need to get there. Now."

Connor checked the time. His expression torn, grave. "I can't leave. Court's due to resume in a few minutes." He spun to Estes. "Have patrol cars sent to Desire Hamilton's house, stat."

He tossed Nick his keys. "Take my Lexus."

Nick made the eight-minute drive to D's house in four, his foot flat on the accelerator, his heart slapping his chest.

He was distressed that no patrol cars had arrived before him, but not surprised to find his sedan hugging the curb. He parked behind it and ran to the porch. He pounded on the door, rang the bell and called her name. When she didn't answer, he raced from window to window peering in. "D, where are you?"

Every damn thing was locked tight. Swearing, frustration a stone against his gut, he tried to think. Maybe she'd gone somewhere in *her* car. God, he prayed not. He scampered to the garage. There were no windows here. He lifted his leg and slammed the door with his foot. Wood cracked. He kicked it again. The hinges creaked and gave. He reared back and smashed it once more. The door popped inward.

The garage was cool and smelled of oil and dust. Her car was gone.

Terror gripped Nick. Using the unlocked garage door, he tore through her house, ignoring everything he'd ever been taught, every rule of caution. "D! D! Where are you?"

He banged open doors, his heart thudding so hard it hurt, his wound pounding. She wasn't here. He reached her bedroom and shoved in. An overwhelmingly sweet scent slammed his nostrils and froze him on the spot. The bed was covered in gardenia petals.

He recoiled, horror slick and icy in his belly, but even

as he stepped back, his practiced eye swept the room, pulling out small details, clues. Pain squeezed his chest, fear so heavy he thought his ribs would collapse as his glance landed on the spot of blood on the floor near the closet.

D's blood?

His pulse filled his throat. He was too late. The stalker had her. Had taken her somewhere. But, God, where? "D?"

"Police! Stop! Or I'll shoot."

Nick shifted around in a daze. Two uniforms, guns trained on him, stood in the hall.

He shook his head. "We're too late. The stalker has her."

"Step away from the door, sir."

"I'm Nick Rossetti, with the LAPD."

The male officer gestured with his gun. "Step away from the door, Mr. Rossetti."

"Detective Rossetti," Nick corrected, sticking his hand into his pants pocket.

"Keep your hands where I can see them."

"May I show you my ID?" Nick asked, irritated that they were following procedure, as he would do if the situation were reversed, frantic that precious minutes were wasted while he convinced them he was unarmed and was allowed to withdraw his ID. "Didn't D.A. Gregg send you to help Desire Hamilton?"

"No, sir. Lady next door called. Said she saw a prowler." The female officer returned his ID and holstered her gun. "What's going on here?"

Nick filled them in, helplessness capturing him, zapping his energy, his spirit, smashing home the realization that no amount of time would bring them closer to D. They had no way to find her. The stalker had outsmarted them. He'd left no clues behind, nothing that would lead them to where he'd taken her.

With all hope slipping from him, Nick staggered back into the kitchen, a man in a fog, his whole life gone like so much mist. The officers called for reinforcements, a crime scene team.

It would do no good, Nick wanted to shout. But it was policy. These two would follow the book. Any other time, Nick would be glad to have such conscientious officers on his team.

His mind was wild, panic zinging through it like a ricocheting bullet. He dropped into one of the dinette chairs, scrubbing his face with his hands. His elbow hit something solid. A glass, he saw. Half-full of watery yellow liquid. It tumbled over. He swore and jerked back, grabbing a pile of papers away from the spreading pool.

As he shook drops of what smelled like lemonade from the damp pages, he noticed the return address on the envelope. These were the papers Connor had given D from Dare's lawyer. D must have been reading them before something interrupted her in the other room. "Oh, God, D, where are you?"

His gaze fell on one of the papers that looked like a deed. The wording swam, then came into focus like a fist hitting him in the gut. He knew this address. The Pacific Palms. Dare had bought the Palms?

He grasped the other deed. Reading, he started to rise.

Chapter Nineteen

Pain pulsed near Desire's right ear. She slitted her eyes, but even that small effort was agonizing. *What happened?* The thought barely occurred when recall stormed in behind it. Her eyelids slammed open. She made to sit up, but was jerked back. What the hell...? Oh, God, no. She was spread-eagle, lashed to a four-poster bed in a room she'd never seen before.

Her naked body wore a gown of gardenia petals.

Revulsion smacked her. Her stomach gave a sick lurch. She gagged, then swallowed hard. *Oh, God, oh, God, oh, God.* Panic, like a fierce insect stinging the underside of her skin, shot through her. Terror, like what Dare must have felt those last minutes of her life.

At least Dare had escaped him. Why had *she,* Desire, thought herself smart enough to outfox the fox? Annie Oakley with a six-gun. Why had she figured she could handle a maniac alone?

Oh, Nick, I need you.

She wrenched against her ties again. A scream climbed her throat. She had to calm down. Had to figure a way out of this. Nick had no idea where she was. He wouldn't be coming to help her. She was alone.

Her breath came in hard heaves. She laid back on the

bed and dug deep inside herself for the source of that Texas grit her mama and daddy had instilled in her. Soon, without her own breath beating against her ears, she heard the sounds around her. Somewhere nearby a shower was running.

Him!

She resisted the panic that threatened anew. What else could she hear? Something outside the house. What was it? Something familiar. Something she'd heard recently. A dull roar. Her breath snagged. The ocean. She was in Eddie Wollinski's Malibu beach house.

Or should she say Dare's Malibu beach house?

In the master bedroom. She tipped her head back and gazed up. Over the bed there was a huge photograph of Dare, but the man who'd been in the picture with her sister had been cut out. Just as he'd been killed. Eddie.

The bathroom door bumped open and Michael Pride stood there, looking nothing like the other times she'd seen him. His usual restaurant "uniform," the floral shirt and khaki pants, had been replaced by a black kimono with a red dragon emblazoned on it. His golden hair was slicked off his high forehead, wet, every hair precise. For once, his foul cigar was missing.

But those eerily intense blue eyes blazed at her, a psychotic lust in their depths. "Ah, you're awake, my love."

Chapter Twenty

Nick nearly ran Connor down as he crashed outside to the squad car. Connor said, "Where's Hamilton?"

"In Malibu." Nick vaulted past him. "The stalker's got her."

Connor swore and chased after Nick. "Where in Malibu?"

"I'll explain on the way." He raced for the Lexus, but an officer stopped them, insisting they could go faster in the squad car. A.D.A. Hamilton was one of their own.

Siren blaring, lights flashing, the four made for Malibu at breakneck speed.

Terror had Nick by the throat, but he was glad someone with quick reflexes was at the wheel. *God, let her be safe,* he prayed.

"Tell me," Connor demanded, his face ashen.

"It was all a lie," Nick said, his voice coming out as hard as the blade of fear against his chest. "One big fat lie. Michael Pride told everyone he was engaged to Dare Hamilton. But he wasn't. If D's sister was going to marry anyone, it was probably her old high-school flame, Eddie Wollinski. He was living in her house, had his studio there. I suspect the two of them invented his Eager Eddie persona to help boost Dare's career, get her into the tabloids.''

Connor shook his head, but there was no doubt in his eyes. "How did Pride get fixated on Dare?"

"If I had to guess, I'd say he met her in one of Dr. Falls's divorce survivors' sessions.'' Nick shoved a trembling hand through his hair, trying to fit the pieces together. Anything to keep his mind off how long it was taking to reach Malibu, anything to keep from conjuring images of what Pride might be doing to D. "The doctor knew he'd lied about being engaged to Dare. After all, Dare was her patient too. I can't figure out why she didn't tell us."

"Desire was convinced that Dr. Falls's brother, Ted, had killed someone and was determined to prove it and put him in jail for life," Connor said.

"So, it was her way of paying D back?" Nick pushed his hair back with both hands. "If she'd told us straight off, she might still be alive."

"Told us what? Saying you're engaged to someone when you're not doesn't make you a stalker, only a liar," Connor said. "She might have had no reason to think Pride was a danger to anyone but himself. Under those circumstances, she wouldn't have broken her code of ethics."

"But if she *knew* it?"

"She'd have told the police. Maybe not you or me, but someone. She had plenty of contacts in the LAPD."

"I wonder if she was going to give him up and made the mistake of telling him so." The blare of the siren was like a scrape against Nick's spine.

"Maybe not. Maybe he just *feared* she'd expose him and decided he couldn't risk it." Connor looked as tense as Nick felt. He said, "The gun will be linked to him. It's the same gun that killed Eddie Wollinski."

Nick leaned forward. "I'd thought Pride meant that bullet for me. But I know now that he had to find and shut Eddie up. Eddie could tell us Pride was never with Dare, not in any of the pictures he'd taken of her. I doubt Pride knew Eager Eddie was a false identity, or that Eddie was Dare's genuine fiancé. I also believe now that the reason Dare maintained the apartment at the Palms was as a front, to keep the stalker she'd never seen from finding out where she really lived."

Connor looked bleak. "He knows now."

Nick scrubbed his face with his hands. When he lifted his head again, he saw they traveled the beach highway. At last. The house loomed ahead. Nick pointed it out, then directed the officer to, "Pull over here."

Connor and the officers agreed to watch the front of the house. Nick tore across the sand and climbed the beach steps as quietly and swiftly as a panther. Breathlessly, he crept across the deck and slipped Eddie's key into the glass door, then biting down the need to rush, inched it open.

The living room was dark, but a light glowed in the kitchen. As he passed the counter he saw an open bottle of wine and noticed that a platter of crackers, cheese and fruit had been prepared. He curled his hands into fists.

A sound from deep within the house startled him. He pressed against the wall, listening. A shower. Training and instinct kicked in. He reached for his gun, momentarily startled to find it missing. Damn it to hell. What if Pride was armed?

Sweat beaded his upper lip. He needed a weapon. Something to subdue the creep. He glanced at the butcher-block holder full of knives, but dismissed the idea. More often than not, knives ended up being used on those who'd meant them for protection.

He retreated to the living room and silently extracted the fireplace poker. Hefting it at his side, he stole into the hall, toward the master bedroom. The door was ajar. From within came the sickening stench that had permeated D's bedroom. He saw her then, splayed out like a Thanksgiving goose on a bed of gardenia petals, tied down, her aqua eyes filled with terror.

His heart filled with rage.

A man moved through his line of vision. Michael Pride. "Ah, you're awake, my love."

Fury pulled Nick forward and into the room. As Pride began untying the belt of the silk kimono he wore, Nick lifted the fireplace poker. "She's not your love, Pride. She's mine."

Pride swung around. He was quicker than Nick expected he'd be. He grabbed the poker, jerked it loose and head-butted Nick in the gut. Pain shot through the bruised rib and air knocked from Nick's lungs. He doubled over. Pride scrambled into the bathroom. Nick sucked in a breath and forced himself up and after the man.

He banged the door against the inside wall. Pride stood spread-legged on the tile floor, a gun aimed at Nick's chest.

"You just won't stay away from her, will you, Rossetti?"

Nick took a step toward him. D shouted, "No, Nick! Don't!"

He pivoted toward her, losing whatever advantage he might have had. Pride swept up behind him and pressed the gun to his temple. "I ought to tie you up and make you watch while I prove to you whose love my only

Desire is, but it's going to be such an intimate moment, I'm not willing to share.''

He cocked the gun and demanded Nick proceed him into the hall. He shoved Nick toward the spiral staircase that led to the studio. Nick went without protest, anything to keep this guy away from D. At the top of the stairs, Pride nudged the gun into his back. ''Down you go, Rossetti.''

''I think you've got that backward,'' Nick muttered.

''What?''

Nick turned as though to glance at Pride. He grabbed the barrel of the gun and yanked with all his might, pulling the startled stalker forward, then up and over the railing. Michael Pride yelped with shock, then fear. His flailing body clattered onto the stand of photographer lights below. Metal clanked. Glass popped and clinked. Pride cried out in pain.

His hand lifted. The gun aimed at Nick. Light flared from the barrel. The shot echoed off the wall, deafening. Nick jerked sideways and the bullet whizzed past his ear so near he felt the accompanying breeze.

The doorbell rang. Shouts from outside. Pounding at the door. ''Rossetti! Let us in!''

Nick ran to the door and opened it. Connor was there, along with four Malibu uniforms.

''He's down there.'' Nick pointed to the stairs, his chest heaving, his ribs aching, his head throbbing. ''And he's armed. So be careful.''

Nick hurried back to D.

Chapter Twenty-One

Nick's bedroom smelled of lemon oil and spicy after-shave, a welcome distraction from the forever-tainted aroma of gardenias that lingered in Desire's nostrils even a week after her ordeal. She would never again wear that scent without thinking of Michael Pride, wanted never again to smell it.

She shoved the nightmarish thoughts from her mind and stared at Nick, her gaze caressing him with all the love in her heart. She could watch him like this forever: sleeping with a slight smile on his sensuous lips, his raven hair mussed, the sheet tugged low on his warm, lightly furred belly. His wounds were still colorful, still evident, but mending.

Joy danced inside her. She stretched and smiled, her body deliciously tender from their voracious lovemaking, her soul as light as a ray of sunshine.

But she feared her newfound happiness was as fragile as a bubble that would burst at any moment.

Soon she would have to choose. Nick Rossetti or her parents. Judd and Marvel Hamilton would never accept him as their son-in-law, but she hadn't had the nerve to tell Nick, hadn't wanted to shatter the wonderment of these past seven days, to destroy the dreams of marriage and children he so vividly described. She yearned to share his excitement, ached for his vision to come true.

But her father had called him "poison" to the Hamilton family. Judd Hamilton wasn't a casual name caller. He meant what he said. Changing his mind was like getting the wind not to blow. He blamed Nick for Dare ending up in Hollywood, for her accident, for her death. He'd consider Nick's saving Desire had settled or evened the score, but it wouldn't put Nick ahead in any way. Especially if her father found out Nick was on suspension for beating up a suspect. She very much doubted her parents would ever completely forgive or accept Nick.

Desire's chest ached. Loving Nick had caused the estrangement with her sister. She couldn't bear the thought of a similar rift between her and her parents. But could she walk away from Nick this time and survive? He stirred, moaned and opened his eyes, the warm brown heating to coffee hues as his gaze landed on her. He reached for her. "Desire. My beautiful, wonderful Desire. God, how I love your name. Good morning."

"It's noon, Nick."

He silenced her with a kiss and the fire for him that had been building in her exploded. She melted against him, laughing, her body exquisitely attuned to his, as though every touch, every stroke was a chord played by a virtuoso on his prize violin, harmonious, intertwined, the melody sweet and resonating.

He rolled her beneath him, her thighs parting in welcome, her hips rising to meet his, and then they were one, the song had begun, it filled her mind, her spirit, her very being, as he filled her. The aria built slowly, each thrust sending it higher, and higher, until the tune consumed her, ringing in her ears, a crescendo of pleasure spilling over her, through her, and she shouted, "Nick, oh, Nick, don't ever stop loving me like this."

"Impossible, my darling, my Desire," he whispered on a husky sigh.

He raised onto his forearms and grinned down at her, making no effort to move away, prolonging the exquisite afterglow. His hair sexily askew over his forehead, he kissed her nose. "But in case you're worried about my commitment to you, let's go pick out your engagement ring."

Oh, yes. Oh, God, no. She would have to tell him. No more putting it off. "Nick, I—"

The doorbell interrupted. Nick looked annoyed. "Somebody has damn bad timing."

They scrambled into their clothes. Connor was at the door. Nick brought him into the kitchen where Desire was making coffee. He gave them a knowing smile, and she'd swear she saw envy in his eyes. Maybe one day Connor would find the kind of love she shared with Nick.

If only he knew it wasn't as perfect as it appeared.

The dripping coffee seemed to punctuate her worry that what she had with Nick could slip away as easily as that water sliding into the glass pot. "What's going on, Connor?"

"You won't believe it." He seemed almost not to believe himself what he was about to tell them. "We found a stash of 'souvenirs' at Pride's house. Something of Dare's, something of yours and a couple of other things. Among them was a bracelet that both Ron Whiting and Ted Gunderson have identified as having belonged to Cindy Whiting.''

''What? Oh my God.'' Desire's hand flew to her mouth, the shock of it slow to sink in. ''What are you saying?''

Nick said, ''Pride stalked and killed Cindy Whiting?''

''Yes.'' Connor's eyebrows lifted.

Desire shook her head. ''How...how did he meet her?''

Nick brought three mugs to the counter. ''At his restaurant?''

''No,'' she said as the connection dropped into place like a puzzle piece she'd had all along and hadn't before been able to see. She looked at her boss for confirmation. ''The divorce survivors' group at the Falls Clinic, right?''

''Bingo.'' Connor gave her his finger-gun gesture. ''Their records show he and Cindy and Dare attended several of the same sessions.''

Nick poured a cup of coffee and handed it to Connor. ''Seems the jerk had a preference for blondes. Has he admitted to anything?''

Connor took a sip of coffee, then said, ''He was denying everything...until we confronted him with the bracelet. Then he fell apart, claiming he didn't mean to strangle Cindy Whiting, but she kept denying their love and she wouldn't stop screaming.''

Desire shuddered, and Nick's arm came reassuringly around her. She nuzzled into him, thanked God for him. ''Then he'll be locked up for a good long time.''

''Yes. It's open-and-shut. He won't be bothering you anymore, Hamilton.''

But Desire knew he could pester her if he wanted—

even from prison. His sort of sickness didn't go away. She would do what it took to protect herself, though. Getting out of California permanently was high on her list of possibilities, something Nick and she *had* discussed—returning to Laredo.

Another hard decision she had to make. They each drank a cup of coffee, then thanked Connor as he left. Nick brought up the subject of the engagement ring again. She said, "Not today, okay? I want to go home for a while."

She had hired cleaners to scour her house, to remove all traces of Michael Pride. Everything he'd left behind. Touched. It was time she faced it. Time she faced everything.

HER HOUSE LOOKED the same as the first time she'd seen it, Desire thought, striding up the walk with Nick behind her. How could she have changed so much and the house so little? On the porch, Desire started. Voices were coming from inside. Frowning, she discovered the door was unlocked. Her heart clutched. Her gun was being held as evidence against Michael Pride and she felt its absence dearly at the moment.

But she would not have shot either the craggy-faced giant wearing a Stetson and Tony Lamas as he paced her living room sipping whiskey, or his petite companion, a forty-something aqua-eyed blonde who had passed her delicate features on to her twin daughters. Desire would, however, have liked to have warned Nick to run back to the car and drive away as fast as he could.

But Nick had already come in behind her.

"Mama. Daddy." She hugged them both, then

stepped back, her nerves ragged ''What are you doing here?''

Her father's steely gaze was sliding over Nick and her heart raced. Her mother looked less hostile. ''Your daddy and I were mightily impressed with your idea to renovate the Pacific Palms and turn it into a shelter for women and children victims of domestic abuse.'' It was a charity her parents had participated in for as long as she could remember, and Desire had hoped they would be willing to invest in the project she had proposed. She just hadn't expected they would be so quick on the uptake.

Judd said, ''I've spoken with the present managers, a Mr. and Mrs. Keray Collins. I'm thinking about asking them to oversee the renovating. Seems he's a carpenter or handyman.''

Recalling how Keray had ''fixed'' the broken window in Dare's apartment, Desire wasn't too sure her father was making a wise choice, but they could discuss that when the project reached the planning stages. ''Sounds good to me.''

''It will be a memorial to Dare,'' Marvel said.

''The Dare Hamilton House, or some such,'' Judd added.

''That's very nice, sir.'' Nick stepped closer to Desire. ''Dare would have liked that.''

''Don't you presume to tell me what Dare would have liked or not liked.'' Judd shook his whiskey glass at him, a scowl on his rugged face. ''You brought her more grief than good.''

''Daddy, Nick—''

''I've checked up on this peckerwood—gathered up all the facts I need to settle my mind about *him*.''

''Daddy, Nick saved my life.''

Her father's scowl deepened. "So I understand. That settled the score. One daughter lost, one saved. Even Steven. Back to square one."

Nick stood tense, but his eyes pleaded for understanding and forgiveness. "I know I hurt this family, sir, ma'am, but it was never my intention. Don't think I haven't paid for it, too."

"I don't care what you've paid. Character is what counts. When I heard you were on suspension, I knew I was right about you." He looked at Desire; her heart felt heavy. "Do you know that he's on suspension?"

"Yes, but—"

"Do you know *why* he's on suspension?"

"Well…" Her pulse wobbled.

"I do. His captain told me."

Nick glanced sharply at her father, but Desire couldn't read his expression.

"According to his boss, Detective Nick Rossetti has no respect for the letter of the law. Right, Rossetti?"

Nick said nothing. Whatever he'd done he made no excuse for it.

"I happen to respect the law," Judd said. "This country would collapse if those hired to enforce its laws all acted as rashly as you did."

Nick's stare hardened. "I'd do it again."

The declaration brought a smile to Judd Hamilton. Desire frowned, confused. "Nick, tell me."

"It's ugly, D." He motioned for her to sit. She chose one of her Danish chairs and he balanced on the slender wooden arm. "My next-door neighbors recently separated. I was glad to see it happen. I suspected the husband had been violently abusive to her and their three little boys for years. I never caught him at it and she denied it, told me what goes on in someone's home is no one else's business.''

Nick's eyes burned. ''The husband left, but he promised he'd be back. I advised her to change all the locks and get a restraining order, but she was afraid of making him more angry. He showed up one night, used his key and went inside. Her screams woke me. The doors were locked. I broke a window. Went in. I pulled him off her. Then I smashed his nose.''

Nick glanced at Judd, then back at Desire. ''He's suing me for breaking and entering and for breaking his nose. She denies her husband was raping her, claims they were making love.'' Nick made a face as though recalling something even more awful than what he'd shared.

Fury washed over her father's face. ''He's not telling you the worst of it.''

Revulsion and anger flushed Desire. She'd seen enough horror to fill in the blanks for herself. This was the sort of crime that had convinced her to become a prosecutor. The more abusive slimeballs she could lock up, the more women and children she could protect. ''You're on suspension for saving that woman and those little boys?''

''And I'd do it again,'' Nick said.

''And I'd want you to,'' she told him, gripping his hands in hers.

''So would I,'' Judd Hamilton said. ''Nick Rossetti does have character, Marvel. The kind of character a man could appreciate in a son-in-law.''

Marvel smiled at Desire. ''The kind of character, Judd, that a mother could wish for in her daughter's husband.''

Her parents exchanged a look of love and devilment.

Desire could not believe her ears. Nick's arm circled her shoulders and the gentle squeeze that accompanied it reassured and sent joy exploding through her.

Nick said, "In that case sir, ma'am, there is something I'd like to ask you…"

"Yes?" Judd and Marvel said in unison.

Nick smiled down at Desire. "Could we hold the wedding at your ranch in Laredo?"

HARLEQUIN®

INTRIGUE®

and HARPER ALLEN present

Bound by the ties they forged as soldiers
of fortune, these agents fearlessly put their
lives on the line for a worthy cause.
But now they're about to face their
greatest challenge—love!

August 2001
GUARDING JANE DOE

September 2001
SULLIVAN'S LAST STAND

Available at your favorite retail outlet.

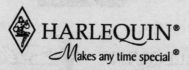

HARLEQUIN®
Makes any time special ®

COMING SOON...

AN EXCITING
OPPORTUNITY TO SAVE
ON THE PURCHASE OF
HARLEQUIN AND
SILHOUETTE BOOKS!

*DETAILS TO FOLLOW
IN OCTOBER 2001!*

YOU WON'T WANT TO MISS IT!

PHQ401

Harlequin truly does make any time special. . . . This year we are celebrating weddings in style!

A Walk Down the Aisle
WEDDING CELEBRATION

To help us celebrate, we want you to tell us how wearing the Harlequin wedding gown will make your wedding day special. As the grand prize, Harlequin will offer one lucky bride the chance to **"Walk Down the Aisle"** in the Harlequin wedding gown!

There's more...

For her honeymoon, she and her groom will spend five nights at the **Hyatt Regency Maui.** As part of this five-night honeymoon at the hotel renowned for its romantic attractions, the couple will enjoy a candlelit dinner for two in Swan Court, a sunset sail on the hotel's catamaran, and duet spa treatments.

Maui • Molokai • Lanai

A HYATT RESORT AND SPA

To enter, please write, in, 250 words or less, how wearing the Harlequin wedding gown will make your wedding day special. The entry will be judged based on its emotionally compelling nature, its originality and creativity, and its sincerity. This contest is open to Canadian and U.S. residents only and to those who are 18 years of age and older. There is no purchase necessary to enter. Void where prohibited. See further contest rules attached. Please send your entry to:

Walk Down the Aisle Contest

In Canada	In U.S.A.
P.O. Box 637	P.O. Box 9076
Fort Erie, Ontario	3010 Walden Ave.
L2A 5X3	Buffalo, NY 14269-9076

You can also enter by visiting www.eHarlequin.com
Win the Harlequin wedding gown and the vacation of a lifetime!
The deadline for entries is October 1, 2001.

HARLEQUIN®
Makes any time special ®

PHWDACONT1

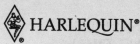
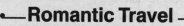

AND YOU THOUGHT TEXAS WAS BIG!

HARLEQUIN®
INTRIGUE®

continues its most secret, seriously sinister and deadly *confidential* series in the Big Sky state with four more sexy cowboy agents guaranteed to take your breath away!

Men bound by love, loyalty and the law—
these specialized government operatives have vowed
to keep their missions and identities confidential....

SOMEONE TO PROTECT HER
PATRICIA ROSEMOOR
September 2001

SPECIAL ASSIGNMENT: BABY
DEBRA WEBB
October 2001

LICENSED TO MARRY
CHARLOTTE DOUGLAS
November 2001

SECRET AGENT HEIRESS
JULIE MILLER
December 2001

Available wherever Harlequin books are sold.

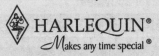

HARLEQUIN®
Makes any time special ®